PRAISE for…

Hit & Mrs.
Crewe's writing has the breathless tenor of a kitchen-table yarn…a cinematic pace and crackling dialogue keep readers hooked.—Quill & Quire

If you're in the mood for a cute chick-lit mystery with some nice gals in Montreal, Hit & Mrs. *is just the ticket.*—Globe and Mail

Shoot Me
Possesses an intelligence and emotional depth that reverberates long after you've stopped laughing.—Halifax Chronicle Herald

Relative Happiness
Her graceful prose…and her ability to turn a familiar story into something with such raw, dramatic power are skills that many veteran novelists have yet to develop.—Halifax Chronicle Herald

Amazing Grace
From the first page to the last, the novel is warm-hearted…It's also funny, alive with Lesley Crewe's trademark wit and ear for dialogue.
—Atlantic Books Today

Amazing Grace *is a fast-paced novel written in Crewe's breezy, chatty style as if Grace were talking over tea in her trailer...Crewe has a gift for creating delightful characters.*
—Halifax Chronicle Herald

Mary, Mary

LESLEY CREWE

Mary, Mary

Vagrant PRESS

Nimbus Publishing Limited
3731 Mackintosh St, Halifax, NS B3K 5A5
(902) 455-4286 nimbus.ca

Printed and bound in Canada

Design: Heather Bryan
Front cover art: Shutterstock; Shelagh Duffett, Halifax, Nova Scotia
Interior illustrations: Heidi Hallett
NB1275

This novel is a work of fiction. Names, characters, places, and incidents are either the product of the author's imagination or are used fictitiously.

Library and Archives Canada Cataloguing in Publication

Crewe, Lesley, 1955-, author
Mary, Mary / Lesley Crewe.

Issued in print and electronic formats.
ISBN 978-1-77108-453-6 (paperback).—ISBN 978-1-77108-454-3 (html)

I. Title.

PS8605.R48M37 2016   C813'.6   C2016-903749-5
                                             C2016-903750-9

Canada   Canada Council   Conseil des arts
            for the Arts   du Canada

Nimbus Publishing acknowledges the financial support for its publishing activities from the Government of Canada through the Canada Book Fund (CBF) and the Canada Council for the Arts, and from the Province of Nova Scotia. We are pleased to work in partnership with the Province of Nova Scotia to develop and promote our creative industries for the benefit of all Nova Scotians.

For my cousin Barbara, who,
once upon a time, planned her wedding
from a bed in our living room.

CHAPTER ONE

IT WAS A SATURDAY NIGHT and Mary Ryan had a hot date with Mrs. Aucoin.

At the age of ninety, Mrs. Aucoin still made her own cookies and was always inviting Mary up to share them in the apartment she rented from Mary's mother.

Despite being twenty-three, Mary had a surprising amount in common with Mrs. Aucoin. There was their shared admiration for a big tomcat named Roscoe, who had to be the ugliest cat on the street but had the loudest purr either of them had ever heard. He was a stray, and Mary tried long and hard to get her mother and grandmother to take him in, but they would not be swayed—so Mrs. Aucoin stepped in and took the chewed-up beast into her home. For that, Mary would love her forever.

Roscoe was purring in Mary's lap as Mrs. Aucoin poured the tea at her kitchen table, a big plate of sugar cookies between them. When she added the milk, Mary noticed it had gone off, but she didn't want to embarrass her hostess so she kept quiet and drank it anyway.

They were two cookies in when Mrs. Aucoin suddenly said, "Did you know my middle name is Mary?"

"Is it? What's your first name? I've only ever known you as Mrs. Aucoin."

"It's Beatrice, but my parents always called me Bea...their bumble-bee, they said."

"That's so sweet. I've always had a bit of a grudge against my mom. She should have known better than to call me Mary. She condemned me to a lifetime of ridicule in school."

"What on earth do you mean?"

"In elementary, I was always asked where my lamb was, and if I was quite contrary. When my boobs got bigger in the middle grades, the boys called me Mary Poppins, but the real fun started in high school, where I was known as the Virgin Mary."

1

"Oh dear." Mrs. Aucoin laughed. "I never thought of that."

"Whenever Mom yells my name, it feels like a commandment: *Marry!* For some strange reason she wants me to get married, even though she never did."

"And do you want to get married?"

"I'm never getting hitched. Why bother? My grandfather walked out on my Gran; my mother didn't know my father's last name; my Aunt Peggy's husband is never home because he's a heart doctor. And then there's my cousin, Sheena. When we were little girls, we played Barbies together and Sheena always turned Barbie into a bride and made me play with the Ken doll. Ken was boring, but at least I had enough self-respect to pretend otherwise. I had Ken climbing up bureaus and bungee-jumping off bedside lamps, while Barbie cried and pouted at the altar."

"Dear me."

"Our friendship was almost destroyed the day I took a pair of scissors and hacked off Barbie's hair and veil. Sheena ran screaming to her mother and Aunt Peggy told me in a very stern voice that it wasn't a very nice thing to do and I should apologize. So I did. I thought I'd get in trouble, but later that day Mom took me out for ice cream. She'd never done that before. I can count on one hand the number of times Mom has taken me anywhere. But really, these days I don't even want to go with her."

Mrs. Aucoin reached out and patted Mary's hand. "Love your mother. You may not always like her, but remember to love her. She's the only one you will ever have. And you'll miss her when she's gone."

Mary trudged home from work in the dark. She was freezing. She'd been cold for eight hours; her cash register was nearest to the sliding doors of the Prince Street Sobeys entrance, and since tomorrow was Christmas Eve, customers had flocked in every few seconds, frantic to pick up last-minute groceries for the holiday season. Everyone tried to get in her line-up with too many items, but Mary didn't say anything. People were stressed out enough. In this season of love, let them fight amongst themselves.

It was a miserable night out, and she had hoped her mom would be outside in their old Dodge Spirit, ready to drive her home, but no. She wrapped a scarf around her head a couple of times. If Sheena had worked on her feet all day and there was a blizzard outside, Aunt Peggy would be idling by the store entrance with her brand new Lexus all warm and toasty for the darling girl to jump right in.

Not for the first time did Mary think how great it would've been if she and Sheena had been switched at birth and Mary was sent home with Aunt Peggy. She always felt a pang of guilt and shut the thought down before it gathered momentum. There was no point in *what ifs*. Life was what it was.

Unfair.

The cold north wind blew wet snow all over Mary's glasses. She couldn't see a thing, so she took them off and put them in her pocket, looking down at her feet to keep her face from being pelted with hail. The route was easy: up to George Street, left, and then straight down George Street, where the large two- and three-storey houses were now apartments with two or more front doors across the wide wooden porches. Crooked mailboxes were nailed beside doorbells, and gravel driveways marked off the properties. The one thing Mary did like about her street was the trees. If you cocked your head at a certain angle, they looked like huge wooden slingshots lined up in an orderly row, thanks to the power company cutting away branches growing near the lines over the years.

The snow kept accumulating and made walking treacherous. Mary slipped on the ice underneath. Thank goodness she was almost up to Dotty's Dairy. Their house was next to the old store, which was both a blessing and a curse. Great if you needed milk, but rotten because the rosebushes on their front lawn gathered litter thrown away by people the minute they left the store—cigarette packs, chocolate bar wrappers, and pop bottles.

Mary mentioned to her gran that perhaps they should cut the scraggly roses down, but Gran said the thorny bushes kept dogs from shitting in the yard.

Thankfully the upstairs apartment windows were glowing through the snow; Mrs. Aucoin didn't like the dark. Mary was grateful to her, because her mother and grandmother never left any lights on at all. It was like walking into a morgue whenever she came home. Only the glare from the television in the living room illuminated a dim pathway as Mary hurried up the back steps and into the porch. She immediately flicked on the light switch.

There were no greetings over the blaring television.

Mary left her sodden outer gear hanging on a hook in the porch and went to throw her purse on the kitchen table, but it was full of dirty dishes. She dropped her purse by the door instead. The sink was also piled high with plates and cutlery, but that didn't stop her from turning on the hot water to thaw out her hands.

While it was understandable that her mother didn't feel like doing housework after standing on her feet all day in her hair salon—a.k.a. their dining room—she often wondered why Gran didn't pitch in a little more often. Sewing hems and the occasional waistband for the neighbours didn't take up a lot of her time, most of which was spent snoring on the couch in front of the TV, a cup of ginny tea in danger of falling to the floor.

The kitchen was a dreary place anyway, whether it was clean or dirty. It was in desperate need of an overhaul. The old cupboards, wallpaper, and chipped lino floor all screamed sixties, with varying shades of orange, lemon, and faded green. You'd think with running a business her mom would make more of an effort, since clients had to walk through the kitchen to get to the "salon," but most of her clientele had been coming for years and they clearly couldn't care less. Carole's Styling Salon was cheap.

"That you?" her mother shouted from the living room.

"Yeah."

Carole appeared in the kitchen with purple jogging pants hanging off her rear and a Winnie-the-Pooh pyjama top stretched across her ample chest. Her salt-and-pepper hair was done up in bobby-pin curls, a change from her usual Velcro rollers. When she did smile, she was attractive enough, but most of the time she scowled. "What's it like out?"

"Didn't you notice the snowstorm? I could've used a drive home."

Carole yawned and reached for her cigarettes. "You're young. You survived." She lit one up and inhaled deeply.

"I can't believe I have so far, breathing in your smoke my whole life."

Carole sat at the kitchen table and pulled a dirty saucer towards her. She flicked her ash in it. "I've got one pleasure in life and this is it."

"You told me you'd quit when you were forty. That was six years ago."

"Jesus. When did that happen? My life is over."

Mary's grandmother, Ethel, shuffled into the kitchen wearing a worn-out pink bathrobe and hairnet. She was only sixty-eight but looked ten years older, thanks to her years of downing booze. She also had a dowager's hump that made her look like she was charging towards you. Arthritis had set up shop in her knees years before, but it seemed to come and go depending on the task at hand. If there was housework to be done, her knees went on strike. If she ran out of gin they'd happily take her to the liquor store, lickety-split.

"Did you pick up my peppermints?"

"Yes, Gran." Mary dried off her hands and opened her purse. She took out a package of large pink peppermints and handed them to her grandmother.

"You'll rot your gut sucking on those things," Carole said.

"Better than sucking on cigarettes."

Mary busied herself getting milk for the bowl of cereal that would be her supper, but there were no clean bowls in the cupboard, so she poured herself a glass of milk and had a piece of bread and peanut butter instead. Then she sat at the table and cracked open the kitchen window in a vain attempt to get rid of the smoke, but the blast of frigid air made her mother screech, so she shut it again with a bang.

Ethel made a racket with the bag of candy. "How the hell do you open these peppermints?"

No one answered her.

"I saw Sheena today," said Mary.

Carole raised her eyebrows. "What's new with her?"

"She's engaged."

Her mother's face registered shock. "Peggy never said anything! How long has she been going out with this bozo? A week?"

5

"Since the summer."

Gran grunted. "She's a tramp."

"She's a hopeless romantic, Gran."

"Same thing." Ethel growled low in her throat and gave the candy package a giant yank, resulting in peppermints flying all over the kitchen.

"For Jesus's sake, Ma!"

"Five-second rule." Ethel gathered up the peppermints that had landed on the counter and table. Mary bent down to scoop up the ones near her feet.

"Don't let her eat those," said Carole. "This floor is filthy."

Ethel popped a mint in her mouth. "You're supposed to eat a pound of dirt before you die. I read that somewhere."

"You'll be dead in the morning." Carole stubbed out her cigarette and immediately lit another. "Great, Peggy planning a wedding. We'll never hear the bloody end of it. And Sheena! She'll be intolerable."

"She was beyond excited," said Mary. "She bought a pack of gum so she could come through the checkout and show me her ring."

"Why can't we be the centre of attention for once? Hurry up and get engaged, will ya?" said Carole.

"You hate men. Why would you want me to marry one?"

"To have a wedding! Peggy had one with a gown and flowers and a honeymoon. What did I get? A life sentence with a souse."

"Living with you is why I drink," Ethel said.

"I've spent my whole life without a man," Carole scofffed. "You made sure you chased Dad away."

Ethel made a face. "My heart bleeds."

Mary looked up. "And *you* chased mine away, apparently," she said to Carole. "I don't see him anywhere."

Carole got up from the table. "Ditto what she said," nodding to Ethel. "I'm going to bed."

Mary pointed. "Put your cigarette out before you do."

Her mother waved her hand vaguely and left the kitchen. Ethel joined Mary at the table and they inspected the peppermints before putting them in a plastic storage bag.

"She's still dripping with jealousy," Mary observed.

"Yep. Always unhappy."

"Why don't I make her happy?"

"You do." Ethel popped two peppermints in her mouth.

Mary took her empty glass over to the sink and decided to do the dishes after all. Her grandmother began rooting through her purse, which caught Mary's attention. "Are those scratch tickets? What did Mom say about that?"

Ethel scratched away like an old hen. "What your ma doesn't know won't hurt her. Besides, it's my money."

"What if you win?"

"I'll be but a fond memory."

Mary grinned. "You'd leave me here all alone with her?"

Ethel pursed her lips. "No one deserves that. I'll give you enough money for a bus ticket outta here."

"Thanks, Gran."

"Oh, before I forget, Mrs. Aucoin wanted to know if you could pick up a few groceries for her tomorrow. That no-good son of hers says he's on back shift and can't take her. You should get her list now. She sleeps late in the morning."

With only a sweater and slippers on, Mary went out into the stormy night and rang Mrs. Aucoin's doorbell. Mary wasn't surprised when she didn't answer; Mrs. Aucoin couldn't hear very well. She couldn't see very well either, so you practically had to be on top of her before she recognized you. Her son had given her a pair of binoculars, but Mrs. Aucoin kept looking through the wrong end and declared them useless. Her son finally installed a can of mace on the wall near the door, but she used it on him one night during a power outage when he came to see if she was okay. He finally told his wife that if they killed her, they killed her. She was going to outlive him anyway.

Mary opened the door and hollered, "Mrs. Aucoin?"

No answer.

She trudged up the steps. "It's Mary. I've come to get your grocery list."

There was a television on in the kitchen, so she walked down the hall but froze in the doorway. Mrs. Aucoin was at the table, face-first in a plate of creamed peas on toast. Roscoe was licking her cheek.

Mary thought she was going to be sick. "Oh no! Mrs. Aucoin!" She hurried over to the woman and moved Roscoe to a chair. Then she gently lifted her neighbour's head and wiped the sauce off her face with a napkin. She pushed the plate away and carefully laid her head back down on the place mat. "I'm sorry. This is awful. Why did you have to be alone?"

Tears fell as Mary patted Mrs. Aucoin's grey hair. She looked around and saw the teapot on the warmer, so she turned it off and noticed the two sugar cookies laid out for Mrs. Aucoin's dessert. That made her cry harder. She didn't want to leave her old friend, so she sat beside her for a while. Mary had never seen a dead body, but it wasn't as scary as she'd imagined. The cat got back up on the table and looked at his mistress quizzically.

"I suppose she wasn't completely alone, Roscoe. Thank goodness you were here."

Mary realized she had better tell someone. She ran downstairs and out onto the front porch, only to find she'd locked herself out of the house. "Shit!"

She banged on the door. "Mom! Gran! Open up! Open this door!"

A light finally came on in the front porch. Her mother screwed up her face trying to see who was outside. "What do you want?"

"Mom! It's me. Let me in!"

Carole opened the door. "What in the name of Jesus…?"

Ethel was behind her with a baseball bat in her hand. Mary tumbled in and tried to catch her breath. "It's Mrs. Aucoin! She's dead!"

"Dead?"

"Yes!" Mary rubbed her cold fingers. "Call the police. Or should we call her son?"

"Don't call him!" Ethel hollered. "That idiot probably murdered her. He'll get us next!"

Carole grabbed the bat from her mother's hand. "Don't be daft. She's probably had a heart attack. Are you sure she's dead? Did you feel for a pulse?"

Mary shook her head. "No. I didn't think of it. I'm pretty sure she's dead."

The three of them charged outside and up Mrs. Aucoin's stairs.

When they reached the kitchen, the cat was curled up beside his mistress. Carole unceremoniously dumped him on the floor. She put her fingers against Mrs. Aucoin's neck and felt for a pulse, but there was nothing. "Call the police, Mary. They should be the ones to contact the family."

Mary ran back downstairs to make the call.

"She owes us two months' rent," Ethel reminded Carole. "Make sure you get it from that louse son of hers." Ethel opened up the sugar bowl on the table and looked inside. "She kept all her cash under her bed. Maybe we should take a look while we have the chance."

"You're an old buzzard."

"And you're the one who always says we have no money."

"So you want me to steal it from a dead woman?"

"It's not stealing when she owes us."

Carole pointed at the door. "Get out now."

It was two in the morning before Mrs. Aucoin's body was finally carted off. The three Ryan women expressed their condolences to her son before Ethel mentioned the outstanding rent. He gave them a filthy look, saying he'd be by with the money in the coming days.

"And by the way, I'm not taking that cat. I don't know where it came from," he added.

"Where is he?" Mary asked.

"I kicked him outside." He stormed off the porch.

Carole shut their front door. "Why did you have to mention the rent, Ma? There's a time and a place, ya know."

"So sue me. Jumpin' Jesus, what a night. I need a drink." Ethel wandered off.

"I have to go out and look for Roscoe." Mary put on her coat and boots.

"You are not going out and looking for that damn cat."

"Yes, I am! And when I find him, he's coming back with me."

"Oh no, he's not."

"Oh yes, he is."

Carole grabbed her cigarettes and lit one. "It's not enough that I have to clean and paint that apartment so we can rent it immediately, now I'm going to be cleaning up after a cat?"

"I'll look after him. And you know darn well I'll be helping you with the apartment. I'm the only one who ever does."

"Who else do you suggest I ask? Your grandmother's useless. I refuse to ask Peggy with her superior attitude, Ted is only handy if he's ripping open someone's chest, and Sheena is God's gift to no one. I don't have a father or a husband I can ask. I don't even have friends, what with the ungodly hours I put in to keep this place afloat."

"How about I do you a huge favour and run away from home? That way you can keep your expenses down."

"Good idea."

"You don't even care that I'm upset about Mrs. Aucoin."

"I do care. I know you liked her."

"Put out that damn cigarette before you go to bed." Mary opened the front door and banged it shut.

It was still blowing a gale, but the hail had stopped. Mary called out into the night for Roscoe. She looked under the front porch and behind the sheds of her neighbours' houses. Tears poured down her face as she marched up and down the street, shouting his name. After an hour she was so cold that she knew she had to head back. All she could think about was how Roscoe had tried to comfort Mrs. Aucoin in her hour of need. And what did he get for it? Thrown out on the street like garbage. Gran was right. She hated Mrs. Aucoin's son.

And then everything changed. Who did she see sitting patiently outside Mrs. Aucoin's door but one familiar mangy cat? She ran up the steps, picked him up, and wrapped him in her coat.

"Thank you for coming home, Roscoe. I really need you tonight."

Roscoe purred.

On the other side of town, in Coxheath, Carole's younger sister, Peggy, was sitting up in bed with a notepad on her lap in her beautifully decorated bedroom, waiting for Sheena to come home. There were already five pages of things to do for her daughter's wedding. She looked at the clock. The bright red numbers glared 2:45. Bright red reminded her of blood. Blood reminded her of car crashes. Car crashes reminded her of hospitals. Hospitals reminded her of her husband. Peggy looked at him.

Ted was snoring his bald head off. That's all he ever did. Ted being twelve years her senior hadn't been an issue when they were married, but now it was a problem. He was boring all day *and* all night. She made a fist and hit him right between the shoulder blades.

"Whaa...whaa?"

"How can you sleep when your only child is in a ditch somewhere?"

He turned over and groaned. "You know this for a fact?"

"Where else would she be at three in the morning during a blizzard?"

"Wake me up when the police get here," he mumbled into his pillow.

"You're pathetic. You have absolutely no parenting skills at all."

"I won't have any medical skills either if you don't let me get some sleep."

Peggy crossed her arms. She didn't know who to throttle first, her husband or her daughter. She had a face full of worry lines that no amount of Estée Lauder could eradicate. And it didn't help that she couldn't rely on her mother or sister. How her niece wasn't a complete loon living with them in that old dump, she'd never know.

Thinking about Mary reminded Peggy that she should encourage her niece to stop dressing like a farmer. Not a good look for the maid of honour. Sheena was the exact opposite; she had a walk-in closet filled with beautiful clothes. But her daughter might never see her closet again if she was frozen in a snow bank on Keltic Drive. Any minute now she'd get a call saying there had been a head-on collision.

Car headlights lit up the bedroom window. Peggy threw off the covers. Thank God. Running down the stairs in bare feet, she made it to the front door just as Sheena came through it.

"Where on earth have you been?"

Not for the first time did Sheena think how great it would've been if she and Mary had been switched at birth and she was sent home with Aunt Carole and Gran. They didn't give a damn what Mary did and had never heard of the word *curfew*. But then she always felt a pang of guilt and shut the thought down before it gathered momentum. There was no point in *what ifs*. Life was what it was.

Unfair.

"Drew and I were just talking about our future, Mother. We lost track of time."

"That's no excuse not to call me."

Sheena pulled off her wet knee-high leather boots and unwrapped the scarf from around her perfectly highlighted blond hair. "I didn't call because I'd wake up Dad. I texted you more than once."

"I wondered what that noise was." Peggy took Sheena's coat and put it in the foyer closet. "Did you have your dinner?"

"Nine hours ago. You wouldn't make me a grilled cheese?" Sheena gave her the pouty look.

"It's the middle of the night."

"So?"

"Oh, all right."

"Thanks, Mommy."

Mother and daughter headed for the kitchen. Whenever Peggy turned on the light, her endorphins buzzed. Ted used to give her the same sensation, but not anymore.

The new renovation was sublime: marble counters, glass tiles, stainless steel appliances, and dark walnut cupboards gave the room a rich, warm feel, while the two crystal chandeliers added sparkle.

Sheena sat at the island while Peggy assembled the ingredients and took out a frying pan. "I might as well make myself a sandwich too."

"I thought you were on Weight Watchers."

"I have lots of points left." That was a bald-faced lie, but the stress of waiting up meant that Peggy deserved every cheesy morsel.

"I showed Mary my ring."

Peggy stopped. "Oh, thanks a lot. I thought we were going to tell them together on Christmas Day."

"I know, but I couldn't wait."

"Great. Now Carole's nose will be out of joint that I didn't tell her first."

"Blame me."

"I will. So did you ask Drew about having a church wedding?"

Sheena reached over and took a handful of grapes from the fruit bowl. "He says he wants what I want. He's so sweet."

"And what do you want?"

"I want everything!"

Peggy buttered the bread and put it in the pan. "It's fine and dandy for him to say that, but you can be sure his mother will have an opinion or two."

"It's my wedding, so I'm in charge." Sheena looked at her ring. "Besides, his mother doesn't care one way or the other. She's having an affair."

Peggy whirled around. "What? I thought Drew's father owned car dealerships."

"Just because he has money doesn't mean his wife likes him. He's a hot mess."

"It's now occurring to me that we know nothing about Drew's family." Peggy flipped the sandwiches rather forcefully.

Sheena sighed. "Listen to yourself. I'm the one who should be worried. How am I going to explain Aunt Carole and Gran?"

Peggy put the sandwiches on plates and cut them in half. She placed one in front of her daughter and then sat on the nearest stool to devour hers. "Don't be rude."

"I'm sorry, but you know what I mean."

"Your grandmother is an alcoholic. It happens in the best of families. It's no reason to be ashamed of her."

Sheena took a bite. "What's Aunt Carole's excuse? I don't think she likes me very much, or Mary, for that matter."

"Carole hasn't had it easy."

"That's her own fault. How many times have you offered to help her fix up that place?"

"I'm not talking about that. I mean she brought me up after our father left because Mom couldn't cope. It's tough looking after a child when you're a child yourself. Imagine a four-year-old making lunch for a two-year-old. I owe Carole a lot."

"Well, she's still a grump. She better not ruin my wedding."

"How could she ruin your wedding?"

"She's coming, isn't she?"

❋

"MA!"

"WHA?"

"Bring me the cash box!"

"Get it yourself!"

Carole shook her head. "I'm going to brain that one."

Her client tsked. "You should put her in a home, Carole."

"Frig that. Let me go to the home and get some rest. Ethel-Alcohol can stay here and let the place fall down around her ears."

"Girl, you just need to join that eHarmony, get yourself a boyfriend, and move."

"Just what I need: a man."

Carole stomped into the living room. Her mother was watching television in her stained bathrobe, stretched out on a maroon horsehair sofa that had belonged to a now dead relative. Some mending was in a pile on the floor and the ever-present tea was on the wonky side table next to her.

"I'm in that salon busting my butt and you can't be bothered to get off your ass and do this one thing for me."

Ethel waved at her. "Get outta the way, will ya? I can't see Marilyn Denis."

"Where's the cash box?"

"How the hell should I know? That's your business."

Carole looked under cushions and newspapers. "You have a nasty habit of taking money out of it to buy gin and lottery tickets."

"When I win, I bet you'll be nice to me then. Look, it's on top of the television."

Carole grabbed it and left. Ethel called after her. "Isn't it Christmas Eve? Where did you put that little fake tree?"

"I don't have time to be looking for that old thing. Try the hall closet."

Ethel took a gulp of her tea before she pushed herself off the couch and weaved her way to said destination. "Ha! No tree in here!"

"Then chop one down!"

Ethel wandered into the "salon," where Carole was making change for her customer. "Hey, girl. What's shakin'?"

"I was telling Carole that she should join an online dating service."

"Acting like some coyote? No thanks."

"That's a cougar, Ma."

The client gave a shout of laughter. "You two kill me! Merry Christmas!"

"Merry Christmas!"

When she left, Ethel said, "Did she give you a tip?"

"Never you mind."

"What's for supper?"

"Kraft Dinner."

"Again?"

Mary was adding up her till when her supervisor came in. "Your grandmother wants you to call her."

"Okay, thanks."

Mary finished counting change and called home. "Hi, Gran."

"Could you bring home some pizza? I can't stomach Kraft Dinner tonight."

"Pizza on Christmas Eve. I can't wait."

"Speaking of which, I didn't have time to go shopping, so pick yourself up some wine and lottery tickets. I'll pay ya back."

"I don't drink wine."

"Well, get yourself some chocolates, then, and some for your mother. And your mom just said to get some cat food and kitty litter for your asshole cat."

Another of Carole's customers was just leaving by the time Mary got home. They exchanged pleasantries and wished each other season's greetings. Mary walked in the kitchen with her boots on because she had too many bags in her hands. Her mother and grandmother were at the table. It was covered with the plastic poinsettia tablecloth they used year after year. They'd even lit one of the emergency candles they kept in the kitchen drawer.

"This looks nice," Mary said as she put the bags on the counter.

"What's all that?" her mother asked.

"These are your Christmas presents. I know we're going over to

Aunt Peggy's tomorrow but I thought we deserved a Christmas dinner here." Mary shrugged off her coat and unpacked the bags. "I bought a big cooked roast chicken, the $9.99 one, and I have instant mashed potatoes and Stove Top Stuffing, a can of baby peas, cranberry sauce and a package of gravy. Oh yeah, and a small fruitcake, because I know you like that, Gran."

"Is it the kind soaked in rum?"

"I think so. And I got an apple pie, candy canes, and eggnog."

"Do we have any rum to put in it?"

"Forget the rum, Ma!"

"Did you get the pizza?"

"No, Gran. I didn't have enough money. Isn't this better than pizza?" Carole kicked Ethel under the table.

"Yes, it's much better. Thank you."

"Where's Roscoe?"

"He was on your bed, so I shut him in there," her mom said. "Jesus, he's got to be the ugliest thing alive."

"I believe he said the same thing about you."

Gran let out a hoot.

Mary left them to open the packages and mix up the food. She opened her bedroom door, or her sanctuary as she called it. A fortress against her crackpot relatives. There was Roscoe, curled up right between her two pillows.

"Hello there, big boy!" She bent down and gave him a kiss right on the top of his head. He immediately started to make a sound like a buzz saw.

"I'm sorry I had to leave you with the warden and her deputy, but you can hide out in here whenever you like. As a matter of fact, it would be better for your mental health if you avoided my roommates altogether. I've got you a first-class litter pan and some Fancy Feast for your dinner. And this."

She ripped open a cat toy package—a mouse with catnip inside. Roscoe took a tentative sniff and then his pupils got enormous. He immediately rubbed his cheek against the furry mouse, then rolled on his back and kicked the shit out of it with his back paws. Once that was accomplished, he nibbled at it with a hint of glee in his eye.

"I'm glad you're happy. Merry Christmas."

Mary loved her room. It was the only cozy space in the joint. Mind you, the wallpaper was stained and peeling in a few places, but she had covered the walls with maps and posters and peg boards so she could pin up items that caught her eye. She'd made her own rugs by braiding old towels together and even sewed her own quilt with all the scraps her Gran had thrown away over the years. She had big pillows and covered foam that created a window seat over the enclosed heat register. Her big closet was a mini refuge—there was a light with a string in there, so she could root around the shelves and shoe boxes of possessions she'd accumulated over the years. But her prized possession was the old wardrobe that stood facing her bed. It reminded her of the one in *The Lion, the Witch, and the Wardrobe.* It was full of secret things, old keys, diaries, notebooks, the flotsam and jetsam of childhood. Her mother and grandmother had been told repeatedly that if they were to ever open the wardrobe, Mary would move to the other side of the world. So far, they hadn't: Mary had rigged it; she would've been able to tell.

Off the work clothes went and she slipped on an old sweater and jogging pants. Her long brown hair was a mess, so she took it out of its ponytail and bent over to brush it. Sometimes she thought about cutting it, but it was a rather nice shade. Almost exactly the colour of her eyes, which one boy had described as dark caramel. She had to wear it in a ponytail at work, and it felt good to let it fall over her shoulders when she got home. Her glasses were dirty, so she sprayed them with cleaner. One day she'd save enough money to buy contact lenses; her glasses always slid down her nose, which was annoying. Just yesterday the stock boy at work said they covered up her cute freckles. When he left her register, she rolled her eyes. Freckles were freckles. There was no such thing as cute ones.

Mary wrapped up the chocolates and lottery tickets for her grandmother with Roscoe's drugged help and gathered the few gifts she'd hidden under the bed.

In the living room the old fake Christmas tree was on top of the coffee table decorated with small red balls, flashing coloured lights, and a rope of gold tinsel. There were even a few gifts around it, so she added hers.

They enjoyed their feast in the kitchen. Mary found the package of Christmas napkins she'd bought one year on top of the fridge, so she took out three and put the package back. They looked nice on the table in the candlelight. Her mom made a show of carving the chicken, until Gran got impatient and ripped off one of the legs to put on her own plate.

"Ma! Hold your horses."

"A body could starve to death waiting for you."

Mary sighed. "Who would like to say grace?"

"We never say grace," Gran replied.

"It's Christmas. It might be a nice gesture."

Gran grabbed a wing and bowed her head. "Dear God, give me strength. Amen."

"I second that emotion," Carole said.

"Motion," Mary muttered.

"Did you say something?" Gran shouted. "Speak up."

After they cleaned their plates, they took their dessert into the living room.

"So what time do we arrive at the palace tomorrow?" Carole said with her mouth full.

"Sheena said anytime."

"I'm not going until supper's ready. Who wants to look at the motherlode of gifts under their tree? Do any of them even need anything? It's obscene."

"Drew's parents are coming for dinner too."

"Oh shit. That means I'll have to babysit."

"I'm not gonna do nothin'." Ethel went to pop a piece of fruitcake in her mouth but missed. It went down the front of her bathrobe, so she dug around until she found it.

Carole pointed at her. "If something spills tomorrow, leave your boobs alone."

Mary put down her plate. "Maybe we should go to church tonight."

Both her mother and grandmother said, "What for?"

"I don't know. It might be nice to listen to Christmas carols."

"I've been on my feet all day and so have you," Carole said. "Put on the radio."

"And the Yule log channel," Ethel added.

The remote and radio were on the other side of the room. Mary had to rock a few times before she could get off the recliner. It was old and went so far back that neither her mother nor grandmother wanted to sit in it.

The three of them watched the flames dance and the wood pop and crackle as they listened to "I Saw Mommy Kissing Santa Claus."

Roscoe came weaving into the living room and sat and looked at them, or at least tried to.

"What is wrong with that animal?" Gran pointed.

"I gave him catnip."

"Can I have some?"

On Christmas Day there was a deluge of snow, only this time it fell gently and made the whole city look like one big Christmas card. Lights twinkled from hedges and trees, front doors, and rooftops. Everything was clean and new, all the dirty snow and litter covered up under a pristine white blanket.

But there was no peace or goodwill in the Ryans' rusty Dodge Spirit that afternoon.

"Ya should've let Mary drive! You're all over the friggin' road."

"Ma, shut the hell up! I'm trying to concentrate."

"Concentrating on crashing into light poles!"

Mary was in the front passenger seat with a Sobeys bag in her lap that contained her relatives' gifts. Her legs were ramrod straight as she tried to brake with a non-existent pedal. "Why *can't* I drive?"

Carole leaned into the steering wheel and wiped at the condensation on the window. "I've been driving since before you were born."

"Mom, don't go so fast. We don't have snow tires."

"Can't afford them."

Ethel was bundled up in the back seat looking like an apple doll. "Oh, here we go. The 'woe is me' speech."

"I'm stating a fact."

"Then why don't you let your sister buy you some?"

Carole swivelled her head back to look at her mother. "I'm not accepting charity!"

"*Mom*, watch where you're going!"

Somehow they managed to make it over to Coxheath without slipping into Blackett's Lake. As they approached Peggy's street, Carole's scowl deepened.

"Look at these places. They have more money than brains."

Peggy's home was perched on a bit of a hill, looking over the water. It was a classic Cape Cod, nestled into the immaculate landscaping with a wide veranda and paver driveway stretching right to the highway.

"I love those twinkle lights in the window boxes," Ethel said. "Your sister always had good taste."

Carole gunned the engine and slipped and slid almost to the top of the hill before the car slowly started to roll backwards. "What kind of moron puts their house on top of a mountain?" she growled.

After several more attempts with everyone also rocking forward to gather a little momentum, they ended up careening down the driveway and landing in the ditch on the other side of the road.

Carole turned off the engine and lit a cigarette. Mary and Ethel knew better than to speak to her. The three of them sat in silence, fogging up the windows and getting colder by the minute. Carole took her last drag and flung the butt outside. "All right. We have no choice but to trudge up the hill. Mary, you're in charge of your grandmother. I'll take the gifts."

Mary had a hard time trying to get her Gran out of the car; the snow bank created by the plow was quite deep and her grandmother was wearing the short zippered ankle boots she'd bought in the 1950s.

"Mary! Get her from the other side. Honestly, I have to think of everything."

"Get back, Gran, and slide over to the other side. It'll be easier."

"Easier? I'm so cold now I can't move my knees."

Mary poked her head out of the car. "You're going to have to help me scoot her over the seat. She can't move on her own."

"Hell's bells."

"Why don't you stay with Gran? I'll go get Uncle Ted."

Mary ran up the long driveway and was out of breath when she got to the front door. She pushed down on the handle but it was locked. She rang the bell over and over again while pounding her fist.

When it finally opened, Aunt Peggy, Uncle Ted, and Sheena were gathered in the foyer looking concerned.

"Mary! What's wrong?"

"Uncle Ted, we couldn't get up the driveway and the car landed in the ditch. We can't get Gran out of the back seat."

Everyone sprang into action, pulling on their winter coats and boots. They skidded down the snow-covered driveway in a pack, Peggy carrying a fleece throw. Carole was leaning on the car door smoking a cigarette.

"Is she all right?" Peggy yelled.

"Of course she's all right," scoffed Carole. "Alcohol doesn't freeze."

While they waited for Drew and his parents to arrive, the family gathered around the spacious Henderson living room. There was what looked like an enormous pine tree in the corner, but it was covered with so many gold and white ornaments and ribbons that Mary wasn't sure if it was really there. A mountain of gifts was on display, as Mom had predicted, and it was hard to look away. You'd think that ten people lived in this house.

Carole was making faces at Mary, so she assumed this meant to give Aunt Peggy, Uncle Ted, and Sheena their gifts, since the Sobeys bag was near her feet. She passed the gifts to her relatives.

"Merry Christmas."

"Thank you, Mary," Aunt Peggy cooed.

She did that every year. Always made the biggest deal out of the Avon bath powder and soap she got. Uncle Ted would rave about his new socks and Sheena would pretend to adore her Walmart necklace and earrings. It made Mary a little sad, but she knew they were trying to be kind.

Then the Ryans would open their elaborately wrapped gifts. The paper and ribbon Aunt Peggy used would cost more than the Ryans' total Christmas budget.

Gran opened hers first. It was a beautiful new bathrobe that Mary knew would be stained by the end of the week. Also a silk nightgown and soft fluffy slippers. Her mother would take the slippers—Gran only liked pit socks on her feet—but maybe she'd give Mary the nightgown, since she only wore flannel. Gran's eyes lit up when she opened a card with a mound of scratch tickets in it.

"I knew you'd like it," Aunt Peggy smiled.

"I'm trying to get her off those damn things," Carole said.

"It's Christmas. Lighten up."

Carole was next and her gifts were a lovely blouse, sweater, and scarf. They would join the others in her drawers at home. Aunt Peggy never clued in that her mother didn't wear any of the stuff she bought her. Or maybe she did know and it was just a power struggle between them. But there were other gifts too, like a new hair dryer, curling iron, and straightener that were obviously destined for the salon. Carole was grateful.

Then it was Mary's turn. Sheena handed her a gift. It was a small box, so it wasn't clothes. She tore open the paper and inside was an iPad. She felt the blood rush to her head. Sheena jumped up and down in front of her.

"Do you like it?"

"I...I...."

"Peggy, that's much too generous," Carole cried.

"Nonsense," said Uncle Ted. "Every kid needs one of these. Let her enjoy it."

"Thank you so much." Mary jumped up and hugged her Uncle Ted first. Sometimes she pretended he was her dad. She always felt safe when he was around. It was too bad she saw so little of him.

"What does it do?" Gran asked.

"Everything!" Mary said. "I can look at the stars at night."

"You could just poke your head out the window, too," Gran said.

Peggy asked if anyone wanted a drink or a nibble, so while the family dispersed to the kitchen, Sheena and Mary went up to Sheena's bedroom and lounged on her canopied bed with two cans of Coke and a bag of Cheetos.

"So it's happening. It's your dream come true."

Sheena looked at her ring. Mary noticed she did that a lot.

"I'm very, very lucky, but one day it'll be your turn."

Mary chugged her drink, the bubbles tickling her nose. She sighed and leaned against one of the ten pillows on Sheena's bed. "I'm not interested."

Her cousin gave her a knowing look. "Everyone's interested. What happened to that guy you used to date in high school? He wasn't bad looking."

"He took me to the prom but left with my best friend."

"That sucks."

"Another guy I dated stole money out of Mom's cash box."

"I never knew that!"

"I didn't say anything. I just put the money back. It was either that or visit Mom in prison after she beat him to death."

"Smart move." Sheena put her can down on the bedside table, stretched out with her hands behind her head, and looked content.

"So when's the big day?"

"Oh, not for another year or so. I want to take my time and have fun planning the wedding."

Mary poked her in the ribs. "You want the wedding more than the marriage."

Sheena grinned.

Uncle Ted shouted up the stairs. "Drew's here!"

Aunt Peggy's dining-room table was covered with tall cut-glass cylinders filled with round Christmas ornaments, cedar boughs, and holly berries. There were several snow-white candles scattered across the lace tablecloth, and each place setting had a crystal wine glass, an enormous gold charger, a slightly smaller silver one, and finally Peggy's exquisite bone china dinner plates. Large cloth napkins held inside pewter rings topped each extravagant pile.

There were swags of real cedar and evergreen boughs braided with little lights draped over the windows, fireplace, and staircase. Mary was sure the greenery on the mantel would catch fire if Uncle Ted didn't stop poking the flames, creating a cascade of sparks.

"Ted, sit down," Peggy said. "We're too warm as it is."

Carole leaned over and whispered to Mary: "Looks chilly to my left."

Drew Corbett and his parents were seated at the far end of the table. When they were introduced to Mary, Drew smirked, his mother gave her a wan smile, and his dad almost dislocated her shoulder shaking her hand.

For most of the meal Mr. Corbett, who asked everyone to call him Chuck, dominated the conversation, and most of it revolved around cars. His wife, Maxine, sat beside him and picked at her food when she wasn't rolling her eyes or staring out the window. Drew chewed with his mouth open while Sheena looked adoringly at him, and the rest of them were busy trying to keep Ethel from drinking out of everyone else's wine glasses.

Chuck finally put a large forkful of turkey dinner in his mouth and Uncle Ted seized the opportunity. He tapped a spoon against his crystal goblet and held it up. "I'd like to propose a toast."

Uncle Ted's ears always turned bright red in social situations, and because of his receding hairline, his ears were now even more prominent. "I'd like to say that Peggy and I are very pleased to welcome Drew into our family. Although Drew and Sheena haven't known each other long—"

"You can say that again," Maxine interjected before downing the wine in her glass.

"—ah, yes…well, it's clear to me they are very much in love. At least, that's what Peggy tells me." He chuckled and everyone dutifully followed suit. "So here's to Sheena and Drew."

"Sheena and Drew." Everyone sipped their wine, but naturally Ethel gulped hers and proceeded to have a coughing fit. Carole hit her on the back until she stopped.

Aunt Peggy cleared her throat. "Maxine, I'm not sure if you're like me, but I was hoping the kids would have a church wedding."

"I don't care if they get married in a barn. I've been through this twice with Drew's older brothers, so knock yourself out. I'm not getting involved."

Drew opened his mouth to say something, but Chuck jumped in. "My wife can be a bit blunt on occasion. I'm sure what she means is that we'll leave that decision up to the kids. It is their day after all."

Sheena glanced at her mother, who looked a little shell-shocked. "Mom, I think we want an outdoor wedding, maybe at the Keltic Lodge...somewhere nice."

"The Keltic Lodge is for old-timers," Drew said.

Sheena made a face. "No, it's not."

"A reception is a party, and I want to party."

"We'll discuss it later," Sheena said, frowning.

"I can provide all the cars," Chuck offered.

Ethel, who could barely see over the table, pointed her finger at Chuck. "Hey, since you're going to be family, how about givin' us a new car? Ours is in a ditch and it's crap anyway."

There was a beat of silence.

"Mom, you're such a kidder!" Aunt Peggy laughed. "Why don't you and Carole come into the kitchen and help me bring out dessert?"

"What's wrong with my granddaughters? You're gonna make an old woman work for her supper? Nuts to that." Ethel held out her wine glass. "Fill 'er up, Teddy, and don't be stingy."

The meal went downhill from there.

All parties were more than relieved when they went their separate ways at the end of the evening. Chuck thanked the Hendersons in a loud, booming voice as Maxine pushed him out the door, clearly impatient to be off. Drew gave Sheena a hasty peck before following them into the night.

The family sat Ethel in a recliner in the family room and she was snoring before the first plate was cleared from the table. Peggy gave the girls a reprieve from the dishes, which annoyed Carole.

"Don't you ever make Sheena do anything around here?"

"Oh, leave them be. I have a dishwasher."

"Yeah. Called Carole."

Peggy put the rinsed dishes into the machine. "I don't want Sheena to hear our conversation. What did you think of Drew's mother?"

Carole picked up a dishtowel. "She's one cold fish."

"Imagine saying, 'Leave me out of it.'"

"I have no doubt that you'll do more than enough to compensate."

"And get this," Peggy said. "Apparently she's having an affair."

Carole picked up a washed pot. "How on earth would you know?"

"Sheena told me."

"Well, how does she know?"

"Don't have a clue."

"Do you like Drew? Looks like a bit of a player, if you ask me."

"No one asked you." Peggy slammed the dishwasher door closed. "He's good-looking, educated, and well-off. What's not to like?"

"She's twenty-two. Why don't they just live together?"

Peggy wiped her hands on her apron. "Why do you care if they get married?"

Carole put down the pot and threw the dish towel on top of it. "You married too young."

"And you're still jealous about it."

"Well, not all of us are lucky enough to have a car accident and marry the doctor on call. I knew Mary's father for one night. After that I was too busy trying to make a living with a colicky baby and drunken mother to look after."

Peggy sank onto the nearest stool. "Are you still sticking to that story? I find it hard to believe you didn't know his last name and you were with him for one night. You weren't fifteen. You were Mary's age."

"Pardon me if I was a late bloomer. I read an article that said fatherless girls are more susceptible to bad men. They crave love in all the wrong places. I'm a classic example."

"Yeah, when you're a teenager, but I'm not going to argue with you. I'm just disappointed that Drew's family isn't as excited as I am."

"Chuck seemed okay."

"Fathers don't know anything about weddings."

"I take it Ted isn't going to have a say in this one?"

"God, no."

CHAPTER TWO

MRS. AUCOIN'S FUNERAL WAS THREE days after Christmas, and Mary made a point of going to both the wake and the service. Both events were packed to the rafters; Mrs. Aucoin had had a lot of children. Mary wanted to avoid the son who had kicked out Roscoe, but it couldn't be helped. He was in the receiving line, along with the others. She gave him a curt nod and he did the same. But the other siblings were lovely.

"We're so grateful you came," said Mrs. Aucoin's daughter, Millie. "Maman always thought you were a lovely girl. If you hadn't gone up there that night, who knows how long she'd have been there."

A very large group of grandchildren and cousins clustered in one of the funeral parlour rooms, but Mary didn't want to speak to them. It was too awkward to say she was the girl who found their grandmother.

When Mary got home, her mother wanted to know who was at the church and was Mrs. Aucoin cremated. Her grandmother wanted to know what the church ladies had served at lunch. "Did they have those asparagus roll-ups? Did you bring me any?"

Mary walked by without answering and shut herself in her room.

Mrs. Aucoin's relatives came by the house in the new year with the keys, the outstanding rent, and a moving truck. It took them all afternoon to cart away her possessions. The stairs to the upper apartment were directly above the hair salon, and the stomping and banging got on Carole's nerves as she put a blue rinse in a client's hair. At one point someone dropped something heavy enough to cause a dusting of plaster to rain down on the lady's head.

The moving truck finally drove away in the late afternoon. Once Mary got home from work and they finished their dinner of beans and wieners, they went up the stairs to see what had to be done before they advertised for a new tenant.

The apartment was rather large: it had an eat-in kitchen, a living room, and two bedrooms. The bathroom was spacious but old-fashioned, and there weren't enough light fixtures in the place so it was a bit dingy now that Mrs. Aucoin's lamps were gone. The three of them wandered about the rooms. Carole looked in the kitchen.

"I'm going to have to paint these cupboards inside and out." There was a pause. "Oh God, you should see the state of the stove and fridge."

"She was old and almost blind," Mary reminded her.

"Her relatives must have seen it. It wouldn't have killed them to at least wipe them out."

"Oh shit," Ethel cried from the bathroom.

"What's wrong?"

"I just told ya. This toilet could use a scrub."

Mary crinkled her nose. "I'm not cleaning that. I'll do anything else, but not that."

It took Carole and Mary a week to paint the living room, the bedrooms, and the bathroom, because they could only pick at it in the evenings. True to form, Carole, who wouldn't ask Peggy to help, was moaning about the fact that Peggy wasn't helping.

Mary, splattered with paint, was on her knees trying to get paint drops off the hardwood. "Then ask her!"

"No. She'll come in here with her holier-than-thou attitude and tell me I'm doing it all wrong. She's not the only one who can decorate."

As things went on, Mary became concerned about her mother's colour choices, but her mom wasn't in a great mood, so Mary kept her mouth shut.

They finished the kitchen near midnight on a Saturday night and when it was dark, the yellow wasn't half bad. It was very bright and achieved the goal of getting rid of the gloomy atmosphere, but when the morning light streamed in through the windows, the redecorating project hit a snag.

Mary woke to her mother swearing loudly.

"What's wrong?"

"If you want to know, follow me."

Mary and Ethel put on their housecoats, and Mary helped her

grandmother up the stairs to the apartment. They walked into the newly painted kitchen.

"Can you believe this?" demanded Carole.

"It's like walking into a nuclear flash! You shoulda let Peggy pick the colour."

"Thanks, Ma. I can always count on you for an honest opinion." Carole turned on her heel and walked out of the apartment.

Mary looked at her Gran. "You shouldn't have said that."

"She must have got this paint from the highway department." They went back downstairs and Ethel called Peggy while Carole was in the bathroom. "Get the Jesus over here, quick."

"Why? What's wrong?"

"You'll see when you get here."

"Why didn't you tell me you were painting the apartment?" Peggy stood in the middle of the small kitchen with her hand shielding her eyes. It was worse than she expected. "There's no way this can be fixed without putting on several coats of primer and then a new paint colour. It might be easier to wallpaper over it." Before Carole could open her mouth, Peggy added, "And I'm picking it out, understand?"

"Be my guest. You can put it up yourself, too. I've got enough to do."

"Don't worry. Sheena can help me."

But when Peggy called Sheena, her daughter made it very clear she could not help; she was busy planning a wedding.

Peggy went back downstairs and sat glumly at her mother's kitchen table. She looked out of place in her pleated wool slacks, leather boots, and tweed blazer. Carole, Ethel, and Mary were still in their bathrobes. Peggy spied something across the room. "What is *that*?"

"That's Roscoe," said Mary.

"Sweet Jesus."

"I second that," Gran said. "He takes some getting used to."

Mary bent down and gave him a piece of cheese. "Ignore these mean women, Roscoe." She scratched behind his ears and he arched his back, purring with pleasure.

Peggy sighed. "Sheena doesn't want to wallpaper."

Carole stood by the toaster, waiting for it to pop. "Listen to yourself, for God's sake."

Mary poured her aunt a cup of coffee. "I'll help you."

Peggy gave her a small smile. "Thank you, dear."

Ethel pointed her finger at Peggy. "There's no way this child is going near that kitchen. Bad enough she helped her mother paint the whole apartment. Your brat could learn a thing or two from this little lady."

"Mom, I have no intention of letting Mary help me. And I don't appreciate you calling my daughter a brat."

"What else do you call someone who doesn't want to help their own kin?"

"Ethel," Carole snickered.

"Shut your pie hole!" Ethel shouted back.

Peggy put her hands over her ears. "Will you two stop for five minutes? Mary, I have no idea how you live with these two. I was lucky to escape at an early age. I recommend you do the same."

Mary poured herself a bowl of cereal. "I don't hear them anymore."

"Carole, are you burning my toast, or what?"

Carole checked the toast. It was burning, so she scraped off the black crumbs, put it on a plate, and plunked it in front of her mother and gave a small bow. "Your Highness."

Ethel rolled her eyes and buttered the toast. "Peggy, give me your cellphone."

Peggy passed it to her. Ethel looked at it and passed it back. "You have to be friggin' Houdini to figure out how to use these things now. Call Sheena for me."

Peggy punched in the numbers. "What are you going to say?"

"Never you mind." Ethel took a bite of toast while she waited for Sheena to pick up. "Hello, Sheena? It's Gran. Fine honey, how are you? Good, good. Listen, I want ya to get off your bum, get dressed, and come down here in a big fat hurry and help your mother buy some wallpaper and fix the upstairs kitchen. And I don't give a Jesus if ya like it or not. Hear me? Don't make me show up at your fiancé's fancy-shmancy house and drag you outta there, 'cause I will. Got that? Good. See ya in twenty minutes."

Ethel gave Peggy the phone. "Your generation is pathetic."

In the end, they all helped because Carole needed a tenant quickly. She was running out of dough.

"I can lend you some money," Peggy told her sister.

"I'd rather starve."

Peggy looked to the heavens.

Sheena was useless at putting up wallpaper and most of the time the other women just pushed her out of the way, but she didn't seem to notice or care. She was too busy talking.

"My friend did her wedding invitations herself. She picked up stuff at Staples and photocopied them. Can you imagine? Mine are going to be on thick, creamy paper with gold lettering. I was also thinking of a swan theme. Feathers are so hot right now. Or I'd like a full ball gown with beading on the top, added lace detail...and it has to be sleeveless with a sweetheart neckline. That, or maybe a form-fitting mermaid style or something with a dropped waist and lots of organza, or maybe even...."

She talked for ten minutes and didn't take a breath. Even her mother looked fed up after a while.

When the ladies were finished, they surveyed their work. The kitchen was normal again. It was time to advertise on Kijiji.

A day later, the horrible wallpaper episode behind her, Sheena hummed as she drove home from work in her Jeep. It had been a gift for her eighteenth birthday four years ago, so she needed a new one. Thankfully her soon-to-be father-in-law said he had just the ticket and would give her a great deal on a new one. Sheena was kind of hoping he might just give her one, but later thought that might be a bit greedy.

Drew worked for his dad and seemed to be just as car crazy. He and Sheena had met when Sheena took the Jeep in to get some work done. Drew was all over her in a matter of minutes. A very smooth operator but he was so darn cute, what could she do?

It seemed strange to think that if she'd received a different car for her birthday, she'd never have met Drew. Her Jeep was her lucky charm. She'd driven it to campus on her first day at Cape Breton University to study business, and drove it back home a week later to burst into tears at the supper table, informing her parents that she was going to kill herself if she had to go back.

Sheena knew her father was disappointed she wasn't going to be a college graduate, but oh well. It was her life, not his. She really didn't need a job if she was going to be married and looked after someday, the way her mother was. And besides, she liked working at La Senza in the mall; most of her paycheque went towards buying all the latest lingerie in the store. Her parents didn't make her pay for food or rent, so she had it made.

When she arrived home for supper, she was amazed to see her father at the dinner table. "Why are you here?"

"I live here." Ted cut into his pork chop.

Sheena sat down and Peggy immediately got up to fetch a plate of food for her.

"You never eat dinner with us."

"A slight exaggeration." Ted scooped a forkful of mashed potato. "How was your day?"

"Great. I asked Riley to be my maid of honour."

"Wait!" Peggy said, setting down the plate. "I thought Mary was going to be your maid of honour."

"No. She's not my sister."

"She's the closest thing you have to a sister. She's your family. I think she should at least be asked."

"Too late. Mary can be a bridesmaid."

"I wish you'd discussed it with me first. How am I going to tell Carole?"

"Aunt Carole won't care, and neither will Mary."

Ted cleared his throat. "It's been decided, Peggy. Leave it alone."

"I want them to feel included, that's all. They're the only family I have. At least Carole is doing your hair."

Sheena's fork clattered onto her plate. "Excuse me? Aunt Carole is *not* doing my hair. Kerrie at Halo Salon and Spa is doing my hair. She always does. She's fabulous."

"How am I going to explain to Carole that she's not styling the bridal party? She told me that was going to be your wedding gift."

"You say, 'Carole, you're not styling the bridal party.'"

Peggy tapped the table with her knife. "Oh, no. If you don't want your aunt to do your hair, you have to tell her."

Sheena looked at her dad. "Can you please tell Mom that since she was the one who got me into this mess, she's the one who should get me out?"

Ted sipped his wine. "She's got a point."

Peggy was incredulous. "Am I going to have no say in this wedding whatsoever? Your father and I are paying for it, missy. Not you."

"Mom! I'm the bride! You have to do what I say. Everyone knows that."

Ted put his hands up. "Enough already. I have something I want to discuss with you both."

"What's wrong?" Peggy asked.

"Nothing. An old university friend who's a member of Doctors Without Borders got in touch with me, asked if I'd like to take a sabbatical and join their organization on the road."

"For how long?"

"At least a year."

"A year!" Peggy sputtered. "Are you joking?"

"I'm dead serious."

"But what about my wedding?" Sheena moaned. "Don't you care about that?"

"Of course I care. I'll be home in plenty of time for the wedding."

"Wonderful," Peggy said. "So I'm supposed to do this all by myself?"

"You know full well the only thing you'd want me to do is hand over my credit cards. I can do that before I go."

"Is this dangerous?" Sheena asked.

"There are always risks, but I'm getting bored with my routine and thought this would be a challenge. I'm not getting any younger."

"Where would you go?"

"Uzbekistan."

"Is that a country?"

"Google it, Sheena."

Peggy looked dismayed. "Isn't that near Afghanistan? Are you crazy?"

"There's a terrible problem with drug-resistant TB in the country. My friend from school is living in Tashkent, and he assures me we'll be safe."

"So you're bored with your life. Who isn't? Your daughter and I aren't enough for you? Thanks a lot, Ted." Her eyes welled up.

Ted's ears began to redden. "Don't be ridiculous. It's got nothing to do with my family. It's my career that needs attention. I feel stale and old and uninterested. This will be the kick in the pants I need to remember why I became a doctor in the first place."

"As long as you come back to walk me down the aisle, I think it's kind of cool. You should go, Dad."

"Thanks, Sheena."

Ted reached over the table and took Peggy's hand. "I hope you'll give me your blessing. You and Sheena will be busy with the wedding and probably won't even notice I'm gone. You're always telling me I'm never around anyway, so what's the difference?"

Peggy wiped her eyes with a napkin. "You have to give me time to think about this. It's not every day your husband swans off for a year to the other side of the planet."

Ted smiled. "It'll be fine. You'll both have a great time here without me, and I'll be back before you know it. I'm leaving in two weeks."

"You complete bastard! You already knew you were going? How is that discussing something with me?"

"Please be happy for me, Peggy. It's the chance of a lifetime. A dream come true, if you will."

Peggy jumped up from the table. "This is how you operate. If I object now, I'm the dream-killer—the bad guy. Boy, you really had this all figured out, didn't you?"

She left the dining room.

Ted looked at his daughter. "Don't worry. She'll be all right."

Sheena made a face. "Ya think?"

Ethel was in Dotty's Dairy buying scratch tickets and shooting the breeze with Dotty, who, rumour had it, knew everything about everyone in Sydney. Her store was small and cramped and hot as blue blazes because she was a thin woman with no meat on her bones. She always wore three sweaters and perched on her stool by the cash machine, seeming never to move all day. She'd point at things people were looking for and kept a baseball bat handy to knock the lights out of anyone she found shoplifting.

Ethel gathered up her tickets. "So my granddaughter is getting married to Chuck Corbett's son. You know him?"

"He owns some car dealerships, doesn't he?"

"Yeah. Apparently his wife is cheating on him."

Dotty dismissed Ethel with a wave of her hand. "Girl, they're all cheating on each other these days. It makes my head spin. You wouldn't believe what I see on a daily basis. Carrying on as if I didn't have eyes. If you ask me, computers are to blame."

"Computers?"

"They hook up with each other over the internet. They don't even need to be in the same room to have sex anymore!"

"That's a good thing if you ask me. See ya later."

"Yep. See ya."

Peggy had a hard time dealing with Ted's decision. She found herself going to Carole's to hash it out a week later. It was the middle of the day so Carole was busy, but Peggy really needed someone to talk to.

Carole's salon was like something out of an old movie set. The pictures of hair styles she'd put up in the early nineties when she first opened were still there in all their curly, overdone glory, the corners peeling upward. The fashion magazines littering the table were just as outdated. The ancient hair dryer's leather seat had cracked open years before, but Carole had simply put a cushion on it and no one was the wiser. Her workspace was a cluttered mess, and even in here there were overflowing ashtrays. Peggy couldn't understand why Carole's clients didn't complain, but then most of them probably smoked as well. The worst thing was Carole's mirror: its frame was crowded with ticket stubs, yellowing Polaroids, thank-you notes, and receipts. With every passing year, the window of reflective glass became smaller and smaller.

Peggy was pleasantly surprised that Carole was free when she arrived. She was in the salon doing their mother's hair. Ethel always insisted on using her old, grey, metal curlers with pink plastic pins. She didn't believe in curling irons, said they were the work of the devil.

Peggy plunked herself down on the small loveseat in the corner of the salon. She always forgot what side the broken spring was on and inevitably sat on that side first. She quickly shifted to the other side and let out a huge sigh.

Carole glanced at her, a cigarette stuck in the side of her mouth. "I know that sound. What's wrong now?"

"Ted's leaving me."

Carole's mouth dropped open, causing the cigarette to fall on the floor. She stepped on it and ground it into the hardwood. "Fuck off!"

"Watch your mouth, Carole," Ethel sputtered before turning around to face Peggy. "What the fuck is wrong with him? Has he got another woman? They all do, according to Dotty."

"That didn't come out right. Ted isn't *leaving me*, leaving me; he's leaving me for a year to go and work in a medical clinic overseas."

"Oh, is that all?" Ethel turned to face the mirror once more.

Carole picked up another curler. "So let me get this straight. You still have the house, the cottage in Ben Eoin, the luxury car, his income, his pension, his credit cards, and his bank accounts? Plus no husband to look after for a year?"

"It's not that simple, you know. I'm not used to being on my own, and I don't want to tell anyone because they'll think this is the beginning of the end of our marriage. Not that I blame them. I don't know of any other husband packing his bags and leaving his family behind. Maybe this is just a convenient way to get rid of me and Sheena."

"Maybe he's gay," Ethel offered. "Dotty says everyone's gay now."

"Who is this Dotty you keep yammering about?" asked Peggy. "Is she some sort of fortune teller?"

"She owns Dotty's Dairy next door."

"The woman who never gets off her stool? Well, she must have a unique perspective on life, seeing as how she's travelled the globe and back."

Ethel shook her finger at Peggy. "Don't be fooled. That woman can tell you a lot. She sees it all and she hears it all. A know-it-all from way back."

"I don't care about Dotty. I'm concerned about my husband. What if he doesn't love me anymore? What if there's someone else?"

Carole pinned the last curler in her mother's wispy hair. "Now you're being ridiculous."

"Of course you are," Ethel agreed. "Who'd want to be with Ted? He's a snooze."

Peggy's shoulders slumped. "Why do I come here?"

Carole lit up a smoke and sat under the hair dryer, since her mother was still in the chair. "I think it's great news. You and Sheena can plan the biggest wedding in history. Your husband isn't here telling you not to. What wife ever gets that lucky?"

"That's a good point."

"You should be grateful for what you've got, instead of snivelling about what you don't," Ethel said. "Carole has wanted to be you for years."

"Shut up, Ma!"

"Well, it's true, ain't it? Ya moan all day about her."

"I do not."

Peggy held up her hand. "Stop, Mom. Carole isn't like that."

"Wanna bet?"

Desperate to change the subject, Peggy pressed on. "I have to tell you something else."

Both Carole and Ethel waited.

"Sheena's asked her best friend, Riley, to be her maid of honour, but wants Mary to be a bridesmaid. I hope that's okay?"

Carole nodded slowly. "Well, I thought family would come first, but whatever."

"And another thing." It spilled out in a rush. "It's my own fault, I didn't check with Sheena first. She's having Kerrie from Halo Salon and Spa do her hair. And the whole bridal party's. I'm really sorry."

Carole nodded again and took a long drag from her cigarette. "Not good enough for her, is that it?"

"Sheena would be more comfortable with someone she's familiar with on her wedding day."

"I used to change her diapers."

Peggy wrung her hands. "I know. I'm sorry."

"It's not your fault."

"It sure as hell is," Ethel piped up. "You've spoiled that girl since the day she was born. You need your head read."

"Speaking of the wedding," Carole said, "how do you want me to do your hair? In an up-do?"

"Oh, I've made an appointment with Sheila at Vallie's in Glace Bay. She's amazing. We'll decide the style once I have my dress."

Carole stared at Peggy. "Get out of my house, you snivelling snot."

Peggy packed Ted's trousers between tissue paper to keep them from wrinkling.

"As if I'm going to have tissue paper floating out of my suitcase when I unpack." He said, unceremoniously pulling the offending material out.

"I can't believe you did that!"

"I'm not worried about wrinkled pants. Will you please let me pack my own luggage?"

Peggy threw his shaving kit on the bed and sat in her reading chair. "Fine. Don't blame me if you forget dental floss. And by the way, you can save space if you roll your socks up and stuff them in your shoes."

Ted looked like he was about to object but then stopped. "That's actually a good idea."

"I do have some from time to time."

Ted walked over and pulled Peggy out of the chair, taking her in his arms. "Thank you for agreeing to this."

"Technically I had no choice." She began to whine. "This is all very scary for me."

"You'll be fine. You're not adrift in the Atlantic. And I'll Skype often."

Peggy reached for the ever-present tissue up her sleeve. "Are you going to miss me?"

"Of course I'll miss you. Especially on your birthday, my birthday, and our anniversary."

She pushed him away. "Don't give me that. You have sex more than three times a year."

"I do?"

"It helps if you stay awake, Ted."

There were genuine tears at the airport between all three of them when it came time for Ted to go through security.

"I'll miss you, Daddy! Make sure you come back to walk me down the aisle! I don't want Mom. That would look stupid."

"I wouldn't miss it for the world."

Peggy and Sheena waited until they saw him walk onto the plane from the airport window. He turned around and blew them a final kiss. They waved and waved.

And then he was gone. They looked at each other.

"What now?" Peggy said.

"Let's go to East Side Mario's. Daddy never wants to eat there."

"Okay."

At dinner, they realized they could go out to eat every night if they wanted to. That cheered them up immensely.

"Where should we eat tomorrow?" Peggy passed Sheena a mint as she paid the bill.

"Drew and I have plans for tomorrow."

"Okay…how about the next night?"

"We're busy."

Peggy pulled on her gloves as they exited the restaurant. "So in actual fact, we won't be having dinner out every night."

"I might be. Just not with you."

"And so it begins," Peggy sighed. "The next year spent all by my lonesome."

Sheena grabbed her mother's arm as they trudged through the snow-covered parking lot. "Don't say that. We'll have lots of fun."

The fun started five minutes later when they couldn't seem to get the car to move properly. They jerked their way towards the exit.

"There is definitely something wrong with the car," Peggy said. "Why is it thrashing about like this?"

"How do I know? It's brand new, isn't it?"

"Get out and look."

"Why me?"

"Because you're younger than I am. Now move!"

Sheena got out of the car, walked around it, and shrugged. Peggy lowered her window and a cold rush of air didn't improve her mood.

"Well?"

"Everything looks fine to me."

Peggy realized that meant nothing. She put the window up and got out of the car herself. She walked around the vehicle and peered at her tires. "How can you tell if your tire is low?"

Sheena stamped her feet and rubbed her mitts together. "Don't ask me."

"Trust your father to leave town just when we need him. What should we do?"

"Call CAA."

"Good idea." Peggy went to open the car door, but it was locked. "*Shit*. I locked the keys in the car! I can't get my phone! Where's yours?"

"In my purse in the car! I can't believe this. It's freaking cold."

"What now?"

"I'll run into the mall and get Riley to call CAA for us."

"Good idea. Hurry up!"

While Peggy waited for help, she grew more resentful of Ted leaving her during a Canadian winter. It was downright inconsiderate, stranding them in the Mayflower Mall parking lot like this. She rehearsed what she'd say to him when he called.

Sheena came running back holding two Tim Hortons coffees. "I had change in my pocket. They're going to be here in a few minutes."

"You darling girl!"

When the tow truck arrived, they opened the locked door and then informed the women that they had a flat tire.

"Thanks a lot, Ted!" Peggy wailed.

"It's not *his* fault," Sheena said.

"It is so! Everything is his fault from now on."

Sheena went to Drew's house the next day to mope about her dad being gone. Maxine opened the door and looked annoyed to see her.

"Hello, Sheena. Drew isn't here."

"He's supposed to be here. He asked me to come over."

"I sent him to the store."

They stood like that for a few seconds. Finally, Sheena said, "Well, can I wait for him?"

"I suppose so."

Maxine didn't move, so Sheena had to slink by her to gain access to the house. If the situation were reversed, Drew would already be sitting on the recliner at Sheena's house with a bag of chips and a pop in his hand.

"You can wait in there." Maxine pointed to the living room. "If you'll excuse me, I'm rather busy."

"Oh, sure." But his mom didn't hear her. She was already gone.

Sheena looked around the room. It was completely different from her house. Sleek. She decided she didn't like it very much and hoped Drew wouldn't want their place to look like this; there was no warmth or comfort here.

Eventually, Drew came home and they headed for the ultra-modern kitchen, where he made them both a plate of tacos. They sat at the island and Sheena told him about seeing her dad off at the airport.

"This whole trip is kind of weird, isn't it?" he asked.

"He's helping people. What's weird is your mom not even sitting with me until you came home."

"Don't start. My mom is the way she is."

"She doesn't like me."

"She doesn't like anyone."

In between bites Sheena moved her hand under the light shining from above to make her ring glitter.

"I love my ring."

"No kidding."

"Don't be mean. You should be flattered I'm so in love with it."

Drew wiped his hands on a napkin. "I'm glad you like it, but you talk about it constantly."

"What a grumpy bear. What should we talk about then?"

"Anything but the wedding."

Sheena leaned back. "I don't understand why you have such an aversion to talking about *our* wedding. It's like you're not even interested. It makes no sense to me."

Drew took a swig of Coke. "Look, Sheena, most guys are just happy to let their girls plan things, and I'm one of those guys. Just tell me when and where, and I'll be there. I'm not interested in making decisions about colours and table settings and cake flavours. I know whatever you decide will be great. I trust you."

Fingering her ring, Sheena frowned. "I just wanted you to be more involved."

"Okay, okay. What do you want me to decide?"

"Should we have an indoor wedding or an outdoor wedding?"

"Indoor."

"Are you sure? It would be so nice to be by the water on a summer day, and the pictures would be awesome."

"Fine. Outdoor."

"How many people should we invite?"

"I want a small wedding. Fifty, maybe."

"Fifty! I have fifty girlfriends alone. I was thinking about two hundred and fifty."

"Whatever you want." Drew threw his pop can in the kitchen sink.

"Should we have a cocktail party beforehand and then the sit-down dinner and dance?"

"I thought you said we'd be outside."

"Not for the whole night!"

"We don't need a cocktail party."

"I'm thinking a cocktail party would be good because we'd be off getting our pictures done and the guests can mill around with drinks and canapés while they wait."

Drew crossed his arms. "Is there anything else I can help you with?"

"What do you want for party favours?"

"What's that?"

"A small gift left at the place settings. Something the guests can take home."

"My brother had matches done with their names on it. Is that what you mean?"

"Oh God. Nothing that tacky. I thought we could have small ornate picture frames. And speaking of cake flavours, what's your favourite?"

"Chocolate."

"I thought a carrot cake with cream cheese icing, or maybe even a coconut flavour. Should it be a three- or five-tier cake?"

"Three."

"Five it is."

Unbeknownst to Drew and Sheena, Maxine was now standing in the doorway listening to this exchange. "Just as I thought. This marriage is going to last."

They both turned their heads at the sound of her voice.

"Mom," Drew said with a warning tone. "Leave it."

"What's that supposed to mean?" Sheena said.

Maxine walked over to the stove. "It means I don't think you two have thought this marriage through. Why the hurry? Marriage is the shits at the best of times...."

"Mom!"

"I'm sorry you're so unhappy Mrs. Corbett, but that's not how we're going to feel about it."

"We'll see."

"I have to go," said Sheena. "Are you coming, Drew?"

"Drew is helping me clean the attic."

"I am?"

His mother gave him a look.

"I better stay here."

Sheena felt tears coming on. "Okay. Have fun." She rushed out of the kitchen, grabbed her coat, and flew out the door.

CHAPTER THREE

MARY HAD A LONG DAY. Government cheques were out and that meant the grocery stores were beyond busy. To amuse herself, Mary took note of what people were eating. It always matched up to what they were wearing and how they carried themselves. The puffy white people always ate puffy white things like bread, chips, and starchy potatoes. The tight, tall people had a garden of veggies at the register and sometimes looked anxious, as if they had forgotten the bok choy or juicing greens on their lists. The people who ate their total grocery order in the car always looked guilty and made jokes about how they were sent on an ice cream run or were stocking up for a birthday party.

Uh-huh.

But Mary loved them. All these people doing what they had to, to get through the day. Everyone worrying about something, distracted and tired, sad or cheerful. Most of them blending in with each other, until you talked to them. Amazing what happened when you smiled at someone.

Mary always took the time to verbalize her thoughts: "I love your coat." "What a sweet baby." "Your hair looks lovely." Old ladies really loved when she said things like that. They all called her "dear" and "honey." It made the day better for everyone. On days like this, Mary missed Mrs. Aucoin.

Today, her favourite customer came through. She was just a bit younger than Mary's mom and was always happy, always horsing around with her teenagers when they were with her. What you noticed about her first was her smile, and then her bright lipstick and crazy, outlandish shoes. Mary wanted to be this woman when she grew up. They had pleasant exchanges, and the woman even commented on Mary's freckles, telling her they came from fairy dust.

"You'll be glad of them when you're older," she grinned one day. "Women with freckles don't seem to get as wrinkly."

Mary's day wasn't over when she got home. Two people had made appointments to see the apartment after work, and her mother didn't want the hassle of interviewing anyone, so she left that job to the youngest in the family.

"You know the drill: no winos, drug dealers, or perverts."

Mary ate her last bite of tuna sandwich. "How am I supposed to figure out who's a pervert?"

Her mom crushed out her cigarette in the overflowing ashtray. "They have shifty eyes. Everyone knows that."

"You watch too much television."

"And make sure they ain't holy rollers!" Gran shouted from the living room. "Nothing gets rid of them pests."

Was it possible Mary's stork got the wrong address? Why did she belong to these people?

The first person asking about the apartment was obviously a wino, drug dealer, and pervert all rolled into one. Mary told him she'd get back to him.

When the doorbell rang a second time, Mary was on edge. *Please let it be a nice old lady.* Instead it was a young man with long hair pulled back in a bun and a backpack slung over his shoulder. He looked like he'd slept in his car. A very dour young woman was at his side, looking like she'd rather be elsewhere.

"Hi. Mary?" He smiled.

"Yes. How do you know my name?"

"My grandmother knew you very well…Mrs. Aucoin. I'm Daniel Hennessy."

Mary took a step back before she stuck out her hand and shook his. "Oh my goodness. I loved your grandmother."

"I know. She talked a lot about you. My mother pointed you out to me at the funeral, but you were gone before I had a chance to thank you…you know…for being there."

"I felt so helpless."

"I can imagine."

The girl beside him sighed. "Is this Old Home Week?"

"Oh, sorry. This is my girlfriend, Amber."

Mary smiled. "Nice to meet you."

"Yeah."

"Please come in," said Mary.

They stepped into the porch, which was very small. The first thing Mary noticed was how good Daniel smelled, despite his rumpled appearance. She stammered, "Are you thinking of renting this place? Silly question. I guess you are if you're here."

"We've decided to move in together to save on rent. This was the first place I thought of."

"Come up and I'll show you around." Mary started up the stairs and realized she was wearing her old ratty sweater that made her look like a butterball. Amber was in skinny leather pants.

The pair followed her upstairs. "I do know what it looks like. I use to visit BeaBea—that's what I called her—but not as much as I should have…and now it's too late."

As they walked through the apartment, Mary wanted him to feel better, because he looked increasingly guilty and sad. "Mrs. Aucoin always said she had the best grandchildren and great-grandchildren in the world…that she had so many she forgot their names!"

He smiled. "That sounds like something she'd say."

"This place is a bit of a dump." Amber wandered around the kitchen. "What's the rent?"

"It's seven hundred, nothing included."

Daniel frowned. "It's not a dump; it's clean. My grandmother was happy here."

"I am not your grandmother."

Mary looked at Amber, trying to figure out what Daniel saw in this girl. "Why don't I leave you two alone to discuss things? I'll be downstairs."

She waited on the last step inside the front door. Mary heard them wander around. Amber did all the talking. As nice as it would be to have one of Mrs. Aucoin's relatives upstairs, she wasn't sure about the girlfriend. Still: money was money.

The couple eventually trooped downstairs and said they'd take it. They gave her two months' rent in cash, and a security deposit besides. They looked like the last people who would be carrying large wads of cash.

Mary shook Daniel's hand. "I look forward to seeing you again soon."

Amber glared at her. "He's taken."

"I know that...." Mary gulped.

Daniel steered Amber down off the porch. "See ya."

Mary decided she didn't like Amber, so when her mom and Gran asked her how it went, she said, "The girl thinks it's a dump."

"A dump! The nerve!" Carole shouted. "Where is she?"

"They left." Mary showed them the fistful of money. "But they're taking it."

Gran grabbed the money out of Mary's hand. Carole grabbed it back.

"And get this. The guy, Daniel Hennessy, is Mrs. Aucoin's grandson."

"You mean to tell me he's related to that jackass son of hers?" Gran grumbled. "I thought we finally got rid of that guy."

"What does Daniel do?" Carole asked.

"I don't have a clue. Don't know what she does either. Maybe they rob banks. It would explain the money."

"Hope they aren't drug dealers," Carole said.

"If they are, it'll be really convenient for me, won't it? Nighty-night."

One afternoon a few weeks later, Drew showed up at Sheena's house unannounced. She was delighted to see him. She'd forgiven him for the fiasco at his house. "I thought you were at work."

Drew took her hand and led her into the comfy family room. "Is your mom home?"

"No."

"Good."

She put her arms around his neck. "Is that...an invitation?"

He smiled. "Not yet. A much bigger surprise! I have to move to Halifax. Can we move the wedding date up? Say to the first of April?"

Sheena's eyes went wide with horror. "What the—"

Drew shook her shoulders in excitement. "Dad wants me to run the new dealership there, and it's an opportunity I can't turn down. I thought he'd be asking my older brother, but he wants me. It's for our future, babe."

"You mean the venues I've booked for next summer are going to have to be cancelled?"

"I guess."

"And how do you know I want to move to Halifax? Did you even ask me first?"

Drew looked puzzled. "Doesn't everyone want to get out of here? It's Halifax."

Sheena wiggled out of his embrace and stared at him. "I'm supposed to leave my life and ride off into the sunset with you?"

"That's what getting married is all about. You planned on leaving your parents to live with me. What difference does it make if it's here or there?"

"It's like starting over! I could kill you!"

Drew put his hand through his hair and gave her an incredulous look. "You know, I was stoked about this promotion. Keep the wedding as it is, then, since that's the only thing you're concerned about," he said, his voice rising. "I'll go live in Halifax for the year and you can stay here. How's that sound?"

Sheena put her hands on her hips. "Stop being such a jerk! You can't just come in here and expect me to be happy," she said desperately. "You have to give me time to think about it."

"You can think about it all you want. I'm going."

"Going where?"

"To get a two-four. After that I'm going to Halifax." Drew banged the front door as he left. Sheena picked up a Dalton figurine and threw it against the wall. When it shattered, she began to sob. Everything was ruined. By the time her mom came home and found her in the kitchen, her eyes were bloodshot and her face blotchy.

Peggy dropped her parcels on the floor. "What's wrong? Is it Daddy?"

"Drew wants the wedding in six weeks! He's moving to Halifax with or without me! He has to run his dad's new dealership."

"Is he out of his mind? We're never going to get a venue on such short notice! What are we supposed to do about the reception?"

"I have no clue. Have it here?"

"Here?" Peggy reached over and put her hand on Sheena's forehead. "You're delirious."

Sheena swatted her mother's hand away. "Mother, I'm as upset as you are, but if I want a wedding it looks like I have no choice. We'll invite fewer people. I suppose it doesn't matter where I am. Everyone's going to be looking at me anyway, whether it's at the Keltic Lodge or here."

Peggy was speechless. And then she wasn't.

"You've waited your whole life to plan your wedding and suddenly you're doing it on the fly? This is worse than if you eloped! Oh, my God. Someone stick a knife in me. I'm done!"

Sheena turned away and stomped up to her bedroom and slammed the door. She threw herself on the bed and groaned.

Peggy stewed in the kitchen. She picked up the phone to call Ted at his office and then remembered he wasn't there. *Goddammit.* She tore up the stairs and barged into Sheena's room without knocking. "You can't have it in six weeks. Your father won't be here to walk you down the aisle."

Sheena sat up. "Can't he fly home for a few days?"

Peggy smacked her own forehead. "He's signed a contract, you silly girl. He can't just leave at a moment's notice. And then there's the other thing."

"What other thing?"

"I didn't want to worry you. There's something going on between the rebels and local authorities. I don't know all the details."

"Oh, my God. Is he being held hostage?"

"No! This sort of thing happens all the time. Your father said he'd be quite safe at the clinic until things calm down."

"And when will that be?"

Peggy threw her hands in the air. "Who knows! The rebels certainly aren't interested in your wedding and whether your dad makes it here or not. They have more pressing things to worry about, like overthrowing the government."

Sheena flopped back on the bed. "This is a catastrophe."

Her mother dropped down beside her. "I've just thought of something else. What about your dress? You told me alterations could take months."

"I'll buy one off the rack."

"This from the girl who had wedding dress cakes for all her birthday parties?"

"Mom, you're going to have to suck it up. And I guess you'll have to walk me down the aisle too."

Peggy shook her head. "I can't believe you're doing this to me. All my hopes and dreams are dashed."

Sheena turned around and grabbed her mother's shoulders. "This is *my* wedding. It's not yours!"

"It's not only *yours* either!"

"Look, can't you see I'm upset? I need your support, Mom. I can't do this if you're shouting!"

Peggy got off the bed and went to the window. "Why the sudden change? His father knew about the wedding at Christmas. He never mentioned the possibility of Drew moving."

"I have a terrible feeling his mother had something to do with this. She doesn't like me. She never even talked to me when I was there waiting for Drew. She just turned her nose up and left the room."

"That miserable woman. Who does she think she is? I'm not putting up with this." She left the bedroom and went to get her cellphone. "What's Drew's number?"

Sheena ran after her. "No, you can't call her! I'd be mortified! Don't you dare let her know this bothers us. That's what she wants. Once Drew and I are married, I never have to see the woman again."

"That's a bit unrealistic, sweetheart. When you marry the man, you marry the family."

"We never see Dad's family."

"Well, they're idiots."

Peggy had to take her mother to the doctor; Carole was busy with clients. At least, that's what Carole always said, but never mind. Peggy's long-standing guilt about her sister taking care of their mother surfaced about once a month. Today was one of those days.

Her mother was waiting in the kitchen with her coat and hat on. "Where were you? We're going to be late."

Carole showed up at the kitchen door with a bottle of Fanci-full hair dye in her hand. "I hope you two will be awhile. Take her to lunch or something. I need a break from her nibs."

Peggy put out her hand for her mother to lean on. "Do you need anything in town, Carole?"

"I need a tummy tuck." She disappeared back into the salon.

As Peggy escorted her mom to the car, she realized with a pang that her mother was getting smaller all the time. She had never taken care of herself, and it was a miracle she was still alive. But because she was, Peggy felt reassured. Didn't matter that Ethel was an alcoholic and as lazy as sin.

As they waited in the crowded doctor's office, Peggy told her mother about Sheena's fiasco. "So the plans have suddenly changed."

"Ya know his mother's against the wedding. Sounds like she convinced hubby to do something about it. I bet she thinks Sheena won't want to go to Halifax and she'll call the wedding off. Poor misguided fool. If only she knew Sheena'd get married in the midst of a tsunami."

"Why do you insist on making snide remarks about Sheena? She's your granddaughter."

Ethel patted Peggy's hand. "I love the kid. It's not her fault. It's yours."

Mothers. God.

Fortunately, Ethel turned her attention to the old lady sitting next to her. As they discussed their various ailments, Peggy tuned out. *Is this what life will be like in twenty-five years?* She wondered. *Comparing ointments for toe fungus?* And now that Sheena was moving away, what would Peggy do? Life just seemed to be a blank space stretching into the future. All at once, Peggy knew she was going to cry. Right here in front of all these strangers, and even worse: in front of her mom. She jumped up.

"Where the hell are ya goin'?" Ethel demanded. "You need to come into the doc's office with me so you'll remember what he says."

"It doesn't matter, Mom. You never listen to him anyway. I'll be right back."

Once locked inside the bathroom, Peggy let her tears fall silently into the sink. Good lord. What was she going to do? A husband who didn't want to be home with her, a daughter who was moving away, a mother who was a temperamental souse, and a sister who moaned and bitched about everything. Right now, Mary was the only person Peggy liked.

Peggy powdered her nose and under her eyes before heading back out. The doctor said what he always said: Ethel's health was not good. She had high blood pressure and high cholesterol and was borderline malnourished.

"Are you a tea and toast kind of person, Ethel?" he asked. "That kind of diet isn't doing you any favours."

"Malnourished? Since when?" Peggy felt like this was a slight on her. "What are you eating, Mom?"

"What I always eat: Kraft Dinner and hot dogs."

"Perhaps you can persuade your mom to spruce up her diet. She also needs to be on Ensure. I'll write a prescription for vitamins."

"I'll do my best, Doctor, but my mother doesn't live with me. It's hard to control her eating habits from across town."

The doctor handed her the prescription. "Try."

Great. Now she was being reprimanded by a snotty youngster. What a dreadful day.

It became worse when she tried to get Ethel to eat a healthy lunch. Peggy took her to Wentworth Perk, hoping the delicious food would entice her, but she was worse than a toddler. "It's a salad, Mom. You're supposed to eat things like this."

"Looks like my front lawn on a plate. It's all bullshit. I can eat what I want, and I want cheesecake and a brownie."

Peggy ended up ordering two slices of cheesecake and two brownies with their tea. It helped a lot.

When Mary got home, she was in for a surprise. Aunt Peggy and Sheena were sitting with Mom and Gran. Boxes of Chinese food littered the kitchen table. Mary was starving, so this was good news. She grabbed a plate and tucked in, but not before giving Roscoe some choice pieces of chicken.

"Why are you guys here?"

"I have to get married in six weeks. Drew and I are moving to Halifax."

Mary stared. "And everyone is okay with this? I thought—"

"Don't say it," Sheena said. "I know it's too soon and I *really* don't want to move to Halifax, but I have no choice."

Mary thought she was hearing things. "And everyone is all right with this?"

"Of course we're not all right with it," Peggy almost shouted. "But since this is what Sheena wants, this is what we'll do."

"But she just said she didn't want to go to Halifax," said Mary, looking around the room for clarification. "How is this doing what she wants?"

Carole lit a cigarette and shook her head. "Don't try and talk to them, Mary. You can't make any sense out of either of them. I think it's insane, but no one's listening to me."

Mary reached for another egg roll. "What does your dad say about this?"

"He doesn't know." Sheena looked at her plate. "I'm not sure I should tell him. I should just let him come home and find me married and gone. Since he can't leave, there's no sense in upsetting him until he gets back."

Ethel grunted her disgust. "Just call the wedding off. It was doomed from the start anyway."

"Thanks a lot, Gran." Sheena stood up. "It's hard enough to make these changes without having my family tell me what a disaster it is. I'm in love with the guy. What's wrong with that?"

"Are you sure you're in love with him? I'm not going through this if it's not for life," Peggy said.

"Of course I am, Mom, God! I have to go." She grabbed the car keys and her coat and was out the door before anyone could object.

"Great, now I need a ride home." Peggy burst into tears and ran to the bathroom.

Ethel leaned over the won ton soup to Carole. "She's going through The Change. That's the only explanation."

"I'll go talk to her." Carole left the table.

"Aren't you eating anything, Gran?" asked Mary.

"Nah, this stuff reminds me of worms and maggots."

Suddenly Mary wasn't very hungry.

Only when the dishes were done did Carole and Peggy emerge from the bathroom. Peggy looked much better, so whatever her sister said to her must have helped. It was at times like this that Mary wished she had a sister to talk to. She did have Sheena, but listening wasn't exactly Sheena's forte.

"I better get back home," sniffed Peggy. "Sorry to be such a mess."

"Do you want me to drive you, Aunt Peggy?" offered Mary. "It's no problem."

"Call Sheena and tell her to get back here with the car," Ethel said.

"I don't want to talk to her right now, Mom. I just want to get home and take a nice hot bath. Thank you, sweetheart, it would be great if you gave me a lift."

While Mary got her coat and boots on, Aunt Peggy said her farewells. When they got outside, there was a skim of snow on the back steps and the car.

"Are we supposed to get more snow?" Aunt Peggy worried. "I hate Sheena driving in this weather."

"I don't think so. Watch your step."

Peggy didn't say much on the drive home, so Mary prattled on about how she was saving up for contact lenses. "I suppose it's vain, but I'm sick of wearing glasses. They always fog up in our house. Mom's too cheap to put in proper ventilation."

"I've bugged her about that for years. The place is rotting under the wallpaper. And no, it's not vain to want to get rid of your glasses." Peggy reached out and touched Mary's knee. "Let me help you with that. Just don't tell your mother."

"I can't let you—"

"You can and you will. You're a wonderful girl, Mary, and I'd like to do something to show you how much I appreciate everything you do for me."

"Thanks, Aunt Peggy."

Mary gunned the car up the driveway and made it to the top of the hill. She kissed her aunt goodbye, waited until she got in the house, and headed back down the driveway.

Peggy let out a big sigh in the foyer. She needed a bath to revive herself before Sheena came home. Maybe then they could talk like civilized adults. But at that moment she remembered she wanted to give Mary some money, so she ran out the door only to see Mary's car heading up the road.

"Damn." She turned back on her heel and felt everything drop away underneath her. She landed on her back and arm. There was a snap. She couldn't scream in pain because the fall had knocked the wind out of her.

As she lay in the cold and dark, it dawned on her that no one knew she was out here. Who knew what time Sheena would get home. Peggy might freeze to death before help arrived. Great. Now she'd even miss the pathetic wedding her daughter was planning. Someone up in the sky must really hate her guts.

"Help!" she squeaked. "Someone help me!"

Total silence.

"Thanks a lot, Ted!"

Realizing that blaming a husband several thousand kilometres away was not going to bring results, she set her sights on the front door. Luckily it was still open. If only she could crawl over and grab her cell out of her purse. She tried to move her arm but it lay there like a broken toy. Naturally, it was her right arm. Goddammit.

Then she tried to slide herself on her back towards the door, but the pain was terrible. She was probably damaging the damage she'd already done. But it couldn't be helped. And she had moved a few inches, so she held her breath and tried again. At this rate she'd get to the door by midnight.

Sheena and Drew went to the early show, just so both of them could be out of their respective houses. They stopped for a burger afterwards and sulked as they ate their fries.

"Why don't we just elope?" Drew suggested. "No one is happy about anything, so what's the point?"

Sheena levelled a fry at him. "The point is I would like some kind of wedding, even if it's a disaster! And I don't want your mother to win, quite frankly. I know she hates me but too damn bad."

"Why don't we just live together? We'll look for an apartment and that will be it."

"Did you not hear me? I want the frigging wedding. Is that too much to ask?"

Drew put his hands up. "Fine. Jeez. Just don't expect anything from my mother. Dad doesn't care one way or the other. He still says he'll supply the cars."

"So you keep saying, but who needs cars at this point? What do we do with them?"

"Don't ask me."

"So we have six weeks."

"Yep. I start work after that. We can stay with my oldest brother in Halifax while we look for an apartment."

"What a fun honeymoon that will be," she said sarcastically. She backpedalled when she saw his look. "Never mind. We'll make it work. Do you love me?"

"Sure."

Sheena was dissatisfied with this response but decided to ignore it. Why start another argument?

When Sheena drove up the driveway a little while later, she wondered why the front door was open. Then she wondered what the lump was on the pavement. When her mother's head popped up, Sheena screamed. In her panic, she put her foot on the gas. She realized her mistake when her mother held up one arm to feebly ward off the Jeep gunning towards her. Sheena slammed on the brakes and jumped out, forgetting to put it in park. The Jeep started to roll backwards.

"Sheena!" Her mom pointed.

Sheena looked around and watched her vehicle careen down the driveway and collide with the big fir tree on their property.

"Oh, my God!"

"Never mind that now! Come and save me!"

"Mommy! What's wrong? What happened?" She bent down and noticed her mother's frozen eyelashes. "You're freezing! I'll go get a blanket!"

"Where the hell were you?" Peggy demanded.

Sheena ignored her and ran into the family room. She looked around wildly and grabbed the same throw they'd used for Gran at Christmastime. She ran back outside and covered her mom. "We need to call 911."

"Just pull me in the house!"

Against her better judgment, Sheena hooked her arms under her mother's armpits, but the minute she tried to pull with any force, her mom screamed.

"Forget this," Sheena said. "I'm calling 911."

"Damn it." Peggy shivered. "I have my old bra on."

"No one gives a shit about your bra."

The ambulance arrived about five minutes later and while they got Peggy on a gurney, Sheena ran down the hill and turned off her Jeep. There was a lot of damage to the back bumper, but there was nothing she could do about it now. She hurried back up to the house and collected her mother's purse, then locked the front door and crawled into the back of the ambulance with her mom.

As they drove, Sheena held her mother's hand. "What happened?"

"What happened was that you decided to leave with the car and Mary had to drive me home."

"Didn't she wait until you got inside the house?"

"She did, as a matter of fact, but I ran out to call her back and slipped. She didn't see me. Call Carole and tell her to meet us at the hospital."

"But I'm with you."

"Just do it!"

Mary, Carole, and Sheena sat in the waiting room for two hours before they were allowed to see Peggy. Mary felt dreadful, Carole was annoyed at Sheena, and Sheena was fretting about her mother and the Jeep.

"If you mention that goddamn Jeep one more time, I'll smack you."

"I'm allowed to worry, Aunt Carole. I need it to go to work. I can't drive Mom's car; it's a stick shift. Why she needed a standard, I'll never know."

The nurse finally motioned them into the outpatients' department. She brought them to an examining room. Peggy lay on the table, looking like hell. Her arm was already in a cast.

"Oh, Aunt Peggy, I feel terrible!" Mary said immediately.

"It wasn't your fault, Mary. I ran out to call you back and slipped. It was a foolish thing to do."

Carole stated the obvious: "So you broke your arm. It could've been your neck. How long were you out there?"

"Seemed like forever."

Everyone looked at Sheena.

"I'm sorry! How was I supposed to know she was lying outside? We were at a movie."

At that point the doctor showed up. "Well, Mrs. Henderson," she said, "it looks like, in addition to your broken arm, you also slipped a disc in your back."

"Wonderful. What does that mean?"

"It means you'll be laid up in bed for six weeks."

Peggy and Sheena screamed together and startled the poor man. "Six weeks! Are you kidding me? I can't be in bed for six weeks. My daughter is getting married in six weeks. This cannot be happening!"

"I'm sure this is distressing, but I think you'll agree that any more damage to your back will make you one sorry lady. Once this kind of thing happens, you might always have trouble with your back, especially when you carry extra weight. You have to be careful. Your health is more important than a wedding."

"It's not, as it happens!" cried Peggy. "Oh, go away." She dismissed the doctor with a wave of her good arm.

The doctor looked incredulous, but she turned and left.

Sheena collapsed into the nearest chair and moaned. "I can't believe it. Daddy's gone. Mom will be stuck in bed and I'm trying to plan a wedding all by myself! Life is so unfair!"

Carole pointed at Peggy. "It's unfair on your mother, not you. It's not going to kill you to do everything by yourself. You're the one who wants this so badly. If it's too much to handle, postpone the wedding."

"Oh no, I can't do that. My mind is made up."

"Frig ya, then. Don't ask for my help."

Peggy waved her good arm around. "Be quiet, Carole! Of course you have to help. You're the only family we have. God. What a depressing thought."

"Excuse me?" Carole frowned.

"I'm sorry...I'm delirious. Can I get some drugs in here?"

CHAPTER FOUR

EARLY THE NEXT MORNING, PEGGY was discharged.

"How am I supposed to get home?" she asked Sheena.

"Well, my car is totalled, and I'd have to take a taxi to the house to get your car, but I can't drive it, remember? Why don't you drive an automatic like the rest of the world?"

"I don't have to explain myself to you."

"Call Aunt Carole."

"I am not going to crawl into that tin can! My back will break in two. I'll have to pay for an ambulance with a gurney, which is ridiculous. Thanks a lot, Ted."

Once they made it back to the house, the paramedics hauled Peggy up the stairs to her bedroom on a narrow gurney. She moaned and groaned in frustration the whole way. She was dozy with pain medication but still managed to be mortified at the sight of her unmade bed, her nightie, and underwear in a pile at the end of it.

When the two burly men finally shut the front door, Peggy hollered for Sheena. She didn't answer, so she hollered again. Nothing.

"This is how it ends," she whispered. "Alone, forgotten...."

The front door banged open.

"Sheena!"

She heard footsteps and Sheena arrived at the bedroom door. "What's wrong?"

"Where were you?"

"I was outside looking at the Jeep. I had to call CAA again. They'll pick it up and take it to a shop. Then hopefully Drew can lend me a car while it's being fixed."

"Well, let me know when you're going outside. I was yelling for you."

"What do you want?"

"I have to go to the bathroom."

"Mother! Why didn't you do that before we left?"

Peggy stared at her offspring. "I'll pretend you didn't say that. Just take my arm. I'm a bit wobbly."

Once Peggy was back in bed, she asked Sheena to grab the laptop on her dresser. "I have to tell your father what's going on."

"I thought we weren't telling him."

"And let him think we're having a fabulous time? No way. Stay here in case I need you."

"Mom, I have got to get some sleep! I've been up all night with you. Let me go."

"Before you do, grab me a few cans of Pepsi, a bag of chips, and that ranch dip in the fridge. Then pass me the remote, my purse, and my cell, also my fluffy socks, tissues, and that *People* magazine on the floor."

"I'm friggin' Cinderella," Sheena moaned as she left the room.

Once Peggy had her supplies and Sheena had disappeared into her bedroom, Peggy turned on Skype. She managed to contact Ted on her first try.

"Hi," he said. "I thought we weren't going to call each other until later in the evening. I've got five minutes to eat my supper before I have to go."

"Well, guess what I'm having for breakfast? Chips and dip, eaten with my left hand since my right arm is broken, and I'm in bed with a slipped a disc in my back. I am bedridden for six weeks!"

"What?"

"And guess who's getting married in six weeks and moving to Halifax?"

"What?"

"And guess who smashed her Jeep last night?"

"Wait a minute! Slow down! Are you joking?"

"I can't believe you're not here to help us. Do you see now how selfish you've been? How life can change in an instant? How about putting your family first, Ted?"

"What a second...I didn't know this would happen."

"What are you going to do about it?"

Peggy could see Ted's ears getting red on the screen. "There's nothing I can do about it right now. We aren't allowed to leave the compound."

Just as Peggy was about to lambaste him for that, a woman appeared on the screen, walked up to Ted, and put her hand on his shoulder. "Say goodbye, Teddy; we have to go." Then she disappeared.

"Who the hell is *that*?"

"She's a colleague."

"A colleague who calls you *Teddy*?"

"My friend introduced us. He calls me Teddy, so that's how I'm known here."

"You son of a bitch. Don't ever speak to me again, Teddy!"

Pressing a finger on a dot on a computer screen wasn't nearly as satisfying as hanging up a phone receiver in someone's ear, but what was satisfying was eating an entire bag of chips and a container of dip and feeling not one bit guilty.

Carole closed up shop for the day and slept until noon. Then she and Ethel picked up a few things at Sobeys before heading over to Peggy's. Ethel was still annoyed that Carole hadn't let her come to the hospital the night before.

They managed to get up the driveway on the first try. Carole helped her mother out of the car and then opened Peggy's front door with her spare key.

"Hello?"

There was complete silence.

"They're both asleep, I bet," Carole said.

"Your mind is a steel trap."

"Ma, don't give me grief. Just sit here until I bring the groceries in."

Once that was accomplished, the two women went up the stairs and stood in the doorway of Peggy's bedroom. There was the poor woman, her head back, mouth open, snoring loudly, her good hand still inside the bag of chips.

Ethel tsked. "No wonder Ted left town. Imagine looking at that all night."

"Can you give the woman a break? She's an invalid at the moment."

Ethel approached Peggy and put her hand on her shoulder. "Peg?"

Peggy grunted and smacked her lips. When Ethel took Peggy's hand out of the chip bag, she opened her eyes. "Who's there? Don't kill me!"

"It's your mother. I'm not going to kill you. However, I can't vouch for your sister."

Peggy blinked. "Ma? Why are you here? You never come over."

"I was here at Christmas. What more do you want? How are ya feeling?"

Peggy looked around groggily and saw her arm in the cast. "I thought I was dreaming. So this really happened?"

"Yep. You're lucky to be alive. What were you thinking, falling down like that?"

"I guess I wanted more drama in my life. Really, Mother, what a stupid question."

Ethel turned to Carole. "She's okay. Let's go."

Carole pulled her mother away and led her to a corner chair. "Just sit and be quiet." She then turned her attention to her sister.

"We brought you a few groceries like milk and bread, but what else do you need? What can we do?"

"There's nothing you can do. It's hopeless."

Carole took Peggy's good hand and gave it a shake. "It's not hopeless. We'll take it one day at a time. Just give yourself a few days to figure out what you need and let us know. We'll do our best to help you. Isn't that right, Ma?"

Ethel was sorting through her scratch tickets. "Yeah, that's right. What she said."

Peggy gave Carole a weary look. "Can you believed we survived our childhood?"

Later that evening, Sheena brought up some supper for her mother on a tray.

"Thank you, dear. What on earth is this? Kraft Dinner?"

"There were ten boxes of it on the kitchen counter."

"This must be what Carole and Ma brought over. I hope they brought something else."

"There's a bunch of bologna too. And white bread! When was the last time you had white bread? It looks kind of great."

Peggy shovelled orange pasta into her mouth. "I wonder how much weight I'll gain in six weeks."

"You can't gain an ounce! You have to look good for my wedding pictures."

"Yeah, well, that ship has sailed."

Daniel and Amber moved into the apartment upstairs. Daniel always had a big smile for Mary when he happened to run into her and they would chat for a few moments before parting ways, but Amber always looked like she'd swallowed a lemon. Mary made it her mission to be as nice as pie, just to bug her.

Unfortunately, an unforeseen problem revealed itself early on. Amber would start yelling at Daniel in the evening and Daniel would play his electric guitar to drown her out. Then Carole and Gran would throw daggers at Mary.

"How was I supposed to know he played guitar? Anyway, you never said anything about musicians, only drug dealers and holy rollers. Next time, you pick the tenant."

"Go upstairs and tell him to knock it off."

"No. You own this place. Tell him yourself."

Gran took a sip of her ginny tea. "Mary likes this kid."

"I do not! Stop bugging me." Mary left the room.

"I rest my case."

Carole got up off the couch and went upstairs. She rang the doorbell, but resorted to pounding on the door when no one answered. Eventually, Amber opened it. "What?"

"I'm the landlord of your dumpy apartment."

"I know who you are."

"Tell your boyfriend to unplug his guitar at night. We can't hear ourselves think."

"Is that all?"

"A word of advice: stop yelling at him, or he won't be your boyfriend for long."

"Get lost." She slammed the door in Carole's face.

"Nice talking to you." Carole went back into the living room and sank into a chair. "People today have no manners."

One week after her fall, Peggy finally consented to speak to Ted again. It took her that long to calm down and stop irrationally blaming him for the accident. Secretly, she still harboured resentment about the "Teddy" issue, but since Sheena thought she was being ridiculous, she decided not to pursue it.

Ted's face filled the screen of Peggy's laptop. "So where do things stand now?"

Sheena sat beside her mother on the bed. "We're having the wedding here at the house because no one in this stupid city ever calls you back."

"I find that hard to believe."

"The minute you say you want something done immediately, they give up. It's ridiculous."

"Have you been shouting at them?"

"No!" Sheena shouted.

"How are you going to have it at the house?"

"I finally found a caterer who's willing to make appetizers and trays of baked hors d'oeuvres," Peggy said. "They'll come in and prepare everything."

"Well, that makes sense. How many do you think are coming?"

"Oh, who knows!" Sheena said, exasperated. "I had to send out emails, for God's sake. So much for my engraved invitations! And naturally, no one emails me back. How long does it take to press *send*? I don't care if anyone comes. I'm going to look like a nightmare anyway, because I can't find a dress, you're stuck in some godforsaken land, and Mom has an ugly cast on her arm. There's not enough chiffon in the world to cover *that* up."

Sheena jumped off the bed and hurried out of the room.

Peggy looked at Ted's dismayed face. "She's not having a good day. She quit her job last week and Drew has been too busy to be of much use. On top of that, hanging around here taking care of me is driving her nuts."

"Are you feeling any better?"

"I guess so. I'm not downing as many painkillers, but then again, I am drinking more wine. And I've gained about ten pounds eating Kraft Dinner."

"Is there anything I can do?"

"Just make sure you're on Skype during the wedding ceremony. I don't want you to miss it."

"I don't want to miss it either. What will you do when they leave for Halifax? Will you be okay by yourself?"

"How should I know? I might jump out the upstairs window into the pool below. If you don't hear from me, you can assume the worst."

"Peggy...."

"Look, Ted, there's no point in asking me what I'm going to do. I've never been in this position. I've never been alone before. Maybe I'll love it. Maybe you can spend the rest of your life over there being happy and fulfilled. I have to go."

"Go where?"

"I have to roll over to your side of the bed to keep it warm."

"I'll call you in a couple of days. Take care of yourself."

"Will do."

Peggy closed the laptop and realized neither one of them had said "I love you."

Carole and Ethel sat at their kitchen window and watched in amusement as Mary and Daniel ran into each other in the driveway on their way to work. Carole noticed Mary was spending a little extra time to on her appearance in the morning. She had even borrowed some mousse from Carole's salon, something she'd never done before.

Carole puffed on her cigarette as she gazed at the pair. "I wonder what he does for a living?"

"Who cares what he does? If she likes him, she likes him. It's not like you were choosy."

Carole took a swig of tea. "I cannot make one lousy comment without you insulting me. Do you really hate me that much?"

Ethel put more sugar in her mug. "I don't hate you. You're my kid. I'm lucky to have you."

Carole froze. "What did you say?"

"You heard me. I love you. I love your sister and I love my granddaughters."

"Ma, are you feeling okay?"

"Goddammit, Carole. No wonder I never say anything."

"Sorry."

The phone rang and Carole reached for it. "It's probably Peggy... Hello?"

"Can you come over here and shoot me?"

"What's wrong?"

"Sheena can't find a wedding dress and she's freaking out. She wants to go to Halifax to look for one."

"So let her go."

"I have to go with her! I'm not missing this quintessential mother-daughter bonding moment."

"You shouldn't sit in a car for that long."

"Can you come with us? In case I need anything?"

Carole put her hand over the receiver. "She wants us to go to Halifax with them to pick out a wedding dress."

Ethel shook her head. "She's nuts."

"Okay, we can go."

"*We?*" Peggy hissed. "I just want you, not Ma!"

"Ma loves you, Peggy. She'd want to be included."

Ethel waved her hands in front of her face. "No thanks. Leave me out of it."

"The more the merrier. I'll ask Mary if she'd like to come too."

"Anyone else you can think of?" said Peggy acidly. "I have to go."

Carole hung up. "There. A nice little family road trip. We should do this more often."

"I'll never tell you I love you again. It's addled your brain."

Her mother's declaration had given Carole an unexpected jolt of *joie de vivre.* She was so used to bickering that she forgot the times they did actually have fun together. At least her mother was a constant in her life, as irritating as she might be.

Carole had laid in bed the other night and felt sorry for Peggy, what with her husband swanning off and her daughter leaving the nest. She didn't think Peggy would handle it very well, and wondered if she would slide into a depression. Carole prided herself in handling whatever came her way without the use of pills. She was also smug about the fact that Mary had turned out to be a sweet and generous girl and not a whiny brat like her niece. Still, it wasn't Sheena's fault her parents spoiled her, and Carole was genuinely happy for her and Drew.

When Mary heard she was expected to go, the first thing she thought of was Roscoe.

"Who will take care of him?"

Her mother made a face. "He's a cat. Leave him a bunch of food and he'll be fine."

"Is that what you did with me?"

"As a matter of fact, yes. Ask the cutie pie upstairs to look in on him," she said with a twinkle in her eye. "I have no doubt he'll agree."

It annoyed Mary that her mother had had a good idea. She asked Daniel that night and he said he'd be happy to.

Roscoe was so lucky.

Carole drove Peggy's Lexus, with Peggy in the front seat, Ethel in the middle, and the girls in the back row. Glancing in the rear-view mirror, Carole saw only grumpy faces.

"This is supposed to be a fun trip! You all look like you're about to be executed. Sheena, aren't we picking up Riley?"

"She backed out at the last minute when she found out old people were coming.

"You could've left that bit out," Gran shouted. "Remind me to spit on her."

"I don't even care anymore. It's all a disaster."

"That's the spirit," Mary said.

Sheena gave her the finger. Mary grabbed it, which made Sheena screech.

"That's enough, you two!" Carole yelled.

When they reached the causeway, they filled up at the Petro-Can and stopped for a coffee at Tim's. Mary was in charge of escorting Gran, and Sheena dragged a slumped-over Peggy, who manoeuvred her bulk into the accessible bathroom stall with much groaning.

"I told you we shouldn't have come," Carole said to her sister.

"Just pass me another painkiller."

Gran couldn't decide what kind of doughnut she wanted and held the whole line up. Carole finally bought a box of twelve to take in the car. It took them a half an hour to get settled back in their seats, with hot coffee being passed around gingerly. Gran eventually picked a doughnut with sprinkles on it and most of them ended up in her dentures.

"Gran," Sheena said, "let me take a selfie with you!" She reached over the seat and stuck the camera in her grandmother's face. "Say cheese!"

When she showed the picture to Mary, the two of them had hysterics in the back.

"What's so funny?" Carole wanted to know.

"Gran looks like a sprinkly Cheshire cat!" They passed up the phone so everyone could have a peek. All five of them giggled for a couple of kilometres.

They stopped laughing when they got to Mount Thom. The snow that had been falling gently for a few hours suddenly decided to switch gears, and now the white stuff was accumulating at a great rate. It didn't help that no other cars seemed to be slowing down any and huge trucks were passing them at a clip.

"This wasn't such a good idea," said Ethel. "Tell me again why you couldn't buy a dress in Sydney?"

"I tried them all. They looked awful."

"No one panic. We'll get to the hotel and have a good sleep and then start early tomorrow morning," Peggy said.

"What if she doesn't find anything?" Mary asked.

"I'll elope."

"If you elope, I'm rewriting my will. I'll leave everything to Mary."

"Thanks, Aunt Peggy."

Several tense hours later, they made it to Halifax and booked into the Prince George Hotel (Peggy's choice). Making Ted pay for it felt good. They had two adjoining rooms, which made it feel like a sleepover. Mary and Sheena decided to go out for a bite and the other three ordered room service.

By the time Mary and Sheena got back to the room, their mothers and grandmother were half in the bag thanks to the minibar. Not only that, they had the porn channel on, and were pointing at the television and killing themselves with laughter.

"Okay, this is disgusting," Sheena said.

"Nonsense!" said her mother. "You think your generation invented sex? Don't be such a prude."

"Go to bed! I don't need three hungover relatives with me tomorrow."

Amazingly, the three women did as they did as they were told. Trouble was, no one got any sleep because the combination of drugs and liquor made Peggy snore like a chainsaw all night. They all mentioned it in the morning.

"Maybe you should go and see if you have sleep apnea," Mary said. "Do you find you're tired all the time?"

"Of course I'm tired, but I have a lot on my plate at the moment."

"You have been getting worse, Mom," Sheena agreed. "I have to leave my television on all night just to drown you out. Maybe that's why Dad left."

"Thanks, sweetheart. You know just what to say."

After breakfast at the hotel, Sheena informed the group she had made appointments in four shops around Halifax and Dartmouth: Chester & Felicity, Always & Forever, Karma Bridal, and David's Bridal.

"I thought we were only going to one store," Peggy said. She frowned. "How long is this going to take?"

"Mother, what's the point of coming all this way if I can't sample everything?"

"Maybe you'll love the first one you try on," Mary said hopefully.

"Not a chance," Ethel muttered.

Ethel was right. They spent almost two hours in each store, Peggy shifting her weight on all the chairs and ottomans, trying to get comfortable while Sheena was in the dressing room.

Every dress looked lovely on her. Sheena was a beautiful woman with a knockout figure, so everything suited her. It made things rather difficult, because the minute they decided they liked one, she'd come out in something else and they'd have to start over. Mary had more fun than she'd anticipated and even wandered off to look at bridesmaid dresses.

There was one gown Sheena loved, but it had a see-through corset on top and Peggy nixed it immediately.

"It looks like you bought it at Victoria's Secret," she said. "It belongs in the bedroom. No way are you wearing that."

"Mother!"

"I don't care. Take it off."

They eventually headed over to David's Bridal in Dartmouth. Ethel decided she was going to take a nap in the car.

"Don't you want to see me pick my dress, Gran?"

"I liked the first fifty you tried on, so why don't you surprise me?"

A young and perky salesgirl named Kelsey took one look at Sheena and said, "You look like a ball gown bride to me."

Sheena's eyes lit up. "I do? How did you know?"

"I'm good at my job. Let me get you the one I'm thinking of."

The minute Sheena walked out in the dress and she saw her reflection, her face lit up and her eyes sparkled. The dress made her look like Cinderella, with its sweetheart neckline and bodice covered with bling. Everyone made noises of approval, even Mary, who knew the layered tulle skirt would be impossible to manoeuvre through Peggy's living room. But that didn't matter: this was obviously Sheena's dress, come what may.

As Sheena preened, Kelsey tucked a full-length veil into her hair with a comb. The veil had embroidered flower petals along the lower half, with crystals around the edging. As they stared with their mouths open, the intrepid Kelsey quickly appeared with a lacy zirconia necklace and dangling earring set, along with creamy satin high heels. "Let's see the whole package!"

For once in her life, Sheena was speechless as she gazed at her image in the mirror.

Peggy blubbered as she struggled out of her chair to hug Sheena. It was mostly because of the pain, but she didn't let on. "You are so beautiful, Sheena. Like a living doll. Oh, I wish your father could see you."

"Me too," Sheena whispered.

Carole looked at Mary with misty eyes. "One day we'll be doing this."

"No. I'm not getting married."

"You'll change your mind."

"No. I won't."

"Honestly. You could pretend for just a moment. I never had a wedding dress...."

That was the moment Peggy cleared her throat. "What's the total for all this?"

Kesley took out a calculator. "Thirty-five hundred for the dress, nine hundred for the veil, a hundred for the jewellery, and three hundred for the shoes. That's forty-eight hundred dollars, plus tax."

Sheena gave her mother a worried look.

"We'll take it," Peggy said.

Sheena jumped into her mother's arms, which made her wince in pain. Carole tsked about the ridiculous amount of money being spent, while Mary smiled, thinking that this was the happiest Mary had ever seen Sheena. The wedding was a hurried mess, so she was glad her cousin would at least have this.

They woke poor Gran trying to get the puffy garment bag into the empty seat next to her.

"What the hell did you buy?" She swatted the plastic back with her hands as it threatened to swallow her face.

"Only the most beautiful gown in the world!" Sheena grinned. "You should see it."

"Can't wait." Gran grimaced. "Can we go home now? My ass is numb."

CHAPTER FIVE

THE WEEKS WERE FLYING BY, all of them fraught and stressful. The closer the wedding got, the more unglued Peggy became. Every morning she woke up and immediately wanted to close her eyes again. Her bedroom was a disaster. She was lucky Sheena had agreed to do the laundry, but the piles of clothes heaped on the bed and dressers made her feel trapped. The thought of hiring a housekeeper crossed her mind, but she didn't want anyone to see how bad things had become.

Carole had said they'd help her but realistically, she had to work and Ethel was useless. Mary came over occasionally but she, too, was busy with her own life. It made Peggy realize how few friends she had. When had that happened? She was so busy with her own little brood, she never included anyone into the fold, and as a result, she had no one who would call her and ask her to lunch or a movie.

Here Peggy was, doing everything so perfectly as a wife and mother, that she had forgotten she existed beyond these roles. Who exactly was she?

Lounging in a bed for weeks on end feeling like a lump of dough didn't help her come to any conclusions. She was the saddest case around. She didn't even care about the wedding anymore. Sheena roared in several times a day to update her on plans, and Peggy would pretend to be interested, but it took everything she had just to nod and smile. Only the mention of Drew's mother, Maxine, drew a spark... and it was usually anger.

"What do you mean, she refuses to hold a rehearsal party? That's the responsibility of the groom's parents."

Sheena flopped onto the bed. "She said, 'What's the point in rehearsing if we're going to be in the house? Just walk into the living room and stand in front of whoever's doing the wedding. Simple enough.' Drew agrees."

"So far they have managed to avoid this wedding altogether."

"Drew's dad—"

"Drew's dad offered cars! Why do we need them? How is that a big frigging deal?"

Sheena got off the bed in a hurry. "I have no idea! I'm just telling you what he said."

"Do you have anyone to marry you yet? I've been asking you every day."

"It's just a matter of calling the Justice Centre and asking for a justice of the peace, or a family judge. We have to get a marriage licence too. Don't worry, I'll do it."

"So it's final then. No minister involved. We're going to hell."

"When was the last time you went to church?"

"That's not the point."

"I think if you asked an actual minister, they'd disagree. Anyway, I have to meet Mary and Riley. They're picking out their bridesmaid dresses today. I won't be back for supper. Do you need anything before I go?"

"Bring me up a quart of ice cream."

"No. I bought you frozen sherbet. You can have that."

"I hate you."

"Oh, Mama, you're being a big baby." Sheena got back on the bed and gave her poor old mother a hug. "Cheer up. You'll feel better soon, I promise."

"I love you, Sheena."

"And I love you. That's never going to change, no matter where I live."

After Sheena left the house, Peggy turned on Netflix and watched a documentary about nursing homes and how the sheer numbers of aging baby boomers would cause a crisis in the industry. It left her sufficiently bereft and certain that this was her future. She sighed and turned off the television.

Then she heard the front door open and Carole yell, "It's only me!"

She arrived at the bedroom door with two Dairy Queen Blizzards in her hands. "Turtle Pecan Cluster—your favourite."

"I could kiss you!"

Peggy's sister passed her the Blizzard and made herself comfortable against the headboard on Ted's side of the bed. "Ma passed out early tonight, and Mary's with Sheena, so I thought I'd pop over. How are you feeling?"

"Physically, a little better. I can move easier, but these painkillers are doing a number on me. And my arm is so itchy under this cast I want to scratch it off. I stuck a knife down there the other day and almost lost it."

"I meant to ask you: do you have a dress for the wedding? We can go shopping if you like."

"I can't be bothered. The dress I bought for Ted's medical conference last year looks better and better. I'll make do with that."

"I never thought I'd hear those words from your lips. How is Ted? Talked to him lately?"

"He talks to Sheena."

Carole stopped spooning her ice cream and gave Peggy a good look. She didn't like what she saw. "Leaving Ted out of the loop isn't going to help things in the long run," she said. "He's not to blame for this. You'd still be sitting here all day even if he was home. He'd be at work."

"I don't think I love him anymore."

Carole froze. "You're not going to do something stupid and walk out of your marriage, are you?"

"Why not?"

"What the hell would you do? You've never worked a day in your life! How would you support yourself? Take it from me, it's not easy struggling by yourself and being all alone in the world. Is there something I don't know about? Does he hit you? Is he a pervert?"

Peggy laughed. "Don't be ridiculous. Poor old Ted is the world's most boring man. He's not a deviant and he wouldn't hurt a fly."

Carole scooped a spoonful of Blizzard into her mouth. "Forget leaving Ted. Just find something to do. You're unfulfilled. So is every woman I know in her forties and fifties. You should hear the way they talk in the salon. Moaning about wasted lives and ungrateful families. I'm surprised women get out of bed in the morning. It's all hormones. Get yourself a shot in the ass. They say that works."

"Pass me a gun."

The bridesmaid dress Sheena eventually decided she liked was a real hit with Riley, but Mary thought it was over the top. It was much too revealing and slinky. The colour was lavender and very nice against her complexion, but Mary thought she looked like a Kardashian without the boobs or butt, so what was the point?

Again, Mary reminded herself, *it doesn't matter.* It was Sheena's day and she was paying for the dress. Mary had been prepared to buy her own, but Sheena generously insisted. Once they were done, Sheena and Riley had driven Mary home and headed out for the evening. Mary knew they'd have a better time without her tagging along. She usually felt like a third wheel around Riley, who was much cooler and always would be. Mary would never possess that particular gene, but thankfully it didn't bother her, like it did so many young girls.

As Sheena's Jeep left the driveway, the headlights revealed Daniel sitting on the top step of the front porch. Kind of crazy on a chilly March evening. Mary always smiled when she saw him. He was the nicest guy. Just like Mrs. Aucoin. And then she realized Roscoe was sitting with him.

"Hey, you two. Shooting the breeze?"

"Ever since your weekend away, Roscoe waits by the door for an invitation upstairs, but now that Amber's decided she's allergic to cats, I come down here and spend time with him on the porch. He's good company."

"Oh, he is that."

Daniel shook his head to get the hair out of his eyes. "Look, I'm sorry about the guitar playing. I didn't realize it was that loud."

"Oh, it didn't bother me, but my Gran is getting old and things upset her. It was no biggie. Do you play in a band?"

"Yeah. We do a few gigs around town, but we're never going to be the Foo Fighters."

"Ah, who needs two?" Mary smiled. "And when you're not playing? Do you go to school?"

"I'll be taking a heavy equipment operator course in August at NSCC. In the meantime, I help out my dad with his machine shop."

"I wish I knew what I wanted to do."

Daniel grinned at her. "You should work with old people. They love you."

Mary laughed. "It's getting young people to love me that's the difficult bit." Mary couldn't believe that had come out of her mouth.

He gave her a sideways glance. "I can't imagine that being a problem."

Before Mary could process the remark, Amber threw open their front door. "What are you doing?" she demanded.

"Talking to Mary."

"Oh, hello, Mary. Funny how I always see you rain, snow, or shine, on the porch or in the driveway. Do you want a timetable for Daniel's arrivals and departures?"

"No need. See you two later. Come on, Roscoe." She and the cat hurried into the house.

She woke up her grandmother when she shut the front door. Gran had been slumped over on the couch in front of the television. She yawned and stretched her skinny legs in front of her. "Where's your mother?"

"I don't know. I thought she was here."

"Probably over at Peggy's. Did you guys find a dress?"

"Yes. And it looks ridiculous."

"Who cares? Wear it for a few hours and then sell it."

Mary plunked herself down on the wonky recliner. Roscoe jumped onto her lap. "I can't do that. Sheena bought it for me."

"Then I'll do it. I need more lotto tickets."

"Gran?"

"Wha?"

"How did you know you liked my grandfather?"

"I never liked him."

Mary pushed against the floor with her feet to keep rocking. "You must have liked him a little bit."

"Not really. I had the hots for him, that's all. He was a good-look-ing man. Much too handsome for the likes of me, which should've tipped me off."

"Tipped you off? To what?"

"Is that the time? I gotta go to bed." Gran pushed herself off the couch and shuffled off, leaving Mary to wonder what secret Gran was keeping. She had almost dozed off despite Roscoe's deafening purr but came to when she heard her mom enter through the back door.

"You home, Mary?"

"Yep."

Carole walked into the living room with her coat hanging off her shoulders. She sat down like she was too tired to take it off. Her mom was nice looking, but she made no effort to spruce herself up, and she dressed like a bag lady. One of these days when her Aunt Peggy wasn't fretting about other matters, Mary would ask her to talk to her sister. Just to give her some friendly advice. Then it occurred to her that Sheena was always trying to give Mary advice. Mary was turning into her mom. That thought was appalling.

"Did you pick a dress?"

"Yep. Sheena likes it."

"I can imagine what it looks like. This poor old wedding is going to be a circus."

"I suppose so." Mary yawned. "I hope Sheena doesn't regret it."

Carole nodded. "Do you think she loves him? I didn't notice any magical sparks at Christmas dinner."

"Everyone's a mystery. Even Gran. Tonight she said she didn't even like your dad. Is that true?"

"I guess so. She made damn sure she drove him out of the house. Which I've never forgiven her for."

"And yet you ended up doing the same thing to me. Is that something I should forgive you for?"

"That's different. You never had a dad. I remember mine."

"So you've suffered more?"

"Obviously."

"Do you have any idea where my father might be?"

"Probably Alberta."

"Should I look for him?"

"Sure. His name was Dave. Good luck with that."

❦

With only a week to go until the wedding, Drew arrived on Sheena's doorstep at seven in the morning because she wasn't returning his texts or phone calls. He banged on the door and shouted her name several times before she finally answered, looking dishevelled and sleepy.

"What are you doing here? What's wrong?"

He walked past her into the porch. "Is your mom home?"

"Of course she's home. She lives in her bedroom. Hug me."

Drew gave her a hug and didn't let her go. "I have to go to Halifax today. I'll be back two days before the wedding."

As Sheena struggled to get out of his arms, he held on for dear life. "Please don't hate me! The bigwigs are coming in from Toronto, and I have to be there. Remember I love you and I didn't plan this, so it's not my fault, okay?"

Sheena was furious. "Ugh! You are the biggest jerk alive! Let me go!"

They tousled around the front entryway. "Say you love me! Say it!"

"I hate you, you miserable boy!"

"Give me a kiss." Drew pursed his lips in her direction and Sheena leaned back as far as she could.

"Never! I'm never kissing you as long as you live!"

Peggy appeared at the top of the stairs. "What is going on? Drew! Let her go."

Drew released his bride-to-be. "I can explain."

"He's going to Halifax!" Sheena cried.

"I'll be back in time! I promise. I swear, Mrs. Henderson. I'll be back for the wedding. I have to attend a meeting. It's about our future. Try and make her understand."

"This is the last straw!" Sheena tore up the stairs and past her mother and, as usual, slammed her bedroom door.

"Drew, could you come up here, please?" Peggy asked. "I'd like to talk to you."

Drew walked up the stairs with all the enthusiasm of a convicted felon. Peggy pointed to her bedroom. "Forgive the mess. Just come in and sit down. And close the door behind you."

Drew sat on Peggy's reading chair nervously running his fingers through his hair while Peggy repositioned herself on the bed.

"We haven't had many occasions to talk, you and I," Peggy started. "Quite frankly, I don't know a lot about you, but I do know my daughter loves you, which is why I'm willing to be here for both of you. You seem like a nice boy, Drew, but I want to ask you something, and I want you to be honest. Is this job an excuse to break you and Sheena up? Are your parents behind this move?"

Drew was about to say something, but he stopped and regrouped. "In a way. It's no secret my mother thinks I'm too young to get married. But Mom thinks marriage stinks anyway. She and my dad are not happy, and she takes it out us. Dad offered me the job away so Sheena and I could start fresh, if that's what we wanted."

"Sheena didn't want it."

He lowered his head. "I need to get out of Sydney, Mrs. Henderson. This is a huge opportunity. It's not like Sheena is leaving Cape Breton forever. She can come back whenever she wants. And I think she'll love Halifax in time. There is so much more to do there. She's just afraid of leaving you."

Peggy recognized his sincerity and was grateful for it. "You're right. She is afraid of leaving me, and I'm afraid of losing her." She sighed. "But in the scheme of things, that's probably why she should go."

"I will be back for the wedding, despite what Sheena thinks. I even ordered tuxes. I told Sheena I was going to wear a suit, so she'll be really pleased to see us on the day."

Peggy smiled. "Don't worry about Sheena. I'll talk to her. You better hit the highway."

Drew walked to the door and turned around. "Thanks, Mrs. H. Sheena's right: you're a great mom."

Peggy basked in the compliment for about ten seconds before Sheena's bedroom door opened. "Did he leave?" she said incredulously.

"Yes."

"I can't believe it!" she shrieked before rushing to Peggy's beside. "You let him go?"

"He's coming back. He has a surprise for you on your wedding day."

Sheena paused and took a breath. She narrowed her eyes. "What surprise?"

"Can't tell you, can I? But you'll be happy."

Sheena stood there debating whether to stay mad. Eventually she decided against it. Her nerves couldn't take much more. "I'm going back to bed," she said with a shrug.

With nothing else to do, Peggy knocked back some more pain medication. She hated the drugs and had considered going to the doctor to get her to change it. She began searching online for alternatives, and came across an article about medical marijuana and pain relief.

Why had she not considered this already?

But then, how would she get it? She couldn't ask Sheena. And Ted would be furious if he found out. Besides, Sheena would probably be horrified.

Peggy racked her brain and thought about the seedy-looking teenager next door—but if his parents found out, they'd call the cops. Who could she trust?

She called Mary.

Mary had a towel wrapped around her head and was brushing her teeth when she heard her cell go off. She walked back into her bedroom and picked up her phone, wondering who it could be. No one called her this early. She was surprised to see her Aunt Peggy's name on the call display.

"Hi. You okay?"

"Hi, honey. Are you alone?"

"Yes...."

"I'm going to ask you something and I don't want you to be...I mean...I don't want you to say anything to your mother or grandmother. They don't need to know."

All kinds of weird scenarios raced through Mary's brain. What on earth could her Aunt Peggy get up to that was so secretive?

Peggy took a deep breath. "Can you get me some pot?"

There was a beat of silence. "Pot?"

"As in weed."

"I know what pot is. I'm just confused."

"I need it for pain relief. These miserable pills are making me constipated. I feel like a hot-air balloon."

"But shouldn't you just ask your doctor for something else?"

"I can do a lot of things, Mary, but I thought this might be faster. I've smoked weed before, but I need someone to get it for me. I can't roam the streets in my condition."

"Why do you think I could get some?"

"Don't tell me you've never tried it?"

"No, I haven't."

"Oh God…I'm corrupting an innocent soul. Forget I said anything," Peggy said hastily.

"No, no. I don't mind helping you, I'd just have to find someone who had some." At that moment, Daniel popped into Mary's head. "Wait, I think I may know someone. Do you want me to ask him?"

"Sure. I'll pay you back."

"Okay. It might not be today."

"That's fine. But soon, okay, sweetheart? Real soon."

The line went dead. Mary looked at the phone. Poor Aunt Peggy was losing her mind.

Mary got dressed in a hurry because she knew Daniel would be leaving for work soon. No time like the present. She assumed he'd know how to get some dope since he played in a band. Wasn't that a prerequisite?

Mary stood in the kitchen window looking out for Daniel. She ate a bowl of cereal while she waited. Her mother came in and plugged in the kettle.

"Who called you so early?"

"It was a telemarketer."

"Those bastards."

Mary saw Daniel head out to his truck. She threw her cereal bowl on the table and scooted out the door, her mother shouting, "Where are you going?"

"Daniel?" Mary headed down the steps as Daniel opened the driver's-side door.

"Good morning."

She raced up to him, looking around to see if they were alone. "Can I talk to you for a minute? Is Amber coming down?"

"No, Amber's upstairs. And I apologize for her comments last night. They were uncalled for."

Mary smiled. "Looks like she was right! I was waiting for you today. I have a question and I hope you don't think I'm being presumptuous, but do you know where I can get some weed?"

"Okay, I wasn't expecting that."

"I know. I'm sorry. I shouldn't automatically assume all guitar players have joints in their back pockets, but I want to buy some for a friend, and I didn't know who to ask."

"A friend?" he smirked.

"Honestly! If I told you who, you'd laugh your head off, but it's kind of serious. It's for pain relief."

"Well, I can get you some, as long as we're talking ounces and not kilos."

"An ounce sounds about right. How much would that be?"

"Hundred and fifty, just to be safe."

"Could you get some today and give it to me tonight? I can meet you on the front porch at eight…as long as Amber lets you out of the house."

Daniel gave her a grin. "I'll be there."

"I owe you," she smiled.

"You do. Remember that."

He jumped in his truck and Mary ran up the back steps, waving as he backed up out of the driveway.

"What on earth was that all about?" her mother wanted to know.

"Nothing. Just saying hi."

"Wipe the smile off your face."

"Jeez, Mom." Mary hurried to her room, her cheeks burning.

At work Mary could hardly concentrate. Nothing this clandestine had ever happened to her. Then it occurred to her that maybe she should buy some dope for herself, but she quickly nixed the idea. She didn't even drink coffee, so drugs didn't loom on her horizon. In this respect she was the exact opposite of her female relatives; she must have inherited some laid-back genes from this Dave character in Alberta.

Her mom and Gran were settled in and watching television at eight, so Mary quietly went out the back door and hurried to the porch. Daniel was there, as promised. She tiptoed up the stairs and stayed away from the living-room window.

"Hi," she whispered.

"Hi," he whispered back.

"I feel like I'm in a movie. Danger lurks everywhere," she said.

"You'd make a great spy."

Mary grinned, "Do you have the *stuff*?"

"Yep." He looked around and took it out of his pocket. "One ounce of Sydney's finest." He handed her a baggie.

She shoved it in her jeans pocket and handed him the money. "If it's more, just tell me. I don't want you losing out on the deal."

"I'm not losing out on anything. I get to talk to you for a few minutes."

Mary forgot all about the dope. "Really?"

"I've been wanting to do this all day." He reached out and took her face in his hands, kissing her for a long moment before letting her go. "I'm sorry. I have no right to do that. I'm not the kind of guy who cheats...just lately, things are a bit difficult and...."

Mary wanted him to do it again, but she nodded. "It's okay. Apparently I've made it more than clear to your girlfriend that I like you, and that's not who I am either. We can be friends, Daniel. I don't want to complicate your life. Thank you so much for this."

She ran down the stairs and around the side of the house, not making any noise as she let herself in. Then she popped her head into the living room. "I'm taking the car for an hour. Stacey at work wants to get a coffee. Her boyfriend broke up with her."

"Okay," her mother mumbled.

When Mary rang the doorbell at Aunt Peggy's, Sheena opened it. She was in her pyjamas. "Oh hey, what are you doing here?"

Mary held up a stack of magazines she had stopped for at the corner store. "Mom thought Aunt Peggy might like these. I also have a couple of chocolate bars."

"Okay. I was just about to jump in the tub."

"No problem. I'll let myself out."

Mary softly knocked on her Aunt Peggy's open door. She was engrossed with something on her computer screen.

"Hi, Aunt Peggy."

Peggy looked up and did a double-take. "Hi! Fancy seeing you here so soon."

Mary walked over to her aunt's bed and sat beside her. "Sheena's taking a bath." She pulled out the bag of dope and put it in her aunt's hand. Peggy took it and put it under the covers.

"I can't thank you enough, sweetheart. And I feel terribly guilty that I even asked. I had no business doing it, but I'm desperate." She reached over and pulled open her bedside table drawer. She picked up a roll of cash. "Now, how much do I owe you?"

"A hundred and fifty."

"Nonsense. Last I heard, dope cost six hundred bucks." She counted out the bills and put them in Mary's hand.

"But this is way too much."

"Buy yourself as many contact lenses as you need. And don't say another word. Now kiss me and go."

Once Mary was home and behind her bedroom door, she jumped on the bed and hugged herself. What a day! She was a drug dealer and a homewrecker all rolled into one. Not that she was proud of that—but it sure made her tingle all over.

And the thought of throwing her glasses away was the icing on the cake.

CHAPTER SIX

THERE IS ONLY SO MUCH you can do before a wedding, and then there is a strange lull. Nothing else can be done until the day of the wedding itself. It's like a deadly calm before the storm. Everyone knows something is coming, but there's no need for action until you see the actual tornado.

The Henderson house was ready, thanks to an army of paid cleaners, florists, and a party decorator that was found at the last minute. Sheena hastily decided she needed balloons, so tanks of helium were used to create a white and cream wonderland, inside and out.

On the morning of the wedding, however, grey skies grumbled overhead and the wind picked up considerably. It did a real number on the balloons lining the driveway, all of them waving hysterically in every direction.

"Okay, this was a ridiculous idea," Carole said. "Look at these poor souls running around."

As the Ryan women navigated up the driveway at eight in the morning, the party planners were frantically trying to tether balloons to weights.

"It would have looked really nice if it was calm," Mary said.

"You always gotta plan for the worst," Ethel told her wisely. "Then you're never disappointed."

"What a horrible philosophy, Gran."

Ethel shrugged. "Works for me."

They had arrived early to help with the last-minute details. The wedding wasn't until mid-afternoon, so they had lots of time to go over everything. Mary carried in their dresses and Carole had bags of hair supplies. While Sheena was still going to her hairdresser, Peggy had called Carole and said she changed her mind about driving to Glace Bay to get hers done. Would Carole mind doing hers as well?

Carole did mind, but she kept her mouth shut.

Only Sheena was up, which surprised the others. "Where's your mother?" Gran asked.

"I can't wake her up."

"Wha?"

"She's alive! She's snoring, that's all. Can you guys give her breakfast? I have to go get my hair and nails done. And if I'm not back before the food people get here, just let them in."

Sheena raced out the door in a hoodie and leggings. Then she turned around. "What's different about you, Mary? Did you get your hair cut?"

"I'm not wearing my glasses."

"Oh. You look nice."

"Mom and Gran haven't noticed."

Sheena continued on her way, but Mary chased after her. "Wait! Your hair will be set. How are you going to get your hoodie off?"

Sheena dithered for half a second. "Shit! Oh, never mind. I'll just cut it off." And away she went. A perfect Sheena solution.

While Mary started breakfast and Gran read the newspaper, Carole went upstairs to wake Peggy. She was surprised Peggy wasn't awake on today of all days, but there she was, on her back, sounding like a locomotive in full throttle.

Carole shook Peggy's shoulder. "Peg. Peggy. PEGGY! Wake up!"

Nothing.

She decided to open the blinds and window to get rid of the stale air. The bedroom smelled a bit off, but she couldn't place the scent. God knew what the woman was eating up here. There were dirty dishes everywhere. She leaned over her sister once more and shouted, "Get up, woman!"

Peggy's eyes popped open in surprise. "Wha? What's wrong?"

"It's me: Carole. It's Sheena's wedding day. Why are you not up and freaking out?"

Peggy struggled in the bedclothes. "I forgot. It's not today, is it?"

"I'm not surprised you don't know what day it is, spending all your time in here. Mary is downstairs making breakfast and Sheena went to her hair appointment. Why don't you have a quick shower and I'll do your hair first, then Mary's, and then I'll worry about Ma and me."

"Okay, thanks." Peggy sat at the edge of the bed. "I can't believe my baby is getting married today. And her father isn't here."

"Don't dwell on that. I'm sure he wishes he were."

Peggy got up slowly. "I don't care anymore."

Carole reached out and put her hand on Peggy's shoulder. "Today is a happy day. You should be happy."

"I will be. In about twenty minutes."

Peggy staggered off to the bathroom and Carole went downstairs to the kitchen. "There is something wrong with that woman." She reached for her cigarettes.

Ethel pointed at her. "You better smoke those outside."

"It's blowing a gale out there!"

"Better than Peggy blowing a gasket in here."

"Jeez, Louise," Carole grumbled as she headed for the back door. "Save me some toast."

By the time Peggy emerged from her shower and got dressed, she was in a much better frame of mind. She ate her eggs with gusto and laughed at everything Gran said, whether it was funny or not.

Carole set up shop in the dining room, making sure to cover the table with a sheet they could whisk away before the caterers arrived.

"So how do you want your hair? Up?"

"Sticking straight up? I don't think so. Can you imagine, Mary? Straight up?"

Mary gave her aunt a worried look.

"Of course not sticking straight up." Carole sighed. "Do you want a bun?"

"I want a chignon."

"Which is just a fancy word for bun."

"Sure...one of those."

As Carole got to work with the blow dryer, Peggy began to sing "Doe, a deer, a female deer," and Mary chimed in to make it seem like Aunt Peggy was just festive and not off her rocker. Soon Carole and even Gran joined in. They went through the entire *Sound of Music* playlist. By the time they were done, Carole had finished. "What do you think?" She gave Peggy a mirror.

"Fantastic! Why don't I come to you more often?"

"I have no idea. You should be supporting me."

Peggy got out of the chair and gave Carole a big hug. "I should. I really should. I've been a snob of the first order, but I'm here to say I've changed my ways and will hereafter only come to you and your marvellous little shop."

Carole stared at her.

"Aunt Peggy, can I speak to you for a second?" interjected Mary.

"Of course, my darling girl. What is it?"

Mary hesitated. "I want to show you my dress. It's in the family room."

Once Mary got her alone, she came straight to the point. "Are you okay? You're not smoking too much, are you?"

"Why on earth do you think that?"

"Because you would never darken the door of Mom's shop ordinarily and now you're saying you're going to have to go there forever."

"Damn, you're right. Do you think anyone suspects? I only had one joint this morning. I was going to have more later."

"Maybe you should stick with Tylenol or something. Just for today. You don't want to make anyone suspicious."

Peggy patted Mary's head. "Good plan. I'm hungry."

She wandered off and Mary tried to get rid of the knot in her stomach.

Sheena arrived back on the scene, Riley in tow, just as the caterers were unpacking the goodies. Her hair was glorious. Some of it was held back with a lace-and-rhinestone headpiece, and the rest fell on her shoulders in soft curls. As promised, she made Mary cut her out of her hoodie and then disappeared upstairs with Riley and the makeup girl. Mary hovered between floors, waiting for her turn to sit in the makeup chair.

The photographer showed up and quickly became a pest. He wanted pictures of shoes and dresses hanging up and he had even snapped one of Gran dozing in a lounger. He tried to get into Peggy's room but she screamed and told him to get lost. She was trying to pour herself into a pair of Spanx with Carole's help. It wasn't going well.

"Okay, forget the Spanx," Carole huffed. "You're going to hurt your back more and all the progress you've made will be for nothing."

"Jesus! I've gained twenty pounds at least!"

"Well, it's no wonder. You have nothing to do but eat all day."

"Are you saying I *have* gained twenty pounds?"

"Not twenty...."

"But a lot?"

"No, Peggy. You haven't gained an ounce. I wouldn't lie to you. Now just suck in or take it off."

There was one more big yank and Peggy somehow managed to hit Carole right between the eyes with her heavy cast. Carole fell to the floor and stayed down, looking dazed.

Peggy hobbled over to her bedroom door and yelled out: "Help! I killed Carole!"

Everyone came running and discovered that, although Carole wasn't dead, she *did* have a big red mark on her forehead. The makeup girl said she'd be able to cover it up.

Peggy was distraught. Nothing anyone said or did could calm her down. Eventually Sheena wound up and slapped her mother across the face.

Everyone held their breath.

"Thanks, honey," Peggy said before she disappeared behind the bathroom door once more.

Gran kept shaking her head and mumbled to Mary, "Somethin' strange going on here. If I didn't know better, I'd say Peggy's come undone in the last six weeks."

Mary almost confessed then and there.

Just as things calmed down and order was being restored, the front door open and a loud voice called, "Is there a wedding here today?"

"Uncle Ted!" Mary raced over to him. "It's so good to see you!"

Uncle Ted was looking rather good. He'd lost weight and had a nice tan. He looked years younger. "Hi, sweetheart." He kissed Mary and gave her a big hug before shouting, "Where's my daughter?"

As they looked up the staircase, Mary wondered if Sheena knew how lucky she was to have a dad who would fly halfway around the world to be with her on her big day.

Sheena came running down the stairs in a bathrobe with *BRIDE* embroidered on the back. She squealed and jumped into her dad's arms. "Daddy! Why didn't you tell me you were coming?"

"I didn't know until the last minute, and I didn't want you fretting if my flights were delayed. I thought it would be better to be a surprise."

The photographer was all over this exciting development, and everyone was tripping over him.

Peggy was in the bathroom with the fan on, standing in the tub with the window open, sucking on a joint and giggling. She knew she had to get it together, but this seemed the only way to go about it. Then she got a horrible feeling that maybe the photographer would creep in here and catch her in the act. She took one more haul off the joint and flushed the remainder down the toilet.

When she sat down to pee she realized she was hallucinating. Oh God, she'd smoked too much. She kept hearing Ted hollering. What was she going to do? Staying calm was the main thing. If she remained poised and gracious, she could get through anything. This was Sheena's wedding day, something Peggy had envisioned all her life. But she certainly never pictured sitting on a toilet unable to wipe herself because her too-tight Spanx wouldn't let her knees open wide enough to do a decent job. Photos be damned. She shimmied the Spanx to the bathroom tiles and kicked them out of her way. The relief was amazing. And then she heard Ted again.

She was overdosing! She needed air! Peggy threw open the bathroom door and rushed out of the room as fast as her back would let her. At the top of the stairs, she looked down and saw her husband standing there.

"Surprise!" Ted yelled. "I made it!"

Peggy stared. "Ted?"

"I'm here! It took a lot of planning and I can't stay long, but they let me go on compassionate grounds."

"You asshole!"

The family, the caterers, and even the photographer instantly melted away from Ted's side. No one wanted to be in on this conversation.

Ted looked confused. "Excuse me?"

Peggy disappeared back into her room, so Ted had no choice but to follow her upstairs. He shut the door behind him. "My God. What happened in here?"

"What happened in here is my life ever since you left. Pretty, isn't it? How dare you not tell me you were coming?"

Ted put his suitcase on the bed. "I literally didn't know until two days ago, and I've been travelling ever since. I thought it would make you happy."

"So now you get to waltz in here after all the work is done and walk her down what little aisle she has and I'll be shoved off to the side like yesterday's leftovers."

"We can both walk her down the aisle if that's what you're worried about. I didn't mean to come back and screw everything up."

"But you're so good at it, Ted." She collapsed into her armchair and stared off into space.

He came closer and took a good look at her. "What medications do they have you on? I think it's too much. You look terrible."

"So now I look terrible on my daughter's wedding day. Thank you for flying a million miles to tell me that."

"And what is that smell? If I didn't know better...." He gave her an incredulous look. "Have you been smoking up?"

"So what if I have? It's none of your business. It helps me relax."

Ted sat back on the bed, dumbfounded. "We haven't had a joint in twenty years."

"Well, it's amazing what happens when your life falls apart. And you know what's really irritating? You look twenty years younger, which I assume is because you're not living here with us."

"That's not true."

"And to top it all off, you can't stay long. Gee, that's too bad."

"Maybe I could stretch it out for a couple of days."

"Please, don't do so on my account. Just go and make sure things run smoothly downstairs. I'd like to have a nap before the ceremony."

She got into bed and pulled the covers over her head, chignon and all.

Ted did as she asked. Sheena told him to stay away from her until she was ready. She wanted her dress to be a surprise. He wandered into the family room because there was mayhem in the kitchen with people he didn't know running around. Mary, Ethel, and Carole were in their finery already, just waiting for guests to arrive.

Ted gave them a sheepish smile. "Looks like I ruined Peggy's day."

Ethel shook her head. "You surprised her, that's all. She's had a really rough go of it since you left. I think she's depressed."

"What she is, is high as a kite. She's been smoking pot up there. Did you know that?"

Mary's stomach did a backflip.

"Frig off!" Ethel said. "Where the hell would she get that?"

"Beats me," replied Ted.

"Well, doesn't that take the cake," Carole mused. "I was wondering why she was singing *The Sound of Music* this morning."

"I'm going to see if Sheena needs anything." Mary left the room in a hurry.

At two o'clock, the Corbett family and wedding guests started showing up. Ted and Carole greeted the guests and ushered in the justice of the peace when he arrived. The house was soon filled to the brim. Servers began offering champagne to the guests. Ted told everyone his wife was up with her daughter, having a moment.

Chuck and Maxine Corbett were surprised to see Ted. Maxine stared at him, holding two glasses of champagne in her hands. "I thought you were AWOL," she said, almost accusing.

"Some things are too important to miss." Ted smiled.

"So right!" Chuck boomed. "So right! I hope you noticed the limousine outside waiting to take the kids to their hotel tonight. Couldn't have them driving in Sheena's old Jeep, could we?"

"That's very generous," Ted said.

Ted made his way over to Drew, who was standing off to the side in the living room with his two brothers, all of them looking very dashing in their tuxes.

"It's great to see you, Mr. Henderson. Sheena must have been so surprised."

"Yes, she was pretty pleased. I'm glad I made it. And I hear you're leaving Sydney to move to Halifax almost immediately."

Drew gave him an sheepish grin. "I hope that's okay."

"You and Sheena have your own life now. Whatever you decide is okay by me."

"Thanks a lot."

Carole pulled Mary over and pointed to the dining room. "Make sure your Gran isn't in there polishing off the champagne. I better go get Peggy, or she's going to miss the whole thing."

Carole opened Peggy's bedroom door, not sure what she was going to see, but when she realized that Peggy had covered up her fresh hairdo, she was livid. She pushed back the covers.

"Peggy Sue Ryan-Henderson. Get out of this bed this minute and behave yourself."

Peggy gave her a filthy look. "I'm hiding."

"Get up." She reached over and grabbed a comb off of Peggy's bureau. "You've made a mess of your hair. Sit still."

Peggy did as she was told. "Can you believe he waltzed in here today like a big hero?"

"I think it's wonderful. Sheena is so happy her dad is here, and why shouldn't she be? You better get over yourself or Sheena will be upset with you. And she'd be furious if she knew you were smoking joints up here."

"He told you? Blabbermouth."

"There. Now go see Sheena. It's all about her right now."

Peggy stood up and took a deep breath, then she walked out of her room and down the hall and knocked on Sheena's door. "It's Mom."

"Come in."

Sheena was as beautiful as Peggy always imagined she'd be, breathtaking in her ivory ball gown with diamond drop earrings shimmering against her cheeks.

"Oh, honey." Peggy started to cry.

"Mom, don't. You'll make me cry. Just hug me."

Mother and daughter hugged each other for a long time. When Ted showed up in the doorway, Peggy forgot she was mad at him. The look on his face as he saw their little baby erased everything. Instantly, she was gratified beyond words that he'd made it home. She reached over and hugged him and he hugged her back.

They heard the violinist and flautist begin to play. Peggy and Carole walked down the staircase together and joined their mother, who was standing by the fireplace holding a champagne flute in her hand. Carole grabbed it from her as soon as they got settled into their seats.

"Meany," Ethel muttered.

As the music played, Mary came down the staircase, followed by Riley. They walked towards the boys, and Mary had to admit that Drew and his brothers, Chris and David, looked spectacular in their tuxes. How was it possible that tubby Mr. Corbett and his miserable wife had managed to produce these three?

Ted walked down the stairs alone and stood at the bottom with his hand held up, waiting for Sheena. It was a good plan, because there was no way the two of them were going to be able to fit on the stairs together with Sheena's skirt.

The sight of Sheena in her finery was something everyone in that room would remember for a long time. She flashed Drew a huge smile when she saw what he was wearing, and Drew shed a few tears as she walked towards him. Mary liked him a whole lot better after that display. She could even forgive him for chewing with his mouth open. And she noticed even Maxine was a little starstruck when she saw Sheena. Mary was proud of Sheena for getting one over on her new mother-in-law.

The officiant then announced that Sheena and Drew had written their own marriage vows. Mary wondered how Sheena had managed to twist Drew's arm on that score. In her opinion it was hokey and cringe-worthy, but she'd only seen it done on television. She hoped it was better when you knew the person.

It wasn't.

Among other things, Sheena promised to always have Drew's favourite beer in the fridge, and Drew said he'd rub her feet whenever she asked. Maxine went back to rolling her eyes.

An exchange of rings, a kiss, and then it was over. Everyone clapped, kissed, and hugged each other.

Mary, Carole, and Gran made their way out to the kitchen to see if they could be of some help so that Ted and Peggy could greet their guests, spend some time with the happy couple, and get some pictures taken. As soon as they walked in, they could tell something was wrong.

"What's the matter?" Carole asked the woman in charge.

"There's no power."

"What do you mean? Of course there's power." She flipped a light switch but nothing happened.

"How did we not notice that?"

"It went off five minutes ago during the ceremony. I have trays that have to go in the oven. I can serve some things, but others need to be warmed up."

"Damn. What do we do?"

"I was hoping you'd know."

"Just give everyone more booze," Ethel suggested.

"Mary, you better tell Peggy and Ted."

When they arrived in the kitchen Peggy looked stricken. "Maxine Corbett will have a field day with this. What do we do?"

"I'll get the barbecue going," said Ted immediately. "And what about our camping stove? I'll set them outside the kitchen door and we'll heat as much as we can."

Having Ted take over was just what Peggy needed. "That's perfect. Frig Maxine. We'll manage.

In the end, they had a blast sitting in the living room in candle-light, most of the young people on the floor, eating and drinking all together because there weren't enough candles or lanterns to light up every room.

Sheena and Drew thanked everyone for coming to the best wedding that anyone had ever had. Cheers went up. Even Maxine Corbett shouted hurray, but she was entirely drunk and swaying in the corner with Gran.

Mary was laughing at Drew's brothers having an arm-wrestling match over the last pig-in-a-blanket on the buffet table when she glanced in the dining-room mirror. She looked actually honest-to-God beautiful. Her bright lipstick brought out her smile and her freckles looked warm and summery. Darn it. Daniel wasn't around to see her and this might not happen again in her lifetime.

"Sheena! Can you take my picture?"

CHAPTER SEVEN

THE NEXT DAY, CAROLE, GRAN, and Mary sat at their kitchen table with a big bottle of Tylenol on the table. Only Mary didn't need it. One thing she'd learned early on was that she would forever be the designated driver in the family; she never bothered learning how to drink.

She poured hot coffee for her mother and grandmother and then fed Roscoe, who was waiting patiently by his dish. "Would you like some eggs?"

The other two shook their heads.

"I'm making some anyway. You need something in your stomachs."

They didn't bother objecting.

While Mary set about making breakfast, the sounds of suffering didn't let up.

"My head," Gran moaned. "I didn't have *that* much to drink."

"Don't make me laugh," Carole scoffed. "You had more than anyone, except maybe Maxine Corbett. What got into her? Chuck had to carry her to one of his fancy cars."

Mary stirred the eggs. "I thought it was a beautiful wedding in the end. Even with the power out. It made it kind of romantic."

"The food wasn't that great," Carole said. "But what do you expect trying to barbecue in a hurricane?"

"I wonder how Aunt Peggy and Uncle Ted are this morning."

"Signing divorce papers is my guess."

"Surely not."

Her mother lit a cigarette. "How else do you explain her reaction to him coming home?"

Gran grunted. "If she's been using wacky-tobacky this whole time, that might have something to do with it. What I want to know is where she got it. There's no way she was cruising Charlotte Street at night."

Mary doled out the eggs on two plates and put them in front of her relatives. "Want some ketchup?"

They shook their heads. Mary put the pan in the sink. "They stopped fighting just before the ceremony, so that has to count for something. I'm sure they'll be fine. I can't see Aunt Peggy and Uncle Ted breaking up. They fit together."

"She was fit to be tied," Gran laughed. "I hope she doesn't do anything stupid."

The Hendersons were having breakfast with the Corbetts that morning because the new Mrs. Sheena Corbett woke up in the hotel honeymoon suite and had a massive panic attack. Not the kind that called attention to itself; just an overwhelming feeling that she would never be able to stay at her parents' house anymore by herself. She'd have to let Drew know first. Not that he would care, but he would now have to be consulted about her every decision. Or at least be informed.

It was suffocating.

What was she doing with a husband? Would she be able to go out with her friends and drink shots? Of course not, because he was taking her off the island and she didn't have any friends in Halifax. What would she do all day while he was working? Did he expect her to cook? She'd have to wash his underwear.

For the rest of her entire life she'd never be able to flirt again or ever go to bed with anyone else. What the hell had she been thinking? Why had she been so impatient to marry a guy who ate with his mouth open? She looked at her expensive wedding dress in a pile on the hotel floor and realized she'd spent about seven hours in it. And after that first hour, no one really saw the exquisite details because of the power outage. What did she do with it now? She'd have to take it to her mom and dad's house. The dress was going to get to live in her bedroom and she wasn't.

Sheena told Drew that she wanted to visit her dad because she didn't know when he would be leaving. Drew believed her and went along with it, even though she could tell he was a little disappointed to be getting out of bed at such an ungodly hour. Her only hope was that she wouldn't cry on the way over.

Peggy was snoring so loud that Ted couldn't sleep, so he set about trying to get the house back in order. The caterers did a good job cleaning up the dishes, but the place was still a tip. Regardless, if you had to have a wedding without power, you couldn't have had a better one.

The front door opened and in walked Sheena and Drew.

"This is a surprise," Ted said.

"It was to me too," Drew replied.

"I was afraid you were going to leave without seeing me." Sheena walked over and hugged her dad.

"I'm here for a few more days. Don't worry. I won't go without telling you."

Ted was about to release her but Sheena clung onto him. "Maybe you shouldn't go back. Mom's had a hard time without you. What will she do when I go too?" She could feel the build-up of tears behind her eyes and knew she had to leave. "I'll go wake her up."

She left Drew downstairs and went up her mom's room. Despite the fact that her mother was sawing wood, she crawled beside her and sobbed her heart out. After a few minutes Peggy realized there was an unfamiliar weight leaning on her. Her eyes opened, and she couldn't believe her baby was in her arms.

"Hey now, hey now. What's this? What's wrong?" She shook herself awake and patted Sheena on the back. "Shhh. It's okay. You can tell me anything."

"Oh, Mama...I've made a terrible mistake! I don't want to be married. Why did you let me do it?"

Peggy had had a rough twenty-four hours, but she wasn't completely insane yet. She pushed Sheena away from her and struggled to sit up in bed. "Oh, no you don't. Don't you dare come in here and decide it's my fault you're married! You wanted this and drove us crazy to make sure it happened. If you weren't sure, you should've let him go to Halifax and delayed the wedding for a year."

"Why didn't I listen to you? Why did you have to be right?"

Now that Peggy was more awake, she saw what was happening. Sheena had on her petrified-little-girl face. She always panicked when faced with a new situation, whether it was school or the first day of ballet class or—apparently—being married. Peggy reached over and took Sheena's hands in her own.

"I want you to take a deep breath. Don't shake your head. Just do it. Deep breaths."

Sheena followed her lead.

"You got married yesterday because you love Drew, and I don't believe for a minute you would've done so if he weren't the one for you. As desperate as you've always been to wear a wedding dress, you're not that crazy. It's a new experience. You're afraid to leave home. You'll be sleeping in a different bed. I had all these same thoughts the day after my wedding. It kind of sneaks up on you and reality hits. But you don't have to be afraid. Your dad and I are always here for you. You'll spend plenty of time here too. Now why don't we go downstairs and get something to eat? You barely had anything last night and that's not helping the situation. I'll make French toast."

Sheena grabbed her mom around the neck. "Thank you for being the best mom ever. I don't know how I got so lucky."

"Remember that. Now let me go. I can't breathe."

They had a nice breakfast together, Ted doing most of the grunt work for Peggy, before the happy couple decided they wanted to meet friends for lunch. They said they'd be back for supper. Ted and Sheena took their coffee into the family room and hashed over the night before.

"I'm sorry I was so rude when you came in. I thought I was hallucinating."

"You were."

"The marijuana actually helped. I've been so lonely and sad and miserable with this cast on and my back always aching. It's been rough. Only now do I feel better. I got out of bed this morning and noticed my back didn't twinge. And I get my cast off tomorrow. That will be a huge relief."

"There's something else I want you to ask the doctor about. You should be checked for sleep apnea. Your snoring has gotten so much worse. I could hardly sleep last night."

"It's that bad?"

"Do you feel tired all the time?"

"Yes, but I thought that was all the drugs I've been taking."

"Just do this for me. You can thank me later."

"Fine. You, on the other hand, look like a million bucks. I hate you for that."

Ted took a sip of his coffee. "I can assure you, I'm not on vacation over there. It's a completely different world; it brings me to tears most days. The only reason I want to stick with it is because they are so desperate for people with medical experience. I really have to go back. I told them I would. And I'll be home by the end of the year. I won't make any more decisions without you."

Peggy sighed. "Is it wrong for me to feel left behind? Especially now that Sheena is leaving town?"

"Of course it will seem lonely, but it doesn't have to be. You should explore what's out there. Take up a hobby. Volunteer. Do things you've never had a chance to do before. You might like it. Change is good, Peggy. And we were definitely in a rut."

"That's true."

"So let's change things up."

"Wanna smoke a joint and go to bed?"

"What about your back?"

"You can do the heavy lifting."

Mary went to work at noon. Everyone noticed she wasn't wearing glasses, even her customers. So how was it that her mom and Gran still hadn't said anything about it? It was probably just because they were hungover, but it bugged Mary to no end. It was like she was part of the furniture to them. Nothing she ever did produced a serious reaction. Was it because she never did anything worth noting?

As she pulled the groceries towards her one after the other in a hypnotic rhythm, she came to the conclusion that for twenty-three years she'd been living like a dull twelve year old. Mary couldn't remember being young and carefree as a kid. There was always too much hollering and upset in the house. Since she didn't have a dad to intervene, she was constantly aware that she needed to be on call in case her grandmother messed up and her mother went into a rage about it. Mary was the buffer between them and they didn't even appreciate it.

At least ditzy Sheena had goals, even if they were only to get a man and have a wedding. But she'd accomplished them. What had Mary ever wanted, besides Roscoe? And Daniel, but she couldn't have him. If she wasn't careful, one day she'd be alone with her face in a plate of creamed peas on toast.

Someone was speaking to her. She shook her head and focused her eyes on...Daniel. He was holding a jumbo box of Captain Crunch and a quart of milk.

"Sorry! I didn't see you."

"You okay?"

She was about to say she was fine, but there was no one behind him in the line up. "Actually, I'm not. Is there any way you can meet me later? I get off work at five. I shouldn't be bothering you, but there's no one I can talk to."

He looked concerned. "Sure, that's not a problem. Do you want me to pick you up? Amber is at her sister's baby shower tonight. We can go somewhere and grab a coffee."

"That would be great. Thank you so much."

She rang in his items and gave him his change. He smiled. "You look great without glasses, by the way. Now I can see your gorgeous eyes."

Mary felt herself blush. "Thanks."

"See ya."

Mary counted down the minutes all afternoon. Normally she was calm and patient at her job, but such was her desire to break free today, that she wasn't her usual pleasant self. She smiled at people, but she didn't speak unless she had to. Eventually Janet sidled up to her.

"This is the first time I've ever seen you unhappy. Is everything all right?"

"I'll be okay. I just don't feel like being here right now."

"God. I feel like that every day. You're always my little ray of sunshine."

"Janet, did you bring your nice red sweater with you today?"

"It's in my locker."

"Could I borrow it tonight?"

"Yes! Girl, how many times have I told you to wear some colour?"

Mary hurried closing up her cash, grabbed Janet's sweater, and went into the ladies' room. She scrubbed her face, brushed her teeth, and took her hair out of her ponytail. She put on the sweater and even she could see it brought colour to her cheeks. For once she didn't look like a little kid. She left the bathroom and went to grab her coat. Janet looked at her.

"Holy Hannah! You look good! Just a sec." She reached into her purse and pulled out a lipstick. "It's the same shade as the sweater."

Mary took it and applied it in front of a small mirror on the wall. "I've never worn lipstick before, except at the wedding yesterday."

"Well, get yourself to Shoppers Drug Mart and buy one. You have lips that need showing off."

Mary realized she looked like her favourite customer with her wacky lip colour. It was exactly the look she was going for. She thanked her fairy godmother and raced down the stairs.

There he was, waiting in his truck near the entrance. She hurried over and climbed in.

"Hi."

He didn't say anything, just stared at her. She worried she had something in her teeth.

"Is it still okay if we go?" she asked.

"Yes! Sorry. You look different…I mean…amazing."

She grinned. "Thanks."

"Where would you like to go?"

"Anywhere."

They didn't go far. They ended up in a quiet corner at Starbucks, drinking coffee and eating lemon loaf.

"What happened today?" he asked. "You looked upset this morning."

"Have you ever had a moment when you wondered what you're doing with your life?"

He chuckled. "Every second day."

"It hit me that I never do anything unexpected. I don't rock the boat. I don't make waves. I stay in my corner and try not to get in trouble.

And I realized the only fun I've had *ever* is when we were exchanging drugs and you kissed me on the porch! How pathetic is that?"

"You're a nice girl."

"That's what everyone says! I don't want to be a nice girl."

"You don't realize how few nice people there are out there. Your niceness is what made my grandmother love you. There's so little kindness in the world. There's nothing wrong with being nice, Mary. I wish Amber were nice. Or nicer to me at least." He looked away and she watched him struggle with his feelings. "I have no business being here with you, because I think you're lovely, and given half a chance, I'd take you in my arms and never let go."

"And I'm saying that I'm always the girl who does the right thing. And I don't want to do the right thing. Now tell me. Is that wrong?"

He pulled her to her feet. "Let's get out of here."

They drove to a quiet dead-end spot and couldn't keep their hands off each other. It was frantic and steamy. Mary had never had such fun in her life, and she was amazed at how well she did. Obviously watching HBO had helped. She cried out, she moaned, she giggled, and when the finale arrived, she got an A+ on her first try.

The cab was about a hundred degrees when it finally stopped rocking. As beads of sweat ran down their faces, they looked at each other with surprise and wonder.

"Am I still a nice girl?"

"You are the baddest girl I've ever met."

Mary raised her arm in triumph. "Yes!"

Ted drove Peggy to the hospital and took the cast off her arm. As he cracked open the hard, dirty shell, she said, "This is the nicest thing you've ever done for me." She sighed. "God, this feels good."

He laughed and gave it a final push. She pulled out her arm and looked at it in horror. "My God, it's so skinny and awful looking! Do they always look like this? Is something wrong?"

"Your arm has been through the wringer. It'll get much better over the coming days. I'm just going to wrap it for now so you don't damage it."

"Wait...I have to scratch it first."

Peggy took great pleasure in rubbing her nails up and down her poor sickly skin. "I've been wanting to do this for so long. This is heaven."

Even better was walking out of the hospital feeling as light as a feather. She swung her arm at her side and relished the feeling of freedom. It was like walking in shoes for the first time after months of winter boots.

Peggy called to tell Carole that, since it was Ted's last night home, he wanted to treat the whole family to dinner. She told her sister to wrangle the troops and meet them at Kiju's Restaurant in Membertou at seven.

Carole hung up and yelled from the kitchen. "We're going to dinner tonight at seven. One last expensive gesture from Teddy boy."

"Seven?" Ethel fired back. "I eat supper at four. I ain't goin'."

"You are so going! It's Ted's last night here."

"That's his problem."

"Did you hear me?" Carole shouted louder.

"I heard you!" Mary hollered back from her bedroom. "I'm sure they heard you upstairs too."

"Make sure you order a couple of appetizers and some dessert. We can wrap them up and take them home."

"Classy, Mom."

Carole immediately got up and walked to Mary's bedroom door. "I'll thank you not to take that tone with me."

Mary kept brushing Roscoe, who was loving his new grooming tool. "There is no other tone to take. Who tells someone to order more food so they can haul it back to their house? That's rude. Isn't it enough they're paying for our dinners?"

"What has gotten into you lately? Everything I say, you bite my head off."

Mary got off the bed and stood in front of her mother. "You are never grateful for anything. You make snide remarks about Aunt Peggy and Uncle Ted all the time. They are unfailingly generous with us but you turn up your nose, saying it's charity or that they're trying to lord it over us somehow." Mary's heart was pounding as she picked up momentum. "Where would we be without them? Why don't you accept anything gracefully? Why can't you be happy? Why do you *insist* everyone else be as miserable as you?"

Carole slapped Mary hard across the face. Mary stood there and never took her eyes off her mother. Carole turned and disappeared behind her bedroom door.

Gran crept down the hall and looked at Mary with big eyes. "You okay?"

Mary sighed. "Yes, Gran. I'm always okay."

Once again, Peggy and Sheena stood together and waved goodbye to Ted at the airport.

Sheena held on to her dad for a long time. "Thank you so much for coming back. It made the wedding really special for me."

"I only have one daughter. I'm happy I made it. Don't fret so much about moving to Halifax. This is the beginning of a new chapter. And don't worry about your mom; she's stronger than you think."

Peggy held on to him too. "Thank you for coming home for the wedding."

"I only have one daughter. I'm happy I made it. Don't fret so much about Sheena moving to Halifax. This is the beginning of a new chapter for both of you. She's stronger than you think."

Two hours later, they waved Drew goodbye from the house. He came over, his car packed with his belongings, ready for his trip to Halifax. He walked over to Peggy and hugged her tightly.

"Thanks for all your help with the wedding and everything. We really appreciate it."

"No problem. We'll spend the week getting her stuff organized for the short term. The rest of her things can stay here until you find somewhere to live."

"Sheena, Dad said to just go over to the dealership tomorrow to sign the papers for the new Jeep. He's already got a buyer for your old one."

"Okay, I will." She smiled. "Love you, Mr. Corbett."

"Love you too, Mrs. Corbett."

They kissed long and hard before he got in the car. They waved until they couldn't see him anymore. Sheena turned to her mother. "I don't like being called Mrs. Corbett."

"Don't worry. No one will call you that. You'd be surprised how few times in your life it happens."

Peggy set about making tuna sandwiches for lunch. Sheena was texting at the island, then suddenly stopped. "What do you think was going on between Mary and Aunt Carole at the restaurant last night?"

"They were pretty quiet."

"Yeah. Did you notice how nice Mary looks without her glasses? She was even wearing lipstick."

Peggy nodded as she cut the sandwiches and put them on plates. "I did notice that. I mentioned it, too. She really is a stunning girl. You should give her some advice about clothes."

"She never wanted any before, but I'll ask her over when I'm cleaning out my closet. Maybe she'd like a few things."

"That's very sweet of you, honey." She placed a plate in front of her daughter.

Sheena smiled and took a bite of sandwich. "Did you give her the money for contacts?"

Peggy sipped her milk. "No...." Sheena gave her a look. "Okay, yes. But don't tell Carole."

"My lips are sealed."

True to her word, Sheena did invite Mary over one night that week, which was a surprise for Mary. Her and Sheena usually only saw each other when their mothers were together or at family functions. She wasn't sure what was up. Maybe it had something to do with the fact that her cousin was moving away.

When she arrived, Aunt Peggy hugged her and told her to go up to Sheena's room. When she got there all of Sheena's clothes were strewn over the room, with most of the stuff on the floor. Sheena was on her knees digging through it.

"Hi..." Mary said uncertainly. "Were you robbed?"

"Oh, hi, Mary. Come sit down."

"Okay...but if you asked me over here to help with your laundry, I'm leaving."

"No. I have to sort through my stuff and figure out what I'm taking with me to Halifax and what's staying behind for now. Who knows how long it will be before we find a place to live?"

Mary joined her on the floor. "Are you excited?"

"I guess, but it'll be hard to leave."

"I can't imagine that. I wish I had somewhere to go."

Sheena stopped in the middle of folding a cashmere sweater and gave Mary a long look. "Is it hard living with Gran?"

"It's hard living with my mother. Gran can be annoying, but she's harmless. Until you add my mother and then the two of them go at it. It's like living with toddlers. I have a constant headache."

"I never really thought about how it must be for you. Why don't you leave? Get your own place?"

"I don't make a lot of money at the grocery store. I'm thinking of going back to school, but I'm not sure what I want to do. Whatever it is, it better pay me enough to leave home."

"When I move to Halifax, maybe you can come and visit me. That would get you out of the house. I'm sure my mom will be coming up every second weekend, so you can hitch a ride with her."

"Thanks! I'll keep that in mind."

"In the meantime there's lots of things I'm giving to Goodwill. Stuff I haven't worn in ages or don't want anymore. Go through the pile and take whatever you like. You have got to stop wearing only black or white T-shirts." Sheena gave her an appraising look. "You're beautiful, Mary. Dress like it."

Mary spent three hours sorting through Sheena's clothes. Mary tried on a few items here and there and her cousin told her what looked good and what didn't. They were at it so long, Aunt Peggy arrived with drinks, crackers, and cheese dip. Then she sat and offered up opinions.

By the time Mary left, she had two huge garbage bags full of clothes, most of them hardly worn twice. She put them in the trunk of her car and stood under the chilly April night sky. Her aunt and cousin were on the doorstep, holding their arms over their chests against the chill.

"Thank you. I…." Mary was lost for words. She wasn't used to being fussed over.

Aunt Peggy gestured for her to come over for a hug. "It's our pleasure, sweetheart. Anything for you."

Even Sheena hugged her. "If I don't see you before I go, don't forget to come visit me."

Mary stopped and bought a small coffee on the drive home, then took it back to the car and drank it in the parking lot.

Something broke inside. Her eyes filled with tears. Aunt Peggy and Sheena had shown her that she was worthy of nice things. And Daniel had shown her that she deserved to be loved.

CHAPTER EIGHT

CAROLE AND ETHEL TOOK THEIR frozen dinners out into the living room to watch Dr. Phil. Today's episode was about a freeloading son who wouldn't get a job or do any work around the house and stole money from his parents.

"You watch," Carole said. "It'll be the mother's fault. It's always the mother's fault."

Ethel ate a forkful of mashed potato. "It generally is."

"Well, it is in your case."

"Hold your horses. You have a job, you work around the house—sort of—and you don't steal money from me, as far as I know. So it looks like I did a great job."

Carole bit into a piece of chewy chicken. "If that's the case, I'm a saint. My kid does it all."

"True, but for someone who's doing such a bang-up job, your kid is pretty miserable."

"She is not."

Exasperated, Ethel threw her tray on the coffee table. "I've got eyes, Carole. Mary has been unhappy for a long time, only you're so wrapped up in your own head you don't notice it. You better do something about it before it's too late." She narrowed her eyes at her daughter. "And for what it's worth, slapping her isn't the way to go."

Carole gave up on her dinner as well. She lit a smoke instead. "I didn't mean to slap her."

"Then tell her you're sorry."

"What was I supposed to do? She was being lippy."

Ethel leaned closer to Carole. "She's not thirteen! She's a young woman and as good as gold. God almighty, why shouldn't she be cranky? I wouldn't want to live with us. Would you?"

Carole didn't bother answering. She knew her mother was right, but she didn't know how to get out of the giant unhappy hole she'd dug for herself. It seemed as though she'd been doomed from the start. And right or wrong, she blamed her mother for all of it. Maybe it would help if she could talk to her mother like a normal person, but that would never happen because Carole was deathly afraid of opening that festering wound. It was better to leave the door closed.

They both heard Mary come in from outside through the kitchen door. She didn't stop to say hello, just kept going until she got to her bedroom and shut the door.

"Go say you're sorry."

Carole stubbed out her cigarette and slowly got up off the couch. She had a headache and felt sick. She needed to stop smoking and start eating right, but the weight of good intentions was too heavy. She didn't have the energy to save herself.

She knocked on Mary's door. "Can I come in?"

"Just a minute."

There were sounds coming from inside the bedroom, like Mary was sliding stuff across the bedroom floor and shutting her wardrobe. The child was a privacy nut.

"Come in."

Carole opened the door and was greeted with Mary sitting on her bed with Roscoe in her lap, as if for protection.

"Can I sit down?"

"Okay."

Roscoe gave a purr-meow, as if giving his consent as well. Carole sat and glanced at him. "He's looking better."

"He was always handsome. He just needed some tender loving care."

"Well, you'd be the one to give him that." She faltered. "I'm sorry about the other night. I shouldn't have hit you. I promise I'll never do it again."

"Thanks."

"Your Gran thinks you're unhappy. Are you?"

"I'm starting to learn that I need to make myself happy. I can't rely on others to do it for me. You should try it."

"I guess I'm not a very good mother, but then again, I didn't have much of a role model."

"Stop it. Stop blaming Gran."

"You don't know everything—"

"And I don't want to." Mary stopped petting Roscoe and he jumped off her lamp, offended. "I'm sorry, I have to get some sleep. Good night."

Carole was dismissed. She felt like a chastised kid as she closed Mary's door. She went back into the living room and sat on the couch.

"Well?" said Gran.

"She loves you more than me."

In fact, Mary loved Daniel.

A week after their first encounter, he asked Mary to meet him at his friend's apartment, which was empty during the day. It was one thing to have a torrid encounter in the spur of the moment; it was another to deliberately have a rendezvous in the middle of the afternoon.

As Mary got ready, she tried to put Amber out of her mind. The girl was insufferable. Mary had heard her screaming at Daniel just last night through her bedroom ceiling. Mary tried to convince herself that if Amber was going to be so mean to him, she didn't deserve him. But she knew that her justification was bullshit. She had no right to be hooking up with Amber's boyfriend.

But it didn't stop her from getting ready.

She pulled on a pair of Sheena's jeans and a cornflower blue top that had tiny white flowers on the gauzy overlay. It was a very pretty blouse and Mary felt quite girly in it. Then she remembered some of the advice Sheena had thrown her way—to always pair opposites— and slipped on a soft leather bomber jacket. *Imagine giving this away!* Mary thought. With her hair in soft waves and her new pink lipstick on, Mary felt like a different woman. She turned to Roscoe, who was curled up on her quilt.

"What do you think?"

Roscoe lifted his head and gazed at her lovingly. She reached over and held his round face in her hands. "I love you, big boy."

Roscoe closed his eyes and settled back in with a contented sigh.

Her mother, between appointments, was at the kitchen table having lunch, which consisted of Pepsi and beef jerky. Gran had her ginny tea and a box of May Wests. They both looked up at the same time.

"You look nice," Gran said.

"You look really nice," Carole said. She surveyed her daughter. "What's different?"

"I'm not wearing glasses, Mother. I haven't worn them for almost two weeks now."

"How can you see?"

"I have contacts."

"What did they cost?"

"I saved up for them."

"Oh. Where did you get that blouse? Is it new? Are you spending a lot of money on clothes?"

"Sheena gave it to me. But if I want to buy new clothes I will."

Gran gave Carole a look and for once, Carole stayed quiet. Mary was beginning to realize that if she asserted herself, her mother backed down. Lesson learned.

"Where are you going?" her mom asked.

"Meeting a girlfriend for lunch."

"Okay. Have fun."

Mary could tell her mother didn't believe her but she couldn't worry about it. She only had one thing on her mind.

Daniel was waiting and opened the door as soon as she knocked. He pulled her inside and kissed her like he'd been deprived of oxygen.

"I'm going crazy without you," he murmured against her mouth.

"I'm here."

Time melted away, as it does when you're in someone's arms. Which was why they both learned the hard way that's it's not a good idea to carry on in someone else's apartment. They heard the door open at the same time and there was a frantic rush to climb back into their clothes. Mary was only halfway dressed when Daniel's friend came into his living room. She turned her back on him and buttoned up her blouse.

"Oh...sorry. I didn't think you'd still be here."

"Hey, sorry man," Daniel said. "We lost track of time. We'll be out of here in a sec."

"Things went well, I see."

Mary wanted to die. She turned back to Daniel's friend with her cheeks burning and said, "Hi. I'm Mary. I'm really sorry for putting you in this position."

"Hey, live and let live," the friend said with a good-natured shrug.

Daniel pointed to his friend. "This is Donny. He's in the band."

"Hi, Donny."

"Hi, Mary. Nice to meet you."

Daniel grabbed his jacket and took Mary by the hand. "We'll see you around."

"You guys can stay for a beer if you want."

Mary cringed inside. The last thing she wanted was to make small talk with someone who'd just seen her half-naked.

"Nah, that's okay, man. We better take off. See ya later."

They hurried out of the apartment and crawled into Daniel's truck. Mary's car was parked behind his.

"I'm so embarrassed," Mary said, her head in her hands.

"Hey, Donny doesn't care. He doesn't even like Amber."

"That makes no difference. Now I feel cheap and definitely in the wrong."

Daniel reached over and tucked a strand of hair behind her ear. "You're priceless."

"Silly boy."

"I'm breaking up with Amber tonight. I want to be with you. I've never felt this way about anyone before. It's almost like I was in love with you before I even met you—like my grandmother wanted this to happen."

Mary grinned at the word *love*. "Now you're just being corny."

He laughed. "That's how I feel. And I think you feel the same way about me."

She reached out and stroked his cheek. "I do. For the first time in my life, I feel alive." She kissed him once more and then reached for the door handle. "Let's stay away from each other until things settle down. But I'll be thinking of you every minute of the day."

"Me too."

Mary got out of his truck and watched him drive away. She got back in her car but knew she didn't want to go home just yet. In the

end, she drove to the theatre and got a ticket to the next show playing. She needed to sit in the dark and give herself a chance to come
back down to earth.

At that moment across town, Sheena's photographer came to Peggy's
house to deliver the wedding pictures. Sheena was leaving in two
days and she and Peggy were anxious to see the photos together. He
gave them a nice box and inside were a few prints of the best shots,
with a memory stick that held all the photos, in both colour and black
and white.

The two of them sat on the family room couch and looked at the
photos on Sheena's tablet.

"Now I feel bad that I thought he was a pest," Peggy said. "I like
these pictures of you girls getting ready…oh, and I love this one of you
and Mary…and…."

Her mother stopped talking. Sheena glanced up. "What's wrong?"

"Look at my hair!" she said, horrified. "What's wrong with my
hair?"

Sheena leaned over the tablet to get a closer look. "It's okay."

"It's terrible! Why is it so flat?"

"You should've gone to Sheila. I told you that."

"But I'm almost positive I asked for a chignon! Oh, God…why
didn't you tell me?"

"To tell you the truth, I didn't really look at you. My focus was
elsewhere."

Peggy lay back against the couch. "Now I remember. I crawled into
bed at one point."

"Why?"

"Who knows? And to think I told Carole I was going to her salon
from now on."

"She won't remember you said that."

"Wanna bet?"

"Never mind your hair! Look at this one of me hugging Daddy."

"Oh, that is lovely. We'll have to send it to him."

They spent a good hour going through all the pictures. The images brought the day back to life and jogged memories that both of them had already forgotten.

"Oh no, look at Gran in this one!" said Sheena. "She's digging her teeth out of her wine glass. The server looks horrified!"

"That doesn't surprise me. And look at Maxine," Peggy pointed. "She's actually smiling in this one!"

"I'll have to make sure Drew gets to see it. God knows the last time he saw her smile."

"Hey, I have an idea. Why don't we take a pizza over to Carole's and show them the pictures? You have to say goodbye to them anyway."

Mary's movie ended at six. She looked in the mirror of the theatre washroom to see if her full-body glow was gone and if she'd stopped smiling. Looking normal was the effect she wanted. Thankfully only her insides seemed to be on fire, so to anyone else she looked like an ordinary person having an ordinary day.

Her heart sank a little when she saw Aunt Peggy's Lexus parked outside the house. She had hoped to slink into her bedroom and stay there, but that wasn't to be. She forgave her aunt when she saw that pizza was on offer; two extra-large ones at that.

"Come look at the wedding pictures!" Sheena cried. "Oh, you're wearing your new blouse and jacket! Great choice."

"Thanks."

They sat around the table and looked through the pictures, pointing to the ones they liked best.

"Look," Mary said. "I don't think I've ever seen a picture of the five of us together."

"You're right," Peggy said. "I'm going to have it blown up and frame one for each of us."

"We don't need three," Carole said.

"I might like to have one for my bedroom," Mary pointed out. "And maybe Gran would like one for hers. Don't tell Aunt Peggy what to do."

"Fine. Don't be so touchy."

At that moment, the front doorbell rang. Mary wanted to get out of the kitchen anyway, so she walked over and opened the door.

Amber was standing there.

Mary felt the blood drain from her face.

"You fucking whore!" Amber screamed. "I knew it! You were after him from the first time you laid eyes on him! Have you been fucking him this whole time?"

Mary couldn't speak.

"Bitch!" Amber lunged and pulled Mary's hair so forcefully that her neck snapped back. Then she clawed at Mary's face.

As Mary tried to protect herself from this raging opponent, she became aware of other bodies and more hollering. Her family was in the middle of the brawl, her mother screeching, "Get that woman out of my house! I never want to see her face in here again!"

Mary curled up into a ball on the rug. She heard Daniel's voice. "Mary! Are you okay?"

"Leave her alone!" Gran cried. "Just leave!"

The front door shut and they heard Amber bawling at Daniel as they struggled up the stairs of their apartment. Her mom and Gran tried to get Mary off the floor, but Mary pushed them away. "Don't. I'm all right. I need to be by myself." She scrambled up and ran to her bedroom, shutting them all out.

The other four were in shock. Things like this didn't happen in real life. All of them went back into the kitchen and sat at the table, trembling. Carole jumped up and put on the kettle before she lit a cigarette and sat back down, the pizza forgotten. They spoke in whispers.

"Do you know who that was?" Aunt Peggy asked.

"Yeah. She's the little madam who lives upstairs," replied Carole.

"Who was the guy?" Sheena wanted to know.

"He lives up there too. He's Mrs. Aucoin's grandson of all people. He's the one renting the apartment and that's his girlfriend."

Aunt Peggy seemed stunned. "But she accused Mary of...our Mary."

Carole and Gran exchanged looks.

"We knew she liked him," Gran said. "And he obviously liked her, but I think this girl is off her rocker. She said Mary's been with him. That doesn't sound like something she'd do."

Sheena made a face. "Why do you guys always make Mary out to be Anne of Green Gables? She's older than I am. She's allowed to sleep with whoever she wants."

"Not someone else's boyfriend," Carole said.

"So she made a mistake. We're all allowed to do that too."

Aunt Peggy looked towards the hallway. "Why don't you go and talk to her, Sheena? I'm sure she doesn't want to face us."

Sheena got up and walked to Mary's bedroom. She knocked on the door. "It's only me."

"Go away."

"Hey, would you rather me or your mom?"

There was a pause. "Come in."

Mary sat cross-legged on the bed, her face swollen and red from crying, Roscoe by her side. Sheena sat on the end of the bed.

"It's not the end of the world. Girls get in fights all the time."

"In front of their whole families?"

"The timing could have been better."

"The trouble is, Amber's right. I had no business going near him."

"You aren't the first to make that mistake and you won't be the last. And excuse me, but her boyfriend isn't blameless. You didn't do it by yourself."

Mary rubbed her nose with her tissue. "But I thought I was better than this."

"Better than what? The rest of the world? You know, Mary, there have been times when I hated your guts. My mother would go on about what a wonderful child you were and how you were too good to be true. It used to make me sick. I felt like the devil child in comparison. It's really nice to know that you're as stupid as the rest of us."

Mary laughed with relief. Sheena laughed with her. "It's too bad we didn't know we had so much in common; we could've been friends."

"I'm glad you're my cousin."

"Me too. Now tell me about this hot guy you're sleeping with."

Mary couldn't help smiling. "Daniel. We hardly know each other but it's like he's belonged to me from the beginning."

"Wow. That would make a great wedding vow."

"He wants to be with me, so he broke up with her tonight. What a terrible scene."

"Well, he *did* break up with her. She's allowed to make a scene."

"But she only ever yelled at him."

"Doesn't matter."

Mary crumpled her tissues in her hand. "Yeah, you're right."

Sheena got off the bed. "I better go. Don't forget to stay in touch. Text me. And look out for my mom."

Mary got up and hugged her cousin. "Thanks for this, Sheena. You've made me feel so much better."

Mary stayed in her room until Sheena and Aunt Peggy left. Aunt Peggy didn't say goodbye to her, which Mary appreciated. Once they were gone, she hurried to the bathroom and locked herself in to take a hot bath. As she lay there, she heard Daniel and Amber still arguing and stomping around. This was much too close for comfort. She wanted to sink into the bubbles and disappear.

At some point she must have dozed off because she was startled by an impatient knock on the bathroom door.

"Are you gonna to be all night?" Gran shouted. "My back teeth are floatin'."

Mary hurriedly got out of the tub and wrapped herself in a towel. When she opened the door, Gran was squirming. "Outta the way!" She pushed Mary aside and slammed the door behind her.

Mary was going to have to say something to her mother, so, resigned, she got into her pyjamas and went out to the kitchen. Carole was looking out the window, and for once she wasn't smoking. Mary sat down and waited for the lecture.

Her mother continued to look out the window. Which was worse than being yelled at.

"I'm sorry," said Mary sheepishly.

Carole turned to face her. "What for? Falling for a guy? People do it every day."

"But—"

"Look, Mary. I have a horrible track record with men, so I can't offer advice on this score. Daniel seems like a nice guy."

Mary nodded. "He is."

"Then I'm happy for you."

"Thanks for coming to my rescue."

"What are mothers for? I saved you some pizza."

CHAPTER NINE

ETHEL WAS AT DOTTY'S DAIRY picking up a box of tea bags. She knew Carole would have a fit because they were more expensive here than at Sobeys, but Mary was on the late shift and Ethel wanted tea now.

"How's she goin'?" Dotty coughed while she sucked on throat lozenges and sipped from a mug of honey and lemon. Today she had on her usual three sweaters, but also a scarf wrapped around her neck and a musty knitted tam on her head.

"Better than you," Ethel said. "Ya still got that lousy cold?"

"Girl, I can't get rid of it. Them jeezly kids don't close that door properly and no amount of hollerin' makes any difference. In my day, we'd take a belt to them, but nowadays if you so much as look at the little christers, their parents have the cops up your arse."

Ethel put the box of tea bags on the counter and opened her wallet. "I'll take my usual scratch tickets too."

"Sure." Dotty lifted the ticket ledger and picked out Emerald 7, Super Crossword, Onyx 8, Lotto Max, Bingo Extra, and Fruit Explosion. She rang up the purchases and Ethel passed her two twenties. "So I heard a rumour about your Mary," said Dotty, trying to sound casual. "I didn't believe it though." Dotty passed Ethel her change.

Ethel straightened her shoulders. "What rumour?"

"That she was sleeping around with your tenant."

"What kind of filthy mind came up with that?"

"Oh, there were a couple of gals here talking about their friend and they swore it was true."

"Who ya gonna believe? A couple of nincompoops or me?"

"You don't have to convince me!" said Dotty, putting her hands up. "Mary's the salt of the earth. There's just one thing I don't understand…."

"What's that?"

"How the hell she's related to you!"

The two of them had a great laugh over that before Ethel took her leave. She hurried as fast as she could to the house so her daughter wouldn't see her through the window, but of course when she walked into the kitchen Carole was there.

"Were you buying scratch tickets again?"

"No."

"I don't believe you."

Ethel decided the tea bags needed to come out of her purse. "I only bought this. We were out."

"I'm missing forty bucks out of my cash box."

"Maybe Mary took it."

"Ma, so help me—"

There was a knock at the door and in walked Carole's two o'clock appointment. "Hey, girls!"

"Hey," they replied.

The customer pointed at her head and walked into the salon. "Look at this! My husband is starting to call me his old grey mare!"

Carole had no choice but to follow the woman, but she turned back and pointed at her mother and muttered, "This isn't over."

Ethel hurried into her bedroom and hid the scratch tickets under her mattress in case Carole decided to search her purse. It was pathetic that she couldn't have one hobby in her life. What else was she supposed to do for excitement?

After the exertion of her foray to the store, Ethel dozed on the couch in front of the television. The doorbell rang.

"Ma! Get the door!"

"Who was your servant last year?" she shouted back, before struggling to her feet.

The door opened and it was Daniel, holding a bouquet of spring flowers. "Hello, Mrs. Ryan."

"Hello, Casanova. Mary isn't home."

He went red in the face. "I actually brought these for you and Mary's mother. To apologize for the other night."

Ethel decided to take pity on him. "Well, you better come in then."

He handed her the flowers, and she pointed at the couch with the bouquet. "Want something to drink?"

"Oh, no thank you." He sat on the edge of the sofa.

"Ma! Who is it?"

"It's Daniel. Brought us flowers."

"Did he bring us a box of chocolates too?" Carole hollered.

Daniel smiled nervously as Ethel sat on the other end of the couch.

"So do you belong to the no-good son that always promised to do things for your grandmother and then never showed up?"

Daniel looked confused for a second and then blurted, "Uncle Gus?"

"Well, you've passed the first test." Ethel reached for her tea. "Now tell me: is that crazy girlfriend of yours gone?"

"Yes."

"Because if I see her around here again, I'll take the broom to her."

"Don't worry, Mrs. Ryan. She never wants to see my face again."

"Call me Ethel. And what are your intentions towards my grand-daughter? You planning on marrying her?"

Daniel looked startled. "Well, I—"

"I'm only kidding," chuckled Ethel. "But do you like her?"

"Oh, I more than like her. She's the sweetest girl I ever met."

Ethel downed the rest of her tea. "Okay, you've passed the second test. Now there's just one more thing."

"Sure," he said.

She reached over and took the front of his shirt in her fist. "If you hurt that girl, I'm coming after you. I'm not here on Earth for much longer, so I'll happily go to prison if I need to. Do you hear me?"

"I hear you, Ethel."

She let him go. "Good. I don't suppose I could borrow forty bucks?"

Sheena packed the last of her things into her new Jeep. Peggy tried to help but she couldn't lift anything too heavy, so she was in charge of Sheena's pillows and comforter. Stripping them off the bed made Peggy's heart ache. Looking around the bedroom and seeing it neat and uncluttered was like a knife to her chest. No more little girls would play in this room. How did one day slip into the next without her noticing that her baby was growing up? All the ordinary hours when mothers don't think anything is happening or life is boring, and yet all along a miracle is unfolding right before their eyes. Why hadn't someone told Peggy to pay attention?

"Mom! I have to go!"

Peggy felt her lip quiver but was determined to keep it together for Sheena's sake. She didn't want her driving on the highway distraught. She took a deep breath and down the stairs she went. Sheena grabbed the comforter and pillows and stuffed them into the back seat.

"Have I got everything?" she fretted in the doorway. "My purse, my cell, my keys, my charger, and my sunglasses. Am I forgetting anything?"

"I made you a lunch to take."

"Oh, that's okay. I'll just grab a coffee and a doughnut. I'm too wired to eat anything right now."

"Are you sure? Because—"

"Mom. I can't eat. I'll be fine." Sheena took her hands and cupped her mother's face. "Tell me you'll be okay."

"I'll be okay."

They hugged each other for a long time, squeezing tighter and tighter. They were both making a great effort not to break down. It was Peggy who finally pushed Sheena from her. "Go. Drew will be waiting."

Sheena got behind the driver's seat, closed the door, and opened the window. "I'll call you when I get there."

"Goodbye, sweetheart! I love you."

"Bye, Mama!" As she drove down the driveway, she waved out the window, and then turned right and drove out of sight, honking her horn. Peggy stood and waved even after she was gone. God knows how long she stood there before she realized her arms were covered with goosebumps.

Into the house and straight to the kitchen. She took Sheena's lunch out of the fridge and ate it at the kitchen island, pretending Sheena was in the other room. Then she tidied up and wandered around the house. It was so quiet. Morgue-like.

"Hello!" she yelled.

There was almost an echo. "Jesus. This sucks."

The only way to distract herself while waiting for Sheena to call was to put on Netflix and eat two huge bags of popcorn. She was almost through the entire first season of *The Mindy Project* when the phone finally rang. It was Sheena.

"Hi honey! Are you there okay?"

She sounded out of breath. "Yes, I made it, and you'll never guess what. Drew found us an apartment so we don't have to stay with his brother. I mean, we will for a few days because we have to buy some furniture for our place, but it will be so much fun picking out stuff."

"Do you need some money? Let me know."

"Drew wants to be independent. I think we'll be fine."

"Why don't you wait until you start shopping? You might change your tune."

"I better go. We have to unpack the car. But I love you and miss you already."

"Bye, honey. Call me when you get a chance. Love you!"

Despite the cloud of loneliness, Peggy was pleased that Sheena sounded so upbeat and happy. Her daughter was a married woman now, with her own decisions and mistakes to make. But gosh, it did her heart good to hear the excitement in Sheena's voice.

The first time Mary went upstairs to visit Daniel, it felt awkward and scary, as if Amber was going to jump out of the closet and beat her to death. Even Daniel seemed a bit uncomfortable.

"This is weird," he said.

"I know. I keep expecting your grandmother to pop out of the kitchen and give me a plate of cookies."

"I'm aware that your mother and grandmother are downstairs." He took her in his arms. "Is it better to make some noise, or be totally quiet?"

She kissed him. "I really don't care."

"I do. Your grandmother said if I hurt you, she'd happily kill me and go to prison."

Mary laughed. "She said that? What a rig."

They heard a loud meow at the same time, coming from outside the apartment door. They looked at each other. "Roscoe."

Daniel ran down the stairs and opened it. Roscoe bounded up and sauntered into the living room. He gave Mary a quick body swipe against her legs and jumped onto the nearest chair.

"He's happy," Mary smiled.

"I wonder who he'll live with?"

"Don't you dare try and take my cat, mister. That will be the end of this relationship."

Daniel took her in his arms again. "Can we not talk?"

Roscoe eventually got annoyed that no one was paying any attention to him, so he jumped up on the sofa and interrupted the proceedings.

"Roscoe, you're messing with my mojo here, buddy." Daniel pushed him to the floor, but Roscoe was not deterred. He jumped back up and snuggled into Mary.

"Leave him alone." She swatted Daniel's hand away and grinned. "He's my first love. I can't abandon him."

"We'll see about that." Daniel jumped off the couch and walked into the kitchen. He grabbed a can of tuna and opened it with an electric can opener. Roscoe was under his feet in seconds. Daniel dumped the tuna on a plate, walked back to Mary, and then led her to the bedroom. He slammed the door shut behind them.

"I will not be outsmarted by a cat," he said.

Then, much to Mary's delight, he pounced.

Peggy was so desperate for occupation that she made an appointment with her family doctor, who was a friend, and what a mistake that was. He made her get on the scale.

"You're over two hundred pounds."

"I most certainly am not!" She was trying not to faint.

Then he took her blood pressure. "This is way too high."

Peggy decided to go on the offense. "I've been stuck in bed since January with a bum back and a broken arm. It's not like I was able to jog or do aerobics."

"What were you eating in bed? Salad?"

"Sometimes."

"Look, Peggy, I like you. I know your family does too. Do all of us a favour and lose some weight so we aren't looking after you when you have a stroke."

"Why are you being such a shithead, Bruce?" Peggy snivelled.

"I told you. I like you."

"Well, I didn't even come in here for any of that. Ted told me to come and ask you about sleep apnea."

Bruce kept writing in her chart. "Okay, we can do that. I trust Ted. How's he doing anyway? I admire him for walking the walk. But I'll miss his annual barbecue this summer."

"You just called me fat. You wouldn't be invited anyway."

He smiled and tore two pages off his prescription pad. "One is for the Snore Shop to have a test, the other is blood work. I want to see your sugars and cholesterol. I can make an appointment with the dietician if you want."

"I'll think about it."

"I want to see you again in a week." He patted her shoulder and walked out. Peggy picked up what was left of her self-esteem and exited the building. Since she had nothing else to do, she went over to the Snore Shop and filled out a questionnaire. Naturally they wanted to know how much she weighed. Jesus. Wasn't it obvious that if you snored like a water buffalo you were overweight? She put down 180. They gave her a device that would measure her oxygen for the night. It was a strap with a box the size of a bar of soap attached to her forehead. If the house caught on fire, she'd have to burn with it because there was no way she'd want another human being to see her in this gizmo.

Since she was only a few minutes away, she drove over to her mother's house. Nothing like gloomy people when you're in that kind of mood.

The back door was unlocked so she let herself in. The place seemed too quiet, despite the blaring television.

"Hello?"

There was no answer. The kitchen table looked like they'd been in the middle of lunch. Peggy reached over and took out a handful of chips from the open bag on the counter. She crunched her way into the living room. The mystery was solved. Carole and Ethel were sound asleep on either side of the couch.

Peggy took a good look at the pair of them while she finished her snack. It was too bad her sister smoked. She had wrinkles forming around her lips. But she was a lot thinner than Peggy, so she was lucky in that regard. Her mother was a round apple on stick legs, blue veins crisscrossing her appendages like a road map.

Getting old was not for the faint of heart.

Peggy reached over, grabbed the remote, and turned off the television. That woke them up.

Carole yawned and smacked her lips. "What are you doing here?"

"Nothing."

Ethel stretched her skinny legs and moaned as she adjusted her position on the couch. "Why did you wake us up?"

"Because I need someone to talk to."

Carole immediately reached for her pack of smokes on the coffee table and lit one. "Don't you have any friends?"

"No, I don't. I had a million acquaintances when Sheena was little and involved in school sports and after-school activities, but then— poof!—they disappeared and I've been left feeling foolish and alone. And now my doctor tells me I'm too fat to live and I have to change my lifestyle."

"They're always yapping about something," Ethel grumbled. "They have nothing better to do than stick their noses and fingers in everyone's business."

Carole blew a smoke ring. "That's their job. Does anyone listen to them? I'm supposed to quit smoking, you're supposed to eat better, and now Peggy has to go on a diet. But will we do it?"

"Maybe we should," Peggy said. "Maybe if we all did it together we could help each other."

The looks on their faces nixed that idea.

"How do other people do it?" Peggy shouted. "The magazines are filled with stories of people losing a hundred pounds or suddenly running a marathon. They're no different than we are."

"Yes they are," Ethel said. "They want to improve. We don't."

Now Peggy got worked up. "And why *is* that? Why do the three of us sit around and moan about our lot, but never try and improve it? And I'm sorry to say, but at least I have tried over the years to change some things about myself. You two are in a time warp." She gestured around the cluttered living room. "Every time I walk into this place, it's exactly the way it was the day before, just another day older and dirtier. The furniture is the same, the decor is the same, your clothes are the same, the food is the same. It's so fucking depressing! How can you stand it?" She jumped up and paced back and forth. "And suddenly I'm starting to feel like you! I'm stuck in this hole and now Sheena is gone and Ted is gone and what do I do with myself? I know I can't get much fatter, so eating can't be my hobby anymore. What the hell do I do with my life? Where the hell did my life go? Why did we never have plans or dreams or goals? Why did we never discuss things or go on picnics or play games? It was always this! Just this! And when I think about that, it makes me so angry!" Peggy started to lose her breath. She saw herself outside her body and she knew she was on the verge of destroying a lot of things, but she was in a vortex of self-hatred and pity.

And then Carole got off the couch and came towards her. Peggy saw her sister's face turn a deep shade of purple. It was frightening.

"You think you had it bad? You think *your* childhood was a never-ending nightmare? And now you—you who have *everything*—are down in the dumps and blame *us* for it? I protected you! I made things better for you! I hid things from you. And you left us the minute you found Ted. You escaped into a better world and you have the nerve to come back and blame us for your rotten life?" Carole was seething. "I have spent my entire life watching you get more than me and I try not to be bitter about it, but I'm angry all the time. I'm angry that you left me alone here. I'm angry that I was left with our mother, who has never acted like a mother. The times I consoled you when Ma would drink and shout and behave like a lunatic. The times I fed you when she was too drunk to wake up. And then you leave and I'm stuck with the woman who made our father leave! The one person I loved more than anyone! She made it so miserable for him to be here that he left all of us. And I'm supposed to forget that and pretend it never happened."

Carole spun around and faced her mother. "How could you? Why did you destroy everything? Why didn't you stop drinking? We could've been a happy family, but you ruined it. I'll never forgive you for that. Never!"

Ethel stood up slowly and put her shoulders back. "I made your wonderful father leave us because he loved you so much. He always wanted to do things with you, like change your diaper and bathe you and sit you on his lap for hours. I thought he was a great dad. Wasn't I lucky woman? And then I had another little girl and he was overjoyed. So overjoyed I caught him peering down into Peggy's crib in the middle of the night and I got a funny feeling but I couldn't be right in thinking that was strange. And then the next night I found him in your bed, Carole, with no clothes on."

She let that sink in.

"And what did I do? I took a baseball bat and fucking hit him and kept hitting him until he fell down the porch steps outside. Then I threw his clothes out the door and told him that if he ever came through that door again, I'd kill him dead.

"And so that's why you don't have a father. And that's when I started to drink. And you know what? I really wish I'd told you this years ago because maybe then you would've spent your whole life hating him instead of me."

Ethel hobbled out of the living room and left her two daughters staring at each other in horror. Both of them grabbed each other's hands and sank into the couch. Carole's tears fell down her face unchecked.

"It can't be true," she whispered. "Not Daddy."

"She has no reason to lie."

"Oh, my God. Oh, my God. I can't believe it."

Peggy held Carole close and let her cry. She had no memories of her father, and couldn't imagine how horrifying it was for her sister to find out the truth about a man she'd loved and pined for all her life. At that moment, Peggy felt like the older sister, and it was enough to make her realize that she'd been acting like an entitled wretch, and that her godawful tantrum was ridiculous. Her life was so privileged, and she had no right to dismiss that out of hand. She felt foolish and chastened. This was one huge kick up the backside from someone up there in the sky. She wasn't going to ignore it.

They heard their mother clear her throat and when they looked up, she was standing by the door with a suitcase at her feet.

"What are you doing?" Carole cried.

"I'm going to live with Peggy. I've been a burden and an irritation to you long enough. Now it's Peggy's turn. I don't want to spend another minute under this roof."

"You can't be serious!" Carole yelled. "Ma! You can't go. I didn't know any of this! You never told me. It's not fair to be mad at me!"

"I'm not mad at you, Carole. I just think we both need a break from each other. Maybe if I was out of the way, you'd find some kind of life for yourself. I don't want you to become a bitter old woman like me. And now that Peggy is looking for something to do, I can be her project. Say goodbye to Mary for me."

Both Peggy and Carole had no words.

"Can we go? I ain't gettin' any younger."

Peggy whispered to Carole. "Let me take her for a few days. You know she'll change her mind. I'll call you tomorrow."

Peggy picked up the suitcase and helped her mother out of the house. They pulled away from the driveway just as Mary pulled in. She wondered where Aunt Peggy and Gran were going.

When she walked in the house her mother was standing in the kitchen looking like the life had been drained from her.

"What's wrong?"

"Gran is going to live with Aunt Peggy."

"Really? She never said anything to me."

"I've lost my mother and my father all in the same day."

Her mother put her hands over her face and let out a wail. Mary was startled. She didn't know what to do. She eventually went over and tried to put her arms around her, but her mother shook her off. "Don't feel sorry for me!"

Carole ran down the hallway and into her bedroom. She slammed the door.

Mary slumped into a kitchen chair. She'd planned on telling her family that she and Daniel wanted to move in together, and she expected an earful because it was a little rushed. What would Mary say now? *Gran's leaving and I'm leaving. You're all alone.* It would be like stabbing her mother in the heart.

Once again, her mother and grandmother came first. When would it end?

Peggy was called to the Snore Shop to discuss her results. She was more nervous than she wanted to admit. It didn't help that the respiratory therapist was a young man who was as cute as a bug.

He shook her hand. "I'm Tom."

She wanted to say, "And I'm a fat, lonely, pathetic housewife." Instead, she smiled. "Peggy."

He sat her down and went over the results. "You stop breathing forty-five times an hour during REM sleep."

"I'm surprised I'm still alive! That sounds bad."

He nodded sympathetically. "It's not good."

She was sent home with a full mask that made her look like a fighter pilot. Tom said they could try others in the weeks ahead to see which one was most suitable for her. As she lay in bed that night and sucked in the machine's air, she realized she sounded like Darth Vader. Her sexy days were over.

CHAPTER TEN

A MONTH LATER IT WAS May, and Ethel still hadn't come home.

Mary got tired of waiting. She spent most of her time upstairs anyway, so what difference would it make if she moved up there permanently? She and Daniel were crazy about each other, and she wanted to sleep in his bed all night, every night.

To get on her mother's good side, she took a couple of garbage bags and a rake outside and began to collect the litter in the rosebushes. It was a good three-hour job. By the end of it, Mary hated humankind. Her back ached and her nails were broken, but the stretching felt good and the air and soil smelled like spring.

Her mother had made pancakes for supper.

"Thanks for doing that. The place looks great."

"You're welcome. I needed the exercise."

"I should get out more," her mother sighed.

"You should. Why don't you plan your appointments so that you give yourself a day off halfway through the week?"

"Well, some customers have their favourite days."

"They won't stop coming to you just because they have to come on a Tuesday instead of a Wednesday."

"I'll think about it."

"There's something else."

Her mother picked up her blasted cigarettes and lit one. "Yeah?"

"I'm moving upstairs with Daniel."

She leaned back in her chair. "You're kidding."

"No, I'm not. I've wanted to do it for a while, but I was hoping Gran would come back so you wouldn't be lonesome. That clearly isn't happening and I can't wait any longer."

"I never asked you to wait around."

"Mom…I know. I just thought I was being nice."

Carole took a drag. "You're making me feel like a pathetic loser."

Mary held her head up with her hand. "I can't win with you."

"If you're up there with him anyway, what difference does it make? Is he bugging you to pay half his rent?"

"If I'm going to be living there, I'll have to contribute something. It's not fair otherwise."

"That's money we could use."

"We have all kinds of money now that we're not paying for Gran's gin, scratch tickets, and food."

Carole gave another mighty sigh. "I suppose it was going to happen some day. At least you're not far away like Sheena."

Mary sat up again and smiled. "So it's okay?"

"How am I going to stop you? Chain you to the bed?"

Mary jumped up and kissed her mother on the cheek. "And just think, Roscoe will be going with me."

"Oh."

Mary was confused. "You sound disappointed."

"He's good company."

"He can visit."

"Just go, will ya? I can't stand all this talking."

Mary laughed and ran out the front door. She gave a brief knock and opened Daniel's front door. "It's only me."

"You better get up here. I'm making hamburgers for supper."

She joined him in the kitchen. "I just had my supper, but guess what?"

He turned over a patty in the frying pan. "What?"

"I'm moving in."

"I love your mother!" Daniel shouted. "But not as much as you."

They forgot about the hamburgers until the smoke alarm went off.

Peggy now daydreamed about her old life when she had been free to come and go and spend her days as she pleased. Her mother moving in had been like instantly acquiring a loud, grouchy hound dog.

"I'm starving! I refuse to eat at six thirty! Just give me some bologna."

"Mother, the doctor said you had to eat better. Now that I'm back on Weight Watchers, I'm planning healthy meals. No more Kraft Dinner."

"Just shoot me now. At least Carole didn't lecture me at every meal."

Now that Peggy's mother wasn't living with her eldest, Carole was suddenly the best daughter ever.

It was a constant stream of complaints. Her bed was too soft. The tub was too hard to get into. The television remote was too damn fancy. There was no corner store she could walk to. You had to drive to the liquor store. The pillows were too thick. The kitchen island chairs were a death trap. There was no candy around.

"If you hate it so much," Peggy finally said, "why don't you go home?"

"I'm teaching Carole a lesson."

"While you're teaching her a lesson, I'm aging rapidly."

"Stop bellyaching. Carole was right. You're a spoiled brat."

Peggy held on to the vegetable peeler and resisted the urge to plunge it into the old gas bag.

One night her mother let out a screech and Peggy forgot that she had her CPAP mask on. She nearly landed on her ass when the hose caught her up short. She unplugged it and hurried into the guest room, turning on the light. "What's the matter?"

Her mother screamed and pointed at her. "What's that?"

Peggy felt her face. "It's my mask."

"You look like Babe."

"Mother, it's a mask that goes over my nose. I can't help that. Comparing me to a pig is not helping my mood. Now what's your problem?"

"I don't know. I had a nightmare, I guess. I don't like it here. I can't find the bathroom in the dark."

"It's not dark. There's a nightlight in your room, one in the hall, and one in the bathroom. If it was any brighter in here you could land a plane."

"It's too quiet. The house doesn't creak. And you can't hear any cars. If someone broke in and killed us, no one would hear our screams for help."

"We have a security system. The alarm would go off if anyone tried to break in."

"I miss Mary."

"She doesn't live at your house anymore. She's upstairs with Daniel."

"She is? What about Roscoe?"

"He's up there with her."

"So Carole is all by herself?"

"Yes."

"She must miss me."

Peggy bit her tongue. "Is there anything else?"

"No. Good night."

"Good night."

Peggy crawled back into her own bed and hooked herself back up to the hose. Too bad it wasn't attached to a car tailpipe.

Peggy and Carole met secretly for lunch one afternoon. Peggy had told her mother that she had to run out for a few groceries, and Ethel asked her to pick up a motherlode of scratch tickets. Anything to keep her happy.

"I know she wants to go home, but for some reason she thinks she's doing you a favour by staying away."

Carole slurped her soup. "I realize she is doing me a favour. I feel much more relaxed."

This is not what Peggy wanted to hear. "So you're not desperate to get her home?"

"Nope."

"Here I was thinking you were pining for her, despite the fact that you fought like cats and dogs."

Carole snorted. "You can keep her."

Peggy's stomach tied itself up in knots. "I can't keep her indefinitely. Ted is coming home at the end of the year."

"We'll revisit that when the time comes."

"Why this sudden change of heart?"

Carole pointed at Peggy with her spoon. "Ma has been like background noise my whole life. And then one day, there's silence. And then another day I turn the radio to a new channel and there's country music. And it's amazing."

Peggy narrowed her eyes. "Country music is amazing?"

"Yes, you stuck-up bitch. I'm hearing another station. And it sounds good."

"This is bad news."

"Why?"

"Because she thinks you're desperate to have her back. It's the only thing she's hanging on to."

"Let her think it." She shrugged.

"But what if she breaks and wants to go home? What do I tell her then?"

Carole smiled. "That's your problem."

"But what about the fact that she saved you as a kid? I thought you loved her for that and you were sorry for everything you thought about her."

"I do love her for that, and I am sorry, but what she did was what any mother would or should do. She doesn't deserve a medal. She's still drinking up a storm. She's not Mary Poppins."

"God. That's for sure."

"I've had her forever. It's not going to kill you to have her for the rest of the year."

"It might."

Sheena was in a foul mood. She hated her new apartment and the smell that permeated the floor they lived on. It was like someone was cooking cabbage, curry, gym socks, and formaldehyde all at once. Drew didn't seem to notice it.

"It's impossible not to notice! You have to walk down the hall to get in here."

"What's the big deal? You're in that hallway for a total of five seconds."

"And today I went out on the balcony and there was a horrid smell of cat pee, not to mention diapers."

Drew went to the fridge and got a beer. "You live in the *world*, Sheena. It's a big bad world filled with disgusting smells. Other people manage to survive it. I'm sure if you put your mind to it, you can overcome this incredible obstacle."

She threw an *InStyle* magazine at him. He pretended not to notice as he dropped in front of his laptop. She sat on the couch beside him. "How was work?" she asked.

"It's insane. If I knew how much shit I had to do I would've let Chris have the dealership. It's like I spend every minute of the day doing a thousand things and it never lets up."

Sheena rubbed the back of his hand. "Aren't you going to ask me about my day?"

He dropped his head to the back of the couch and looked her way. "How was your day?"

She jumped up. "I bought bamboo sheets! They're gorgeous."

"Swell." His attention went back to the computer.

"Drew."

He didn't answer.

"Drew?"

He reluctantly raised his eyeballs. "What?"

"I'm alone all day. I need someone to talk to at night."

"You're going to have to join a chat room. I need five minutes of peace."

Sheena stormed out of the room. He shouted, "Don't get mad!"

She was mad. She was angry and alone and upset. This was the time when she missed her parents the most. It was like no one cared what happened to her. Filling the time shopping had been great for a while, but when Drew hardly looked at what she bought, the thrill went out of it.

It was time to call her mother on Skype. She curled up on their bed and waited for her mom to answer. The familiar jingle sounded and kept going. Maybe she wasn't home. Damn.

And then up popped the picture. Her mother came on the screen looking frazzled. "Hi, honey."

"Hi, Mom. I miss you."

"I miss you too. What's going on?"

"I bought bamboo sheets today."

"Oh, they're lovely. I won't buy anything else."

Sheena noticed her Gran walk up behind her mom. "Hi, Gran! Are you staying out of trouble?"

"There's no goddamn trouble to get into. This is the most boring place on earth."

"But all you did at home was watch television and sit at the kitchen table. Can't you do that at our house?"

"Ain't the same. I'm afraid to spill something on your mother's rug, or knock over one of those prissy china figurines she's got all over the house. It's like an obstacle course in here," Ethel grumbled.

Sheena tried not to laugh. She could tell her mother was about to boil over. "Well, it was nice talking to you, Gran. See you later?"

"Yeah, see ya. Tell Drew to send me a car and get me outta here."

"Will do."

Gran wandered out of the room.

Sheena grinned. "Oh my God. What is up with her?"

"I have no fucking idea!" Peggy hissed. "It's like I can't do a thing right."

"Mom, you look stressed. You're going to have to send her back to Aunt Carole."

"Carole doesn't want her anymore. She's suddenly seen the light and Ethel ain't in it."

"Poor Mommy. Do you want me to come home?"

Her mother's face lit up. "I'd love that! But I thought you were going to try and find a job."

"I will once we find a house. I'm not staying in this stinking apartment forever. And at the moment Drew doesn't care if I'm here or not. He's so tired when he comes home from work, he just ignores me. Maybe if I take off for a bit, he'll appreciate me more."

"Oh, I don't like the sounds of that. Don't start coming home every time you're mad at your husband. You need to stay and work it out."

"Do you want me home or not? I'd only come for a few days. I'm not deserting him."

Peggy hesitated. "Okay," she said with a smile. "Yes, that would be awesome."

Mary and Daniel spent a whole weekend dragging the stuff out of her room into the upstairs apartment, but the minute Mary pointed at the wardrobe, Daniel knew it wouldn't fit up the stairs.

Mary's face fell. "But that's my favourite thing in the whole world."

Carole was standing in the doorway. "You can come down and hug it every night."

The last items they collected were Roscoe's bits and bobs.

"Can't you leave a couple of food dishes here in case he wants to visit?" her mom said.

That made Mary smile. "You like him."

"He doesn't give me grief like you do."

Daniel and Roscoe went out the door and up the stairs. Mary looked back at her mom. "Are you going to be okay? I'm just upstairs if you need me."

"Get out of here. I have things to do."

"Okay. Bye. I'll see you tomorrow."

Once the kids left, Carole looked around and wondered what she should do. Even with the television on, there was a silence that seemed deafening. She grabbed her jacket and went for a stroll. She ended up on the boardwalk and sat on a bench to watch the water in Sydney Harbour. There were couples out walking together after supper, some of them arm in arm. What was that like? To have someone to share your day with, to talk over the past hours while watching the setting sun?

With her mother gone, Carole had a chance to mull over the shocking truth about her father.

It still didn't seem real. She'd spent so much of her life wishing he would come back and save her from her mother and now she had to reverse the narrative. There was never going to be a happy reunion. Turns out her mother was the hero all along. A drunk, flawed hero, but you can't have everything.

And now she was the guilty party. It never occurred to her that Mary would resent not having a dad—she'd never had one to miss. Mary never said anything growing up, but maybe that was because Carole didn't spend a lot of her time talking to her. She was always too busy trying to make a living and keeping Ethel from imploding.

And now that Carole finally did have some time, Mary was as good as gone. As Carole and her sister were finding out, babies grow up and leave home and if you have nothing else in your life, the world is a cruel place.

She was about to get up and return to the house when she saw a woman walking towards her with a little dog on a leash. He was wearing a Cape Breton tartan jacket, this Scottie dog who walked as if he was extremely proud of himself. Carole wasn't the type to make comments to strangers, but there was something about this little dog's face that moved her.

"He's awfully cute," she said to the woman.

The woman stopped and the dog walked over and sniffed Carole's hand.

"He's quite a character," she agreed.

"What's his name?"

"Billy."

"Hi, Billy."

Billy gave her a lick and then continued on his way. The woman smiled over her shoulder. "Good night."

"Good night."

First thing tomorrow morning, Carole was going to the SPCA to find herself a Billy.

Mary didn't have to go to work until the afternoon, so after a long and scrumptious goodbye to her man that morning, she decided to go see Gran at Aunt Peggy's. Mary missed her like crazy and couldn't believe she was still holding out over there in Coxheath. She knew Gran well enough to know that she'd be missing everything about the old house and her daughter. They might have hated each other's guts at times, but they didn't realize how much they depended on each other.

It crossed Mary's mind that she was so wrapped up in Daniel she'd let her Gran's situation stay on the back burner, but today, she would go and see for herself how she was doing.

The drive up to Aunt Peggy's house was so easy to navigate without snow. Beside the Lexus, there was a new Jeep in the driveway. Was Sheena home from Halifax already?

She knocked on the door and pushed against it. It was open.

"Hello!" she called. "It's just me."

"That you, Mary?" Gran shouted.

"The one and only!"

Gran came racing out of the kitchen at a lopsided clip, her arms stretched out in front of her. "Let me see ya." She grabbed hold of her and patted her back with enthusiastic thumps. "You're looking good, girl. Love agrees with you."

They walked into the kitchen, where Aunt Peggy and Sheena were making a big salad.

"Hey, Sheena. What are you doing here?"

"Marriage is a bore. I needed a break, so I came home."

"Jeez."

"No, Mom needed some help." Sheena tossed her head at Gran and Mary understood. "And Drew is really busy, so I knew he wouldn't miss me for a few days. How's it going with the hunk upstairs?"

Mary couldn't hide her smile. "It's good. Really good."

"Sit down, honey," Aunt Peggy said. "Would you like some chicken salad?"

"Yeah, that would be great."

Gran sat in the seat beside her.

"How's it going, Gran?"

"I'm bored outta my tree."

"You are? Well, why don't you go home? I'm sure Mom is missing you."

"If she was, she'd have been over here by now. So she can get stuffed, because I don't need her."

It was plainly obvious to all of them that Gran needed Carole very badly, but since she was such a stubborn old coot, this situation might drag on into the foreseeable future.

"Maybe she's just not sure if she should come over because you haven't been in touch. Have you ever thought of that? It can't be easy not hearing from you. You can imagine what she's thinking."

"I have no damn idea what she's thinkin', and I'm tired of thinkin' about it. I gotta go take a shit."

Gran got off the stool and charged out of the kitchen. The other three looked at each other.

"This is ridiculous," Mary said.

Aunt Peggy put a plate of salad in front of her and whispered, "Have you talked to your mother? Because the last time I did, she didn't want her back."

Mary was incredulous. "Are you serious?"

Peggy nodded. "That's what she said, and I'm going crazy because if Gran does ask to go back, I don't know what to tell her. My blood pressure goes through the roof just thinking about it."

Sheena brought over the forks. "That's why I came back. The look on Mom's face the other day, I thought she was going to have a breakdown. What should we do?" She looked at Mary. "You know Gran better than we do. You've lived with her your whole life."

Mary shook her head. "I'm not sure what to do. Maybe it would be a good idea just to get them together in the same room and see what happens."

"You'd have to be there, Mary," Aunt Peggy begged. "I wouldn't want to attempt this without you. Did you know that my hair is falling out in clumps?"

After lunch, Gran cornered Mary in the family room. "Did you know my hair is falling out in clumps?"

"Really?"

"Yes! I was in that goddamned bathtub the other night and there was a big ball of it. This place is doing my head in."

"Umm...was the hair grey or brown?

Gran thought about it. "Brown, I guess."

"And is your hair brown?"

"It would be if your goddamned mother would dye it for me."

"Gran, come sit with me." She pulled her grandmother into the loveseat. "You're blaming this house and Aunt Peggy for your misery, but it's not the house or the things in it that are upsetting you. You're missing your home and Mom." Ethel stiffened, but Mary plowed on: "And why wouldn't you? They've been your life. It's like you've been pulled up and planted in a different spot, but this spot doesn't have enough sunlight or water. You belong on George Street. That's the only reason you're sad. Why don't we go tell Mom that?"

Her grandmother nodded.

Mary looked at her watch. She still had two hours before she had to be at work. "Go get your coat."

While her grandmother went to collect her coat and purse, Mary rushed back into the kitchen, where Aunt Peggy and Sheena were hiding while Mary worked her magic.

"I've convinced her to go and see Mom. Let's roll."

"Sweet Jesus!" Aunt Peggy cried out, relieved. "If this works, you are definitely going in my will."

Mary put Gran in her car and Sheena drove her mother in the Jeep. They followed each other across town. Gran didn't say anything, so Mary knew she was nervous.

When they pulled up to the house, Gran surveyed the rosebushes. "You did a nice job cleaning up that litter. I know damn well your mother didn't do it."

Mary gave her grandmother a stern look. "Be nice."

The four of them gathered outside the vehicles, as if to catch their collective breath. Aunt Peggy and Sheena were holding hands. What the heck had been happening with this family while she was busy making love to Daniel? Was she the only sane one in the group?

They walked into the porch and stepped across the kitchen threshold, but they didn't get any farther than that. A huge Newfoundland dog galloped out of the living room with drool coming out of his mouth, two itsy-bitsy snarling Chihuahuas at his heels. Everyone screamed and rushed out of the house, trying not to be trampled or nipped to death.

Carole came charging behind them. "Stop screaming, for God's sake! They're rescue dogs, and they're emotionally unbalanced!" She struggled with one thick leash and two stringy ones, trying to corral the dogs as they zeroed in on Gran, who was running around in circles.

Aunt Peggy and Sheena found refuge in the Jeep. Gran continued to scream, "Fucking little bastards!" so Mary shoved her in the car and helped her mother put the leashes on the dog's collars. By then she'd figured out that the Newfoundland dog was just trying to kiss everyone and the Chihuahuas were very excitable.

Mary and Carole stood in the driveway, chests heaving. The other three eventually emerged from their vehicles.

"I've seen it all now," Gran hollered. "I can't leave you alone for five minutes and you're up to something ridiculous! Do these beasts belong to you?"

"As a matter of fact they do."

"Mom," said Mary, "what were you thinking?"

Carole faced them down. "I was thinking that everyone else has a life, so why not me? Do you know how many unwanted animals there are in the world?"

"Yes!" Mary shouted. "Which is why I always wanted some but you would never let me!"

"People can change their minds."

"But three?" Aunt Peggy cried. "Three?"

"I went in for one but apparently these three are best friends and I couldn't just leave the other two behind. Look at them."

They did. Big bug-eyed Chihuahua rats, who were now shivering and looking pathetic.

Gran stood with her hands on her hips. "I've seen some pretty stupid things in my day...."

Carole pointed at her mother. "Ma, shut your mouth. This has nothing to do with you. You made up your mind and you're living with Peggy. These are my pets and they now live in my house. What you think about it doesn't matter one iota, have you got that?"

Gran blinked a few times.

"But Carole," Peggy whined. "This is Mom's house. She wants to come back because she's very unhappy with me. We came here today to tell you she wants to come home."

"That's too damn bad. She made her bed. Now she can lie in it. Come on, boys."

Amazingly, the dogs followed her obediently into the house.

The four of them stared at each other.

"Don't worry, Gran," said Mary. "I'll talk to her."

"I'm not going near that place. She thinks she can kick me out of my own house and then fill it up with hairy beasts, then let her do it. I hope she chokes on dog shit."

Gran got in the back of the Jeep.

Aunt Peggy looked stunned. "What happened? What happened here?"

Sheena took her by the arm. "Never mind, Mom. Let's get you home. See ya, Mary."

"Yeah. See ya."

The Jeep drove away, and Mary got into her car and drove to work.

CHAPTER ELEVEN

SHEENA STAYED FOR A WHOLE week, which was awfully kind of her. Sometimes Peggy forgot that her daughter had even moved away. When she bounced down the stairs for breakfast in the morning, it was just like old times. That is until Misery Guts showed up and dampened the mood.

Both Peggy and Sheena were almost afraid of Gran. They knew she was temperamental, but they'd never seen her in such a foul mood. They put their heads together and tried to help lift her spirits.

"Gran, I have to go to the mall today and stop in to see Riley. Would you like to go with Mom and me? We'll buy you a treat."

"Pink peppermints?"

"Sure."

"And scratch tickets."

"Of course."

"Well, I got nothin' else to do."

With that gracious nod, they headed to the Mayflower Mall. Because it was slow going with Gran in tow, Peggy told Sheena to run ahead and see her friend, that they'd be along. They didn't get too far. Gran wanted a cup of tea at Tim Hortons and an apple fritter. Peggy sat with her and privately hankered for the apple fritter, but sipped her coffee with sweetener instead. She was down six pounds and felt good about it, but that didn't stop her from resenting all the skinny people in her peripheral vision.

When she was done, Peggy helped her mother out of the chair and then took her by the arm. She pointed at The Bay. "I have to run in and get some night cream."

"Do they have afternoon cream too? It's all bullshit. Cream is cream."

Peggy steered her over to the Estée Lauder counter. Thank goodness Joan was working today.

"Hi, Joan!"

A lovely and very attractive blond woman with a British accent smiled at the two of them. "Hello, Peggy."

"Joan, this is my mother, Ethel."

"Nice to meet you, Ethel. Are you looking for anything in particular?"

"I'm looking for sweet F-A. It's this one who spends her money like there's no tomorrow," she said, jabbing her thumb at Peggy.

Joan hid a smile. "Peggy is one of my best customers. Her skin is lovely; don't you agree?"

"I never noticed."

Peggy made a face at Joan. "Could I get some more Revitalizing Supreme, the Global Anti-Aging Crème?"

"Of course." She took out the box from under the counter. "I must tell you, we just got in our New Dimension Shape + Fill Expert Serum. You'll love it. Just tap it under the eye and across the cheekbone, like this." She demonstrated by tapping her ring finger across her face. Her nails were always an exquisite colour. If Peggy could put makeup on like Joan, maybe Ted would still be at home.

"Sure, I'll take that too." Peggy handed Joan her credit card.

"How much is all that?" Ethel asked.

"None of your business."

"All ya need is Ivory soap. I've been using it for years."

Joan put the purchases in a bag and gave them a big smile. "Thank you, ladies. Enjoy the rest of your day."

"Bye, Joan. Thanks again."

They continued up the mall at a snail's pace. "Mom, why don't we buy you some new slacks and a top?"

"Don't need them."

"What about a sweater?"

"Got one. The trouble with this generation is that they think they need a hundred times more than they do. You can only wear one sweater at a time. It's a waste. Everyone is greedy these days. My mother had two dresses: one for working in and one to go to church. End of story. Did that stop her from being happy?"

"It must have. You always said your mother was a jerk."

"Stop changing the subject."

They eventually arrived at La Senza. Sheena and Riley were nattering at the back of the store while Riley fiddled with the hangers, pretending she was working. Ethel wandered over to the tray of thongs and picked one up.

"Might as well put a string of dental floss up your bum."

"The bras are pretty," Peggy said.

"How would these tissue-paper-thin bits of lace hold up two sacks of flesh weighing five pounds each? Only the exceptionally deluded would buy this shit."

Sheena and Riley saw them and walked over to the counter, Sheena carrying a handful of bras. "I have to buy these."

"Hi, Mrs. Henderson. You must miss Sheena a lot. I know I do." Riley entered the codes into the cash register.

"I certainly do miss her. And having you running in and out of the house."

Riley rang up Sheena's bras, and the girls said goodbye to each other. Ethel, Peggy, and Sheena continued on their way, stopping at Indigo.

"Hey Mom," said Sheena, "you know what they say is really relaxing? Adult colouring books. Why don't you buy some?"

"I heard about that. Let's take a look."

Ethel wasn't interested. "I'm going up to the Rocky Mountain Chocolate shop."

"Oh, Mom, don't buy a ton of chocolate; I'm on a diet."

"Who said you were getting any?"

Ethel wandered up to the store and stood in front of the shelves filled with sweets. She'd heard chocolate could kill dogs. She picked up a big box and brought it over to the counter.

"I'll take this."

Once it was wrapped up, Ethel tucked it under her arm and went out the mall door. She made her way over to the bus stop and waited for the bus to George Street.

Peggy and Sheena took a lot longer than they realized picking out their colouring books and coloured pencils. Sheena bought *Animal Kingdom* and Peggy chose *Secret Garden*.

"This will help me pass the time when Mom starts ranting about my useless TV remote," Peggy laughed. "Anything to keep calm. Honestly, I don't know how Carole didn't strangle her years ago."

They walked up the mall side by side.

"Poor Gran. She hasn't had a very happy life, has she?"

"Well, I wouldn't say it was totally unhappy," reasoned Peggy. "There were lots of times when we laughed about silly things. She used to embarrass us horribly when we were kids, always dressing up for Halloween and scaring the pants off little kids in the rose bushes. She loved that. And then there was the time she hauled off and hit a guy who rammed into our car bumper. She jumped around in the street, yelling, 'You nearly killed my kids, you fat asshole!' Carole made me crouch down in the seat in case the guy came after us. And then there was the time she took us to the movies and let us buy theatre popcorn. That was a huge treat. You'd think Carole and I had won the lottery, we were so excited. No, it wasn't all bad."

They arrived at the chocolate shop and didn't see Gran, so they assumed she was wandering around somewhere close by. Five minutes of looking turned into ten, ten to fifteen, and now they were a bit concerned. Sheena and Peggy hurried back to the chocolate store and confirmed with the salesgirl that yes, an elderly lady had bought a big box of chocolates.

As they continued to race up and down the mall, Peggy panicked. "Carole is going to kill me! She never once lost Mom."

"She couldn't have gone far," Sheena panted. "Let's look in the washrooms."

They looked in every bathroom stall and hollered her name, but no one answered.

"Goddammit!" Peggy fretted. "I'm calling Carole."

Carole could not believe how much her life had changed in a week. She was busy from dawn till dusk but had never been happier. Billy, the big black Newfoundland dog, was as gentle as a bear, and he insisted on sleeping in Carole's bed because, as she soon learned, he was afraid of the dark. Will and Liam, the Chihuahuas, went everywhere Billy went, so they made themselves at home on Carole's bed too.

Surprisingly, her customers loved the boys. They held the two little ones when they were in the chair, and Billy lay beside Carole like a fluffy rug. She just stepped over him instead of on him.

The first time she took them for a walk together, they pulled her down the street at such a clip that she almost passed out, she was so winded. And then when she sat down to a cup of tea and a cigarette, the minute she lit it up, the three of them gave her hangdog looks and wrinkled their noses at the smell of the smoke. Liam even coughed.

She quit smoking there and then.

Her evenings were now spent brushing Billy, and the fur she pulled out of that dog was not fit. She found it relaxing, sitting on the floor with that big lug stretched out, clearly loving the feeling of the brush. Maybe she should get into dog grooming? The idea excited her. Imagine being able to do hair and not have clients talk your face off or bitch and complain about everything under the sun.

What would she call her new business? Pooch Palace? Mutt Central? Doggy Style? Well, maybe not the last one.

She went to bed every night looking forward to getting up. She'd meet Daniel and Mary going off to work in the morning. They would pet the dogs and make a fuss over them, but Roscoe kept clear. He'd sit on the roof of the shed out back, watching the proceedings with a healthy skepticism.

Before Mary got in the car one morning she commented on her mother's bright new outlook.

"You seem really happy."

"I can't begin to tell you what a difference it's made to have three sane beings in the house with me. They give off a positive and loving energy, unlike the Toxic Wonder."

"Mom, don't be mean. Gran isn't all bad."

"She isn't all good either. Did you know I quit smoking? I think Liam is allergic to it."

Mary stamped her foot. "Say that again."

"I think Liam is allergic to smoke."

"I've had to use puffers all my life because of your smoking!"

"Sorry. Let's go, boys."

She and her boys ambled up the street and out of sight. Mary watched them go, then she turned to Roscoe. "Have you ever felt like killing someone?"

Gran enjoyed the freedom of the bus ride. She hadn't been by herself in a long time. It was fun to watch the neighbourhoods go by, remembering old friends and how they would meet at Ashby Corner and get into all sorts of trouble. She wondered where they were now. None of them had been any good at keeping in touch. Ethel didn't realize until now how she'd isolated herself her whole life. Would her friends know she ended up being a drunk? Probably. Dotty and her Dairy never missed a trick.

It was too late to worry about it now. She was too old to remedy anything and would no doubt die with lots of regrets. So be it. Let someone else try to frantically repair their ways before their time was up. Ethel didn't think God would care one way or the other. Human beings were so good at punishing themselves, why would he bother?

She got off the bus on Dorchester Street and walked down George Street towards the old house. She stopped at Dotty's to buy pink peppermints since Peggy and Sheena had lied about getting some for her. There was a young man with a pimply face behind the counter.

Ethel dropped her peppermints in front of him. "Where's Dotty?"

"She's dead."

Ethel felt her heart shudder. "What? When did that happen?"

"Just a couple of days ago. Her funeral was this afternoon at Forest Haven."

Ethel paid for the peppermints and walked out of the store in a daze. Dotty was about the closest thing she had to a friend. And there Ethel was, living over in Coxheath, blissfully unaware of this tragic event. She should've been here. She should've gone to the funeral. Instead she was waltzing up and down the damn mall watching her idiot daughter and granddaughter buy shit they didn't need.

Ethel looked at her house and knew it wasn't Carole's fault she wasn't living there any more. It was her own fault. She was the one who'd packed her bags and said she was moving in with Peggy. If she hadn't made that grand gesture, she'd still be home and she probably would've seen Dotty a few more times.

She trudged back up to Dorchester Street and waited for another bus. Once it arrived, she sat in the back seat and opened the box of chocolates. She ate one after the other, not even tasting them. Dotty had loved chocolates. She'd eat them for her.

Carole was doing a blow-dry when her client suddenly said, "Did you hear about Dotty?"

"Next-door Dotty?"

"Yes, she died two days ago. Her funeral was today at Forest Haven."

"Jesus Murphy! What happened? I can't believe I didn't know."

"They say it was heart failure."

"That poor woman. Gosh, the place isn't going to be the same without her."

"That's for sure. She was a real institution around here. I can remember her sitting on that stool when I was a kid."

Carole's cell went off. She looked over her client's shoulder and saw it was Peggy. "Do you mind if I take this? It's my sister."

"Go ahead," the woman said.

"Hi. What do you want? You never call when I'm working."

"Mom is missing!"

"What?" Carole stepped away from the chair and headed out into the kitchen. The boys followed her. "What do you mean, missing?"

"Missing! As in missing-person posters! We took her to the mall and she went up to buy some chocolates and that's the last we saw of her. We've scoured the mall. We were hoping she was with you."

"No, she didn't come here. Of course, why would she? I practically banished her from the property. You don't think she did something stupid, do you?"

"She's always doing something stupid," Peggy yelled. "Why would now be any different?"

"Call the police!"

"We can't. She would have to be missing for twenty-four hours."

"I think this is a little different. You had her at the mall and she disappeared. Maybe they'll put out an Amber Alert. God, that reminds me of that horrible ex-girlfriend of Daniel's."

"Call Mary! Perhaps Mom just went to Sobeys."

"How could she walk all the way to Sobeys?"

"Maybe she took a taxi!"

"Okay, I'll call you back."

The client was now out of the chair. "Look, you clearly have a family emergency. My hair is dry anyway." She passed Carole some money.

"Oh, thank you!"

"Is it Ethel?"

Carole nodded, her eyes welling up.

"I'm sure she's fine," soothed the customer. "She'll be home before you know it." She left with a small smile.

"Yes, thanks."

Once the door closed, Carole called Sobeys. "I need to speak to my daughter, Mary Ryan."

"She's on cash at the moment. Can you leave a message?"

"No, I bloody well can't leave a message! This is an emergency!"

"Sorry. I'll go get her."

While Carole waited, Billy nudged her tummy with his big head. "It's okay, Billy. Don't be scared." She scratched behind his floppy ears.

Mary sounded breathless. "What's wrong?"

"Is Gran with you?"

"No! Why would she be here with me? I'm working."

"Peggy and Sheena had her at the mall this afternoon and they lost her! How do you lose an old cranky woman?"

"Are you sure she's not just wandering around the mall? Maybe they keep missing each other."

"They put it over the intercom, but she never showed up. Where would she be if she's not with them or me or you? She has no one else."

"Should we call the police?"

"Frig it. That's what I'm going to do. Get home now!"

Carole called Peggy back. "I'm calling the police. Get over here."

She was still on the phone with the police when Mary and then Peggy and Sheena showed up. Carole passed the phone to Peggy. They wanted to talk to her since she was the last one with Ethel. They sat around the kitchen table, with the dogs close by. They were as good as gold, obviously sensing something wasn't right. At one point, Sheena even picked Will up and put him in her lap, and she always said she wasn't a dog person.

Peggy finally hung up and sat down with the others. "They said to stay here, because she will probably wander home. They have her description and they've alerted patrol cars to keep an eye out for her, but I don't think they're particularly worried."

"They don't know her like we do," Carole said. "She never goes anywhere. It's not like she has a long list of friends."

The minute she said "friends," Carole thought of something. "Did Ma know that Dotty died?"

"Dotty who?" Peggy asked.

"You mean Dotty's Dairy Dotty?" Mary cried. "When was this?"

"Two days ago, apparently. She and Ma always got along like a house on fire."

"How would she know?" Sheena said. "She's been with us the whole time."

Carole snapped her fingers. "Maybe she ran into someone at the mall who told her."

Peggy shook her head. "Why does it matter?"

"Because Dotty's funeral was today at Forest Haven. I bet she's there."

All four of them scrambled to their feet and jumped into Peggy's Lexus. They drove as fast as they dared up Prince Street, then passed the Mayflower Mall and on down the Sydney–Glace Bay Highway. They turned into Forest Haven and drove all over the cemetery looking for a stubby, skinny-legged woman holding a box of chocolates.

Sheena and Mary even put their back windows down and shouted her name as they drove. They couldn't see anyone and were starting to despair when Mary pointed. "Is that someone on the ground?"

"Where?"

"Way up there! It looks like a bundle on the ground. Let me out!"

They stopped the car and the four of them ran towards the rumpled shape, all of them shouting, "Gran! Mom! Ma!"

It was her.

"Is she dead?" Carole screamed. "Please, *please* tell me she's not dead!"

Mary knelt down and put her ear to her Gran's mouth, and then felt for a pulse. "I think she's breathing."

"Sheena! Call 911!" Peggy shouted. "Call 911!"

There was a dark foam coming out of Ethel's mouth.

"Oh my God, she's dying!"

They took off their jackets and bundled her up as best they could. The sirens could be heard in the distance.

"Stay with us, Ma!" urged Carole. "Don't you dare leave me, or I'll kill ya!"

"I smell chocolate," Sheena sniffed. Then she pointed to the ground. "Look, there's an empty chocolate box on the ground. She *was* saying goodbye to Dotty."

"Hang on, Gran," Mary whispered in her ear. "Hang on."

CHAPTER TWELVE

GRAN WAS NOT SUPPOSED TO live through the night. Her heart attack had been severe. Then she wasn't supposed to make it through the week. She fooled them. The family was warned that the prognosis was not good and she could easily succumb within the month.

Three full moons later it was August and she was still eating cheese and crackers in the hospital while they tried to find a bed in a nearby nursing home. She was a beloved character on the cardiac floor. The nurses humoured her and listened with rapt attention to her stories of drunken mischief. Ethel thrived on the attention. She hadn't had this much fun in years. After a while she ran out of her own stories and made stuff up. She'd ask anyone who dropped by if they'd do her a favour and run to the liquor store for gin. Even the misery of detox wasn't enough to quell her thirst for booze.

Peggy, Carole, and Mary had a nice schedule worked out to visit her. Daniel would drop by on his lunch hour to bring her pink peppermints. Even Sheena would stop in now and again, since she always managed to find some excuse to come home. Drew, for the most part, was used to it. Sheena would get a look in her eye and before he knew it, she and her Jeep were gone.

But she and Drew did buy a house that summer in the Hydrostone district of Halifax. It was pricey but both sets of parents helped them with a big down payment. Sheena had spent a frantic few weeks decorating, and her mother had made the trek down to help her with it. Drew had no say in the matter, but he was happy to let them choose. In his downtime he was involved with fantasy football and wrestling. Peggy took a page out of the book *How to Be a Good Mother-in-Law* and didn't comment on how ridiculous wrestling was. He could be frequenting bars instead, so she left well enough alone.

It was Mary whom Gran was always the happiest to see. The women who shared her room at different intervals loved Mary because she would make a point of going over to sit with them and ask them how they were. She'd inquire about their families and was interested to hear their stories. After Mary would leave, Gran would beam with pride as they told her what a special girl Mary was.

"Oh, she's a little honey. Always was. I haven't the faintest idea where she came from; her mother is basket case."

"She must take after you, Ethel!" one of them would hoot.

Mary lounged on the couch after supper. Her feet were on Daniel's lap and Roscoe was on her chest. Daniel was flicking through his cell as his fingers absentmindedly brushed the bottoms of Mary's feet. He thought it was crazy that she wasn't ticklish, but no matter how hard he tried, she never cracked a smile, so he'd given up long ago.

Mary smoothed out Roscoe's whiskers. "You know what?"

"What?"

"I think I know what I'd like to do."

"When? Tonight? Tomorrow? Fifty years from now?"

"What I'd like to do with my life."

"I hope it's spend it with me."

"That's a given." She smiled. "I think I'd like to be an RPN. A Registered Practical Nurse," she added when Daniel gave her a blank look. "I don't want to spend four years becoming an RN, but I think an RPN would be up my alley. I've watched them come in and out of Gran's room, and they're such an important part of a person's recovery. It must be amazing to help someone like that."

Daniel gripped her toes. "You would be terrific! I think that's perfect."

"It's too late to get into this year's program, but if I save up my money, I'm sure I'll have enough for next year's tuition."

Daniel grinned at her. "Look at us. I'm heading to NSCC in a couple of weeks for my heavy equipment diploma and you'll be a nurse. We're so grown up and responsible. We're turning into boring people."

"Boring people are the folks who make this world a better place." She rubbed Roscoe's nose. "Isn't that right, you handsome devil?"

Roscoe agreed.

Peggy had lost twenty-five pounds and she was looking mighty fine. She was proud of herself, even though her mother never said anything. Her sister, niece, and daughter did, so that was enough. And Ted was very happy with her progress, asking her to do a striptease for him in front of the computer one morning before he went to bed. Only after he swore that there was no one in the building and all the citizens of the city had vanished did she concede.

It felt ridiculous. She had no music to help her along, so she sang as she cavorted around the end of the bed. "Da da da...da...da da da...da da da...dada...da da...dun dun...wop! Dun...wop! Dun...wop!" She threw her bra at the screen and wrenched her back doing it. "Ow ow ow!"

Ted was in hysterics on the other side of the screen. He held his glasses in his hand as tears ran down his face. "Stop! Stop! You're going to kill yourself! Oh my God...that was priceless!"

Peggy hobbled to the side of the bed. "You're supposed to be turned on, you big jerk!"

She'd talk to him at night before he headed out for the day. They hadn't talked like that in years. He'd pour his heart out about some of the things he'd seen and Peggy would cry about how unfair life was. It was all about where you were born on this planet. Just plain stinking luck made the difference in whether your life was hell or not.

When Peggy wasn't running up to the hospital to visit her mother, she was taking sewing classes with a woman who was highly recommended. It came to her one night in a dream. She remembered that she used to love to watch her mother sew, and Mom would give her small scraps and a needle and thread to make dresses for her doll.

Naturally, Peggy ran out and got the most expensive sewing machine available, and soon regretted her decision when she saw the two-inch-thick manual that came with it. But she had long evenings to fill, so she set about the Herculean task of learning every trick this machine had. Even her instructor couldn't believe the bells and whistles.

She started with sewing covers for cushions. Peggy would hold up material in front of the computer screen and Sheena would pick out which ones she liked. Then Sheena wanted a duvet cover, so Peggy set to work sewing that. Mary happened to call her one day for a recipe, and Peggy asked her if she wanted a couple of aprons. Mary said sure.

The days flew by. One afternoon another sewing student got the wrong time for her appointment, and the instructor asked if it was okay if they did it together. That's how Peggy met Lynne, and they got along so well that they went out for coffee afterward and talked about sewing techniques for three hours. Turned out Lynne lived just down the road. Pretty soon they were shopping for fabric together and meeting for lunch. Peggy found herself humming during the day, even when she was eating celery and carrots for a snack. She'd come a long way, baby.

Carole spent every second evening sitting with her mom in the hospital room. She would take videos of the boys throughout the day and play them back for her. "Look at Liam! He jumped up on the table and knocked the package of cookies on the floor so Will and Billy could have some. He's so thoughtful."

Ethel was not impressed.

"I bet the house is a shambles. How can you live with all the fur floatin' around?"

"I clean up the fur and brush my dogs. The place is spotless."

"They better not lie on that couch in the living room. That's my spot. When I get home I want those dogs on the floor."

This was a delicate subject. The doctor had told Carole that her mother could never live at home again and no matter how many times it was explained to her, she refused to listen. At first Carole thought her mother was being deliberately wilful about it, but the doctor also explained that some of Ethel's brain function had deteriorated with the heart attack.

"I didn't know she had any brain function left!" Carole had joked.

The doctor didn't think it was funny.

"Lighten up!" she said to his retreating back. Jesus, some of these medical types were such tight-asses.

So Carole would go over it again. "Ma, you can't come home. I can't take care of you all by myself. We're trying to find you a room in a nursing home."

"One of those vegetable plots?" Ethel shook her head. "I ain't goin'."

"You have to go somewhere. The hospital can't keep you forever. They need these beds for really sick people."

"Carole, go home. You're beginning to depress me."

Carole loved going home. Her boys were always overjoyed to see her. They looked at her as if she was the best person on the planet. She wanted to be that for them. Looking around on the internet she found places around town where dog people met to have play dates with their dogs. Carole had never known this existed. She started meeting other owners, and naturally if your dog was the same breed, you tended to gravitate to them to compare notes or offer suggestions.

Carole was obviously new to this game, but her boys never let on. They did their best to be perfect gentlemen when they were in a crowd. She couldn't have been more proud.

And then one day the SPCA called to say another little dog had come in overnight and was it possible she had room for him too?

"Aw, nuts. Don't do this to me."

"I'm sure we'll have no trouble adopting him. He's a little black pug. I thought you might like first dibs, since your last adoption was such a resounding success. He's awfully cute. I'd take him myself if I didn't have six already."

"I'm not promising anything. I'll just take a quick peek."

That's how she came home with Weechee.

But Weechee upset the delicate balance in the household. Billy ran and hid on Carole's bed and Will and Liam were chased around the house until they dropped with exhaustion.

Carole picked up Weechee and tried to scold him but she couldn't get him to focus on her. His eyes looked in two different directions. His curly pink tongue stuck out almost to his chin, and his face was split in half with his goofy grin.

"You can't beat up other dogs. You'll have to go back. I'm sorry, but my boys come first. Do you hear me?"

He licked her face all over and snuggled into her neck.

"Well, shit."

And so began the impossible task of trying to fit Weechee into the mix, but it didn't go well. Billy was still cowering on top the bed and Will and Liam spent the day under it. By nine o'clock that night, she knew the dog had to go back.

The trouble was that she was completely mad about him.

Carole rang Mary's doorbell. She came down the stairs wearing her favourite flannel pyjamas. When she opened the door she made a face.

"Who is this?"

"This is Weechee. You have to take him. The boys don't like him but I'm in love with him. Please don't make me take him back."

"Mom, I have a cat."

"So? Cats and dogs aren't assholes like people. They actually get along."

Mary looked at him. Weechee was snorting.

"Hold him. Just for a minute."

Mary reached out and Weechee engulfed her face with pug kisses. He wiggled and snorted and tried to bury his face in her boobs. Both Mary and her mother started laughing.

"This dog is ridiculous!" Mary shouted.

Daniel came down the stairs. "What are you two doing?"

Mary held Weechee up. "Look at this monster."

Daniel took one look and grabbed him. "This is the cutest dog I've ever seen!"

"That's great. He's yours. I'll bring you some food." Carole disappeared into her house.

"We can't keep this dog," Mary said. "What about Roscoe?"

"Roscoe will give him a big scratch on the nose and that will be that." Daniel could barely keep the wiggly bundle in his arms. "He's saying, 'Please Mommy! Please take me in! I'm just a poor boy...nobody loves me....'"

Carole arrived back and shoved a dog dish and a bag of food in Mary's hands.

"Perfect. See ya tomorrow." She slammed her front door shut.

Daniel ran up the stairs with the dog and left Mary to lock up. How had this happened in the space of one minute? She followed him up the stairs and watched Daniel put Weechee on the floor and gaze at him like he was the best thing that had ever happened.

"Look at this guy! He's like a stuffed toy. Hey, Weechee!"

The dog hunkered down with his two front paws stretched in front of him on the floor and his curly-tailed bum waving in the air. When Daniel took a step nearer, he took off like a shot and ran down the hall into the kitchen, only to appear a second later and run back up the hall. Then he spied Roscoe on the couch and hurled himself into the air and landed right on him. Roscoe did exactly what Daniel predicted: he puffed up and swatted Weechee right across the face. Weechee yelped and made a beeline for Daniel, who picked him up and nestled him under his chin.

"Poor little guy. Don't be so mean, Roscoe."

Mary hurried over to her cat. "Hey, don't say that. This is his house."

"There's more than enough room for them both."

Mary wondered about that.

CHAPTER THIRTEEN

IN SEPTEMBER, CAROLE MET JERRY Hawco at a fundraiser for the SPCA. All pets were welcome, and Jerry walked in with a gorgeous black-and-white Newfoundland dog named Ruth. It was love at first sight for Billy, who pulled Carole over to check out the new babe.

Jerry was a carpenter, divorced with two grown kids who lived away. He was shy and easy-going, completely the opposite of Carole, but he didn't need to know that. They spent the entire time talking about dogs and then he asked if she wanted to have a coffee with him later that week. She agreed, and decided she ought to touch up her roots.

She was in the middle of that when the phone rang. It never failed. The phone number looked unfamiliar, so she took off one of her rubber gloves and picked it up.

It was the Seaview Manor. They had a bed for her mother.

"But it's in Glace Bay," Carole said.

"When a spot becomes available, you either take it or go back to the bottom of the list."

"I see. We'll obviously take it. What do we do now?"

Carole got off the phone and called her sister. "Peggy, they have a bed for Ma at Seaview Manor. We have to go tell her."

The sisters vowed to stay strong as they walked in their mother's hospital room. It didn't help that she looked very small and vulnerable lying there. She was gazing out the window and didn't see them come in.

"Hi, Ma."

Ethel turned her head. "What's wrong? The two of you are never here together."

"Nothing's wrong," Peggy said brightly. "How are you feeling?"

"Like a butthole, how d'ya think? I'm sick and tired of being here."

Peggy clapped her hands. "Well, we have good news. They've found you another bed. You can leave here tomorrow."

"I'm going home?"

The sisters glanced at each other. Carole cleared her throat. "You're going to a nice room at the Seaview Manor in Glace Bay."

"Glace Bay? Who the Jesus wants to go there? I had a cousin from Glace Bay and he was a first-class eejit."

"They assure me it's a lovely room—"

"I ain't goin', I tell ya! You can't make me go. I want to go home. Please take me home." Ethel began to cry. "I won't make no trouble. I swear."

Carole and Peggy couldn't hold back their tears. Peggy looked to Carol in desperation. "What do we do?"

Carole reached out and took her mother's hand. "It's for your own good, Ma. They can't keep you here. But we'll come and visit you every day. You won't be alone, I swear. I promise. Do you hear me?"

"Why are you doing this? Where's Mary? She'll take me home. " Ethel twisted away from her daughters. "Mary! Mary!"

Ethel's voice got louder and her agitation extreme. Peggy ran out the door and headed for the nurses' station. "Could you help me, please? Our mother is very upset."

Eventually a nurse gave Ethel a shot to calm her down, and she drifted off to sleep, tears still on her cheeks. The sisters were beside themselves, but a social worker came in and explained that it was always distressing to make this kind of move, and they weren't to blame. They were helping their mother. Carole and Peggy still felt like monsters, no matter how the woman tried to explain it.

The social worker said it would be better if Carole and Peggy weren't there when they moved Ethel in the morning, but waiting in the new room to greet their mom when she arrived. Carole asked Mary if she could be there too, so Mary switched shifts with Janet.

The three of them drove out to Glace Bay and parked in the Seaview Manor parking lot. The blue waves sparkled on this perfect September morning, and the breeze was warm. All Mary wanted to do was run to the bottom of the street and throw herself into the water so she could swim away and leave this heartache behind. Her grandmother would hate it here. Not that there was anything wrong with the facility, but she wasn't in her own community. She would feel a thousand kilometres away, even though it was only twenty minutes.

They gathered in the lobby and someone came and took them to Ethel's room. They'd hoped she'd be next to a window, but that side of the room was occupied.

Peggy panicked. "Is there any way she could be upgraded to a single room?"

The administrator tried to be patient. "Mrs. Henderson, this isn't a hotel. We only have so many rooms and there are lots of people on waiting lists. It's a very slow process. And in your case, you're lucky. Your mother could have been sent anywhere in the province. Try to be grateful she's so close to home."

Peggy sat in a hard chair, Carole sat on the hospital bed, and Mary stood against the wall while they waited. Every time it sounded like someone was coming, they held their breaths.

Eventually, the noise out in the hall indicated that several people were coming. Carole and Peggy stood up and joined Mary by the wall. Two paramedics came through the door with Ethel bundled up in blankets. She looked so small, her frightened face not knowing where to look. A couple of nurses and the administrator came in as well. Then came the soothing, loud voice of the head nurse, as the men unbuckled the straps holding her on the gurney.

"Now, Mrs. Ryan, we'll fix you up in no time and have you comfy in just a minute. Then you can visit with your family."

Mary heard Gran's voice tremble. "Where are they?"

"They're right here, Mrs. Ryan."

Mary stepped forward. "Gran? It's me."

"Mary? Mary!"

They placed Ethel in the bed and the paramedics moved off with the gurney. Mary reached out and grabbed Gran's hand. "It's okay."

Her grandmother had aged in the three days since she'd seen her. Mary couldn't believe her eyes.

"Mary, get me outta here! I've been kidnapped. Those bastards wouldn't listen to me. I told them to leave me alone but they just bundled me up like a bag of old trash."

Mary was aware that her mother now had her face buried in Aunt Peggy's shoulder. "Listen, Gran. I want you to lie back and take a deep breath. You're not alone. I'm here, and Mom's here and Aunt Peggy too. We all came to see you, to welcome you to this new room. All these people are here to help you. We won't let them hurt you."

"But why can't I go home with you? You can take care of me."

"You can't go home right now because you're too ill. But I can come and take you outside for a walk when the weather's good. I can put you in a wheelchair and we can do wheelies in the hallway," said Mary with a smile. "And I'll smuggle in pizza. How does that sound?'

"What about some gin? I could use a stiff drink."

"We'll see."

Ethel's eyes landed on her daughters. "You two did this! You couldn't wait to get rid of me. I hate you both. Go away! Get out!"

Peggy and Carole had no choice but to leave the room. They were distraught. The social worker took them down to one of the sitting areas. "Fear of the unknown comes out as anger. She doesn't hate you. But she needs someone to blame. So far Mary seems to be a calming influence, so at least we have that."

"But when we leave, what will happen?"

"We know how to deal with it. We've had plenty of experience and she will be well looked after. This is one of the hardest things you'll ever do. There's no denying it. All you can do is your best."

Mary sat with Gran for the rest of the day. Peggy and Carole tried to come back in, but Gran kept telling them to get lost. They signalled to Mary from the hallway that they would get lunch and bring something back for her and Gran. Mary nodded.

Her grandmother never let go of her hand. At one point Mary knew it had fallen asleep and she was aching to move it, but didn't dare. Every time she thought about how she'd have to leave this bedside, her stomach tightened. It ran though her mind that maybe they shouldn't have rushed to save Gran that day in the cemetery. Maybe they should've just let her go.

Did anyone ever know the right thing to do?

When the sisters came back with soup and sandwiches, Ethel let them come in. She was hungry. After half an egg sandwich and a few spoons of tomato soup, her eyes closed and she was breathing deeply.

The nurse came in and suggested they go. They didn't dare lean down to kiss her in case she woke up. All of them tiptoed out and walked wearily back to the car, but Mary kept going.

"I need a minute."

She continued down to the water and stood there in the sunshine, trying to get her breath. Her chest heaved as she sucked in the fresh salt air and the aroma of grass and flowers. Why wasn't her grandmother outside smelling this too? Of course her grandmother never went outside unless she had to, but still. That wasn't the point.

And to think that maybe someday in the future she might have to go through this with her own mother. Was it wrong to hope that someone just dropped dead or died in their sleep? What was worse, the shock of someone suddenly not being there, or the agony of long, drawn-out goodbyes?

Why was life so hard? Why couldn't people just stay in their own homes and when the time came go to sleep in their own beds? Humans made things so complicated. Animals knew to wander off when their time came and find safe, quiet places to rest their weary heads. They dissolved back into the earth with no fuss or fanfare.

People could learn a lot from animals.

But in the meantime, Mary still had to deal with her mother and aunt. She took a deep breath and walked back to the car. She could tell they'd been crying.

"Thank God you were there," Aunt Peggy said. "How do you do it?"

"Do what?"

"Always say the right thing."

"I suppose I just think about what I'd like someone to say to me."

"Well, you're a genius at it."

Her mother nodded. "You are wasted in that grocery store."

"Actually, I think I'm going to apply to become an RPN at NSCC next year. I'll have enough money saved by then."

"Frig that!" Aunt Peggy said. "Ted and I will pay your tuition. And don't you dare say anything, Carole, because you know I have money and if it can help this girl, then it should. She'll make a fantastic nurse."

"I wasn't going to say anything," Carole sniffed. "I'm over that. If you can help her, by all means, do it. And it would make Ma happy."

Mary was overwhelmed. "Gosh! I don't know what to say. Thank you, Aunt Peggy. But I still can't get in this year. The course is already starting."

"Never mind. The year will go fast enough."

Mary looked out the window going home. Two minutes ago she was miserable, and now she was happy.

What a strange world.

CHAPTER FOURTEEN

SHEENA NEVER GOT AROUND TO getting a job, because she always had something to do instead. She made new friends, the wives and partners of Drew's employees. It was empowering to be thought of as the boss's wife. Then they met the couple over the fence who'd moved in just six months before they did. Justin and Alisha were almost clones of Sheena and Drew. They dressed more or less the same, drove the same cars, and drank the same beer and wine. The couples barbecued together on weekends or went downtown on Saturday nights for dinner at their favourite Thai restaurant.

Sheena was truly settling in to her new life in Halifax. She didn't feel the need to go up to Cape Breton as often, and surprisingly her mother didn't bug her to come anymore.

Their first Halloween together in their new house, Drew helped her decorate the outside of the house with lights and cobwebs. Sheena had a lot of different pumpkins on her steps, all of them glowing with weird and wonderful faces she'd found on Pinterest.

They even dressed up together as Baby and Johnny from *Dirty Dancing*. They were going to a party at Justin and Alisha's once the trick-or-treaters stopped coming. While Drew was used to kids coming to his house in Sydney, children had never come to Sheena's house because of the long driveway, so she couldn't wait to pass out the candy. She looked at the enormous bowl of treats she'd accumulated and the boxes of chips on the floor. "Do you think we have enough?"

Once five o'clock hit, the doorbell rang and never stopped until seven-thirty. They finally had to shut the porch light off because they didn't have a single piece of candy left.

"That was wild," Sheena said. "My back is aching. Maybe we should just go to the movies next year."

Drew's cell went off and he hurried over to the dining-room table to answer it.

"Hi, Mom."

And then he didn't say anything for ten minutes. Sheena could tell by the look on his face that it was something serious, so she sat on the living-room couch and watched him quietly.

He eventually said goodbye, put the phone down, and then sat on the nearest chair.

"My parents are getting a divorce."

Sheena's heart sank. "Oh, Drew, I'm so sorry."

"Hey, it's not like I'm surprised. I just wish they'd done it years ago, so we didn't have to be in the middle of their fighting when we were growing up."

"I wonder why they decided to do it now?"

"She wants to marry someone else," Drew said dully.

"Oh gosh, your poor dad."

He shrugged. "I think he has a woman too, so he'll be all right."

Drew sounded matter-of-fact, but his face betrayed him. Sheena got up, walked over to him, and put her arms around his head as he sat there, his cheek against her tummy. He cried, and it killed Sheena to hear it. It must be a terrible feeling to have your parents divorce no matter how old you were. She was glad he felt comfortable enough with her to let it out.

Sheena called Alisha and said something had come up and they couldn't make the party. Alisha understood. Maybe next time.

Mary shouldn't have worried about having a cat and a dog. Weechee and Roscoe became fast friends, but they spent their time running around the apartment in a perpetual game of chase. It never stopped. Worse, they loved to jump on and off the bed at lightning speed. If you happened to be sleeping on your stomach, God help you. They had no regard for your comfort whatsoever. Even Daniel had to yell at them from time to time, and that was unheard of because Daniel didn't think Weechee ever put a foot wrong.

The only time Mary and Daniel ever argued was about their pets.

"Roscoe was here long before this mutt, so he has rights. Weechee is the usurper," Mary reasoned.

"So if we have kids, whatever the first baby does is above reproach and the next kid will be treated like a second-class citizen? That's your logic."

Mary threw a pillow at him while she laughed. "It is not! But what happens if the second baby is a first-class moron? Do we still let him do whatever he wants? Even if he wants to jump out the second-floor window, like you-know-who"—she jabbed her thumb at Weechee—"the other day?"

"You-know-who was having a fit because those idiots Will and Liam were chasing Roscoe around the yard. He was being a hero."

The two of them snorted with laughter. Mary wiped her eyes. "I can't believe I fought my mother my whole life trying to have a pet and right now this house is like an ark. Mom's got Jerry's dog Ruth down there because she gets lonesome during the day. And she still has clients who come to see her despite all that. I'm not sure who's loonier."

Carole decided she was going to be coy with Jerry. She wasn't going to rush into anything, because God knew she made that mistake the last time someone took her to bed. Considering that was twenty-three years ago, maybe she should be in a hurry. But she'd managed without men her whole life and took a weird, resentful pride in that.

Truth be told, she was more in love with Ruth than with her dad, but Jerry was an awfully nice man and the last time he came around for supper, he'd given her good advice.

"So you say you're thinking of opening a dog-grooming business?"

"It crossed my mind. Sometimes I can't stand the thought of cutting one more head of hair. It's always the same thing. I could do it in my sleep. Maybe I need a change. I love grooming the boys, so it seems a natural progression."

"Do you have the money to renovate the place? I could always give you a quote. Anything done today isn't cheap, but I could give you a good deal because this hamburger is delicious."

She wondered if he knew it was a frozen patty.

"I was only thinking about it."

Jerry wiped his mouth with his paper napkin. "Seems to me you have a nice little set-up here as it is. You and the dogs always have such a good time together. Everyone at the park mentions it. How do you think your boys would feel having canine strangers demanding your attention eight hours a day?"

Carole looked at the dogs. Her three and Ruth were sitting in a semi-circle around the table, eyeing every move, and now they thought scraps might be in the offing. All of them perked up.

"You know, Jerry, you're right. Why ruin a good thing? Thanks."

"You're welcome."

"Would you like some dessert? I have an apple pie."

"Sounds wonderful."

She hoped he wouldn't know it was frozen too.

Peggy drove out to Glace Bay to visit her mother with a gift in hand. She'd sewn a throw cover for her bed in various shades of blue, Ethel's favourite. Peggy selfishly longed to keep it herself. One day it would be returned to her when the inevitable happened, but Peggy didn't like to think about what shape it would be in then or what kind of fluids would stain it in the interim. No, this throw would be staying in the manor.

By now Peggy recognized some of the residents lining the hallway outside their rooms. They'd nod or try to get Peggy to come and talk to them. She always felt like a scoundrel when she'd pretend to be in a big rush. Too bad she wasn't a nice person like Mary.

There was one elderly lady who dressed like a prim librarian. She stood ramrod straight, too. Peggy wondered at first why she was in here since she seemed so put together, but once you talked to her for five minutes, it was pretty clear. The nurses said she knew everyone's business. They affectionately called her the town snoop.

Her name was also Ethel and she always remembered that Peggy was there to see her mother Ethel. This pleased the other Ethel to no end.

"Hello!" Ethel waved her hand as Peggy approached. "Are you going to see Ethel today?"

"Yes, I sure am."

"Did you know there are three Ethels on this floor?"

"No, I didn't."

"I'm Ethel, there's your mother Ethel, and then there's the Ethel who shits a lot."

Lord. Peggy moved on in a hurry. She poked her head around the door of her mother's room. Her mom never ventured outside it. It was like she had lost the will to do anything, and Peggy's guilt was suffocating.

Ethel was in bed curled up on her side. Her eyes were closed, but that didn't mean she was sleeping.

"Hi, Mom."

Ethel opened her eyes and scowled. "Got nothing better to do than come in here and see me?"

Peggy leaned over and kissed her mom's cheek. "As I matter of fact, I came to give you a present. And you'll never guess. I made it myself."

"Bully for you."

So it was going to be that kind of a day. Peggy sat on the chair and put the gift on her lap.

"Would you like to open it?"

"No."

"Mom, please. I'm so excited to show it to you."

"Do what you want then."

Peggy opened the tissue paper and proceeded to shake out the blanket. She had to stand up so it wouldn't hit the ground. "What do you think? Do you like it?"

"It's nice."

"All your favourite colours of blue."

"I hate blue."

Peggy folded it up and sat down. "No, you don't."

"I fuckin' hate blue! Carole likes blue."

Poor Peggy was heartsick. "Really? I was sure it was...well, it doesn't matter. It will still look nice on your bed."

"I don't want it."

"Mom—"

Her mother got up on her elbow. "I don't want the fuckin' thing.

Give it to Carole. Why is it when a person is old and in bed that no one pays attention to what they're saying?"

"I'm sorry. You're right." Peggy folded it back into the tissue paper. There was no way this was going to end up a dog's blanket. It was coming home with her after all.

"So how are you feeling, Mom?"

Ethel looked at her and Peggy didn't ask again.

"Ted made his reservations for his flight home. He'll be here for Christmas. Only six weeks away. I can't believe how fast the year went. Remember last Christmas?"

"You mean when I was happy and living at home? Yeah, it rings a bell."

Peggy looked down at her lap. "I'm sorry. I'm so sorry that this has happened to you. I don't know what to do."

"You could take this goddamned pillow and smother me with it. No one would care, and I'd be eternally grateful."

Peggy tried not to cry but she couldn't help it. This was unbearably sad. "If I wasn't so afraid, I'd do it for you. But I can't, Mom. I can't."

Ethel turned on her back and sighed. "I know. How's Sheena?"

They talked a little about Sheena and Drew, and then her mother wanted to know about Mary and Daniel.

"They are the cutest couple," Peggy said. "They look happy all the time."

"They come to see me."

"Did you know Carole is dating?"

Her mother gaped at her and struggled to sit up. Peggy had to help her. Once she was sorted, she looked more like her old self. "Tell me all about it."

Peggy told her what she knew.

"Do you like him?"

"Yes, he's very nice. A quiet kind of fellow."

"How the hell did he get mixed up with Carole?"

"They both own Newfoundland dogs. They met at the park."

Ethel put her head back on the pillow. "She'll ruin it. She ruins everything."

Peggy felt a prick of resentment. "No, she won't. She's changed a lot over the last few months. Haven't you noticed?"

"The only thing she does when she's in here is show me videos of those damn dogs. You mark my words; she'll talk herself out of it. She'll think up some stupid excuse and send the guy packing."

"I don't think you're being fair."

Ethel pointed her finger at Peggy. "Now I'm not there, so you're going to have to be on the lookout for it. Don't let this guy slip through her fingers. It might be her last chance at happiness. She doesn't think she's good enough, but she is."

"Have you ever said that to her?"

Her mother gave her a filthy look but then turned away. "Probably not."

"Why don't you? While you still have time?"

Sheena lay on her bamboo sheets and drew up a list. For a second she felt like her mother but then dismissed the terrifying thought. Drew was in the shower getting ready for work. She loved this time of morning, listening to Drew hum in his own off-key way. Over the last few months, she'd grown to really like him, not just love him. Now that he had his own home, he was more relaxed and playful. He enjoyed spending time with his brothers but was always grateful to throw his keys in the dish by the door, flop onto the sofa, and check his computer. Or snuggle up with her.

It was a big decision as to whether they should go home for Christmas or spend it here in their new home, but Sheena was looking forward to seeing her dad and made the case that they would have lots of Christmases in this house. Drew agreed, thinking he should probably see both his parents, even though he was dreading it.

"They sold our house so my brothers and I have nowhere to go. None of us wants to spend Christmas with the new partners. I'm glad I'm staying at your place."

"Once we come home we'll have our first dinner party on New Year's Eve. We'll invite Justin and Alisha and the gang at work. It'll be fun."

Sheena put two Pop-Tarts in the toaster and a coffee pod in the

Keurig: breakfast was served. Drew always took it with him. She told him more than once that she could make a proper breakfast for him, but Drew didn't like eggs, so Pop-Tarts it was.

He gave her a long kiss. "See ya later."

"Bye, honey." Now she did sound like her mom. Sheena took her list and sat down to call home on Skype. Her mother appeared on the screen. "Hey, what's up?"

"I'm planning my first dinner party on New Year's Eve."

"Ambitious. What are you serving?"

"That's why I'm calling you. I don't have any idea."

"I'm not going to make the menu for you. I'm busy."

"Doing what?"

"Lynne and I are going to an art show, then out for lunch."

"Oh. Well, just give me some quick suggestions."

Peggy sighed. "Most people like roast beef. That's easy."

"What kind of roast beef?"

"What kind? A prime rib is usually what you'd serve company."

"How much do I get?"

"How many people are coming?"

"I don't know."

"Then I can't help you."

"If I have potatoes, should I buy the little ones? The three-pound bag?"

"Unless your guests are mice, that's a tad stingy."

"Oh, this is hopeless. Why did I think this was a good idea?"

"You're giving up already? Sheena, my love, it will come. You're not going to learn these things overnight."

"But you make it all look so easy."

"Ah yes…the underappreciated housewife who goes unnoticed until her family realizes she was a genius all along. Unfortunately, they never catch on until they've moved out."

"I always knew you were a genius."

"I'm still not planning your menu. Love you. Bye!"

This was annoying. Her mother used to hang on her every word when she first moved away. Now Sheena was lucky to catch her at home.

There was only one thing to do: Christmas retail therapy. She stood up and was immediately dizzy; so dizzy that she fell down. Sheena was astonished that she was on the floor. She stayed where she was because she realized she wasn't feeling well. A small stab of fear tickled the back of her neck. But it was probably nothing. She was overreacting.

When she tried to get up, she knew she was going to be sick. She crawled to the bathroom off the kitchen and vomited in the toilet. Three times. As she lay against the cool porcelain it hit her. She started to count back in her head and then got confused and started over. How long had it been?

She just might be. It had never occurred to her because it wasn't in her long-term plan just yet. They were supposed to be married for three years at least and take a few trips before babies came on the scene. They were good at making sure it didn't happen.

And then she remembered the night they'd polished off that third bottle of wine.

In the movies, girls in this position would look horrified but then their faces would soften and they'd make doe-eyes in the bathroom mirror. Sheena just burst into tears. This was scary. She couldn't have a baby here all by herself. How would she look after it alone? Drew would be working. All her friends worked. She wouldn't be able to drink. What if she killed it? She was alone in the universe with this parasite clinging to her looking for attention. She was just a kid! How could she have a kid?

After a half an hour, she was freezing on the tile floor and moved gingerly upstairs to take a shower. She gathered herself under the hot steaming water. Maybe she was being premature. The first thing to do was take a pregnancy test. Stop panicking until she knew for sure.

Driving to the drugstore, she was on autopilot. Coming home with three boxes and not remembering how she got back made her wince. Hopefully she hadn't run anyone over. She held her breath as she peed on the stick, left it on the side of the tub, and zoomed into the bedroom to crawl under the covers.

After a few minutes she peeked out to look at the clock radio. It was time. She hid under the sheets anyway.

"Get a grip, Sheena!" she yelled in the empty house.

She tossed the sheets aside and marched into the bathroom and picked up the stick.

Yes.

She peed on another stick.

Yes.

She opened the third box.

Yes.

A few hours later, Drew found her wrapped in her favourite chenille throw on the couch, wads of used tissues surrounding her body and a bucket in her lap.

"My God, what's wrong?"

"I'm having a baby!"

"What?"

"I know! Can you believe it? I'm mortified. I wanted to wait until I was like, thirty-two. I'm too young to be a mom! I don't even like kids. I never babysat kids because they were too gross. And now I have one growing under my shirt and I'll get big and fat and then the kid won't like me because it'll know I didn't want it and how do you talk to it then? What would I say? 'Sorry, kid?' It's impossible! This is the worst day of my life!"

She waited for Drew to say something.

He smiled. "It's the best day of mine."

CHAPTER FIFTEEN

IT WAS PEGGY'S TURN TO visit her mom, but Lynne had invited her to play bridge with her friends.

"I don't know how to play bridge."

This didn't bother Lynne. "We're only just starting ourselves. One of the group had to drop out. Her son is in rehab and she's not dealing with it very well."

"But isn't rehab a good thing?"

"Not when you've pretended your whole life that your son never drank or did drugs."

Peggy tsked. "Poor woman."

She called Carole because she knew her sister was rescheduling her appointments and now had Wednesdays off.

"I hate to do this to you, but would you mind popping in to see Mom? I've been invited out to play bridge and I'd like to go."

"There's no such thing as popping in to see her. The experience puts you in a coma of despair for the rest of the day."

"I know. Sorry. I'll take two days in a row."

"That's okay. Honestly, Peggy, I wish the poor woman would die. She'd be so much happier."

"It's almost like she's waiting for something, isn't it?" mused Peggy. "The doctors still can't figure out how she's still here."

"I can't believe I'm saying this, but maybe I'll buy a bunch of scratch tickets. That'll cheer her up. I gotta go; Jerry's here with Ruth."

Ruth galloped through the door and had a great reunion with her pals as if she hadn't just seen them the day before.

"If you don't mind," Carole said to Jerry, "I have to head over to Glace Bay. I'll walk the dogs when I get home."

"I actually came to say that I have an easy schedule today. Want me to come with you?"

Carole had to think fast. Did she want Jerry to meet her mother? If he did, would he pick up Ruth and never come back? Would she care if he never came back? What if....

"Carole?"

"Sorry. Look, I have to visit my mother in a nursing home. It's very depressing and I'm sure that's not how you want to spend your afternoon."

"If it would make the day easier for you, I'd like to come."

Was this guy for real? Had he actually said that?

"Okay. Thanks."

They decided to walk the dogs before they left, in case they were delayed. Jerry took Billy and Ruth, and Carole pushed Will and Liam in a cheap baby stroller she'd found in someone's trash. They were often worn out trying to keep up with Billy on their jaunts, so this was a great solution. Weechee sometimes joined them. Carole would tie his leash to the buggy handle and he'd trot along, but one day she looked down and he'd jumped into the netting at the bottom and enjoyed a free ride. Looking at their faces brought Carole such joy. How had she never noticed dogs her whole life? She must have been sleepwalking through the years.

Jerry insisted on stopping at the grocery store so he could buy Ethel a bouquet of flowers. Carole picked up the scratch tickets. He asked whether Ethel liked chocolates, and Carole suggested pink peppermints instead.

She was incredibly nervous when they walked into the manor together. Would people think they were together? Wait, they were together. Who was she? Carole didn't recognize herself anymore.

When they got to her room, Ethel was sitting up in bed having her lunch. She picked up her food with her fingers, but a lot of it rolled across the sheets. Her hair was flat and godawful.

"Hi, Ma."

"You never visit me."

"I do so! I was here two days ago."

Ethel grunted. "Who's he?"

"Ma, this is my friend Jerry Hawco."

Jerry stepped forward and held out the flowers. "It's very nice to meet you, Mrs. Ryan."

Ethel took the flowers, slightly mollified. "Nice to meet you." She looked around. "I don't know where to put these."

"I'll get a vase with some water. I'll be right back." Carole left and Ethel stared at Jerry. He kept smiling.

"So sit your ass down and tell me about yourself."

Jerry pulled up a chair and folded his hands across his flannel shirt. "Not much to tell. I was born in the Pier—"

"The Pier, dear."

Jerry laughed. "That's right. No better place in the world."

"Who's your father?"

"Wilfred Hawco. He worked at the steel plant, until he died of cancer."

"Wilfred? The name rings a bell. I probably knew him."

"I'm divorced—"

"Did you cheat on her?"

"No, ma'am. One of those cases of marrying right out of high school. We're still good friends. We love our kids. I have two boys. They're working out west, like a lot of youngsters these days."

"What do you do?"

"I'm a carpenter."

"Like Jesus."

Jerry chuckled. "I can guarantee I'm not like Jesus."

"Do ya drink?"

"No, ma'am."

"Too bad. Do ya smoke?"

"No, ma'am."

"Gamble?"

"Nope."

"What do you do?"

"I love my dog. We go hiking together. She's good company."

"I'm not a dog person. They shit too much."

"Don't we all," Jerry quipped.

Ethel chuckled. "I like you."

Carole came back into the room and was shocked to see her mother smiling. She put the vase on the table beside her bed. "Well, now. Looks like you two have become friends."

"Don't get carried away." Ethel put her head back on the pillow. "I have to do a background check. Make sure he doesn't forge signatures or steal cutlery."

They chatted easily for a couple of hours and then Ethel's eyes started to close. Carole and Jerry got up to leave.

"Goodbye, Mrs. Ryan. I hope you don't mind if I come to visit you again."

"You can come anytime. Leave that one at home."

Carole leaned over her mother and kissed her forehead. "See ya, Ma."

Her mother grabbed her hand and whispered, "Don't frig this up."

"Gee, thanks."

"You deserve him."

As Carole walked down the hall with Jerry, she realized her mother had just given her blessing.

When they got back to Jerry's truck, Carole leaned over and kissed Jerry on the mouth. He was surprised, but not as much as she was. It felt comfortable and nice.

"Thank you. You are the only person my mother has been nice to in years. What on earth did you say to her?"

"Nothing. But she reminded me of my mom, all bluster and show. I find people like that are very insecure. Always waiting for the other shoe to drop, so they can never relax. It's a hard way to live."

Yes, it was a hard way to live.

"You're a miracle worker, and for that I'll make you supper."

"How about we pick up supper and take it back to my place? It might be nice to have a few hours away from the kids."

Carole grinned and put her hand in his. He drove out of the parking lot with one hand on the wheel.

Peggy arrived at Lynne's house looking forward to a fun afternoon. She was a little nervous to meet Lynne's friends and hoped she'd like them. What if she didn't? How did one back out of a bridge foursome?

Lynne's house was almost an exact replica of Peggy's, every room decorated within an inch of its life.

Lynne was pleased to see her. She ushered her into the living room where a bridge table had been set up in the middle of the rug.

"Everyone, this is my new friend Peggy. Peggy, this is Linda, Vera, and Maxine."

Linda and Vera turned their heads and smiled hello. Maxine turned around in her chair. Good gravy. Maxine Corbett, the mother-in-law.

Maxine gave Peggy a pretend smile. "Actually, we know each other. My Drew is married to Peggy's daughter."

Everyone gasped with delight. Lynne clapped her hands. "What a small world! Oh, this is perfect. We'll get along famously."

Peggy wanted to crawl into a hole.

She decided that Maxine was not going to ruin a perfectly good day and after a while, learning the rules of bridge made her forget about Maxine. Her concentration was fixed on her cards. Too bad she hadn't listened harder in math class.

At one point Lynne and the others went into the kitchen to prepare snacks. Maxine shuffled the deck.

"I suppose Sheena told you that Chuck and I are getting a divorce."

Peggy lied. "No, she didn't, actually. I'm sorry to hear that."

"Don't be. It should've happened years ago. I think the boys are relieved, although they're annoyed at us for selling their childhood home. The two older ones aren't coming home for Christmas. I'm glad Drew can stay with you and Ted. It'll be nice to see him over the holidays."

"They can hardly expect you and Chuck to keep the house."

Maxine shrugged. "Your kids think everything has to stay the same. They get to go away and make a new life, but God forbid their parents aren't in exactly the same spot when they want to drop in."

Peggy nodded. "I'm just learning how difficult it is to reinvent yourself once you stop being Mom. We only had Sheena, and when she left I couldn't believe how sad I was. You'd think I was never going to see her again, but in those first few days, that's how it felt."

Maxine looked thoughtful. "Maybe it's different having a daughter. My boys were involved in sports and their father handled all that. I don't think I was ever as hands-on as you are."

"I realize now I just about ruined that child trying to give her everything. It's only after they're gone that you have enough room to breathe and look at it sensibly."

"None of us is perfect."

They nodded at each other. The other women came back laden

with trays and they enjoyed some refreshment before having another game. By the time the afternoon was over, Maxine and Peggy
smiled at each other and said they'd see each other next week at
Vera's house.

Lynne held Peggy back. "I'm so glad you and Maxine already
knew each other. I was a little worried about what you'd think of her.
She has a reputation for being standoffish, but once you get to know
her she's fine. We go way back."

"She's family now. So I guess I have to like her."

"Not necessarily," Lynne said.

Two weeks before Christmas, Mary was in a terrible rush. She'd
slept in, which was not like her at all. Daniel had already left for
school. He'd left a Post-It note on the dresser mirror: "I need cereal.
And you. XO."

She hopped in the shower, and got dressed while eating a banana. Weechee followed her around until she gave him the last
piece. Roscoe was still snoring under the quilt. She grabbed her cell
and called her mom.

"I'm late for work. Could you come and take Weechee out after I
leave?"

"Sure."

"Thanks."

She put on her boots and coat, grabbed her purse, and gave
Weechee a kiss on the snout. "Your grandmother will be up in a bit.
See ya."

He cocked his head. Mary always took him out before she left.

"God! Don't make me feel so guilty!"

She rushed down the stairs and shut the door.

Janet saw her run in through the Sobeys sliding doors and tapped
her wrist.

"I know, I know!"

Once on cash, Mary was completely out of sorts. The entire morning felt wrong somehow. She didn't even try to be pleasant, just kept
her head down and did her job.

It was nearly lunchtime when she looked up and saw her mother and Jerry come in together. She knew instantly something was wrong. Mary left her cash and ran over to them.

"Is it Gran?"

Her mother was crying and couldn't talk. Jerry took her by the arm. "It's Weechee. He was hit by a car." He paused. "He's dead."

Mary burst into tears and covered her face. "Oh no! Oh no! How am I going to tell Daniel?"

"I'm so sorry, Mary," Jerry said.

She looked at her mom. "Did you take him off his leash? You know how crazy he gets. You should've watched him better!"

Her mother wiped her eyes and looked at her sadly. "I went up to get him and the door was already open. He was gone."

Mary almost fainted. "I didn't close it properly. Is that what you're saying?"

"We went looking for him for hours. We scoured the neighbourhood. And then we found him by the side of the road. The bastard who did it didn't even stop."

Mary doubled over. "It's all my fault. Daniel will hate me."

Janet came over to see what was the matter. She told Carole and Jerry to take Mary home.

"Where is he?" Mary cried.

"We wrapped him in a blanket. He's in the truck."

Mary was inconsolable. She went back to the apartment and held Weechee in her arms like a baby. She couldn't look at him, just rocked him in his blanket back and forth. Her mother sat with her. Jerry said he'd be downstairs.

Roscoe sat in the hallway, not wanting to come in the room but not taking his eyes off the blanket.

"I didn't even want him! I complained about him all the time. He just wanted to kiss people. Even when I was mad at him, he'd just kiss me."

As the afternoon grew longer, Mary knew Daniel would be home. She couldn't bear it.

"Stay with me, Mom."

"I will."

They heard Daniel's truck pull up and then the door open and shut. He whistled coming up the stairs, bounding into the room.

"There's my girl! This is a surprise. Did you get off early?"

When no one answered him, he looked closer. "What's wrong? What's that?"

Mary cried and cried. Carole got up and put her hand on Daniel's shoulder. Her voice quivered. "It's Weechee. He was hit by a car. I'm so sorry."

Daniel's face crumpled. "No," he whispered. "No." He reached out and took the bundle from Mary's arms and then walked around the room with him cradled on his shoulder. "It's okay, buddy. I've got you. You're going to be all right."

Mary grabbed her coat and purse and ran down the stairs. She jumped into the car and took off. She saw her mother in the rear-view mirror on the porch, with her arm in the air, calling her back.

It was hard to drive when tears kept blinding her. The only thought she had was to get away from everyone. It was her fault Weechee was dead. Why hadn't she called Janet to say she was sick or that she'd be in later? Why was she rushing? Why didn't she just take a minute and let him out to pee? Why? Why? Why?

Mary eventually got to her destination. She walked into Gran's room and stood by her bed. Gran opened her eyes and held out her hand.

"Can I lie with you?"

Gran pushed over and Mary crawled into bed with her, hiding her face against her saggy breasts. Her grandmother pulled up the covers and tucked her in. They didn't talk. Mary felt safe.

She must have fallen asleep. The room was in shadows. Her breath was calm and her heartbeat steady, but she wasn't sure where she was for a split second. And then it all came rushing back.

Mary had run away when Daniel needed her. She had thought only of herself. Maybe she wasn't such a nice person after all. She needed to apologize to him.

"Gran. Gran?"

She moved her head and lifted it away from Gran's chest. "Are you awake?"

There was no movement. Mary got up on her elbow and looked at Gran's face. She'd seen it before.

Gran was gone.

Mary nestled back into her chest and held her close. There were no tears. Gran was where she wanted to be and Mary had helped her get there.

She got off the bed gingerly and stroked her grandmother's face. Then she went out to the nurses' station and told them. They immediately went into action, and asked Mary if she was okay. She assured them she was fine.

"Don't call my house or Aunt Peggy's, please. I'd like to tell them myself."

She drove home and saw the lights were on upstairs and downstairs. When she walked into her mother's kitchen, Mom and Jerry stood up, their furry kids beside them.

"Are you all right?" Mom asked.

"Yes. I'm sorry—"

"That's okay."

"Is Daniel—"

"He's better. He's worried about you. Where did you go?"

"Gran's."

"I should've thought of that."

"She's dead, Mom. She died in her sleep, in my arms. It was beautiful. I felt only peace." Mary walked over to her mom and hugged her.

"Thank you, Mary."

Then she walked up the stairs to her apartment. Daniel held out his arms and gathered her close. "Gran died. She and Weechee went to heaven on the same day."

Daniel held her for a few moments, then said, "Heaven?"

Mary smiled despite herself. "You're right. They'll give the devil a run for his money."

CHAPTER SIXTEEN

CAROLE DROVE OVER TO PEGGY'S. News like this wasn't delivered over the phone.

The moment Peggy opened the door, she knew.

"Was she alone? Goddammit."

"Mary was with her."

"Thank the lord for that girl. Come in. I'll make some tea." Peggy reached out and hugged her sister. They stayed like that for a few minutes, letting reality sink in.

Two cups of tea and a slice of low-fat banana bread later, they felt a bit better about facing the job ahead. Peggy was going to call Sheena after Carole left. Right now they needed to call the manor and the funeral home and think about the arrangements.

"You write the obituary," Carole said. "That's more up your alley."

"I've never written one in my life. What should we say?"

"Not the truth, that's for sure."

"Of course the truth. She raised two daughters, has two grand-daughters, liked to sew and—"

"—drink, gamble, and swear?" interjected Carole.

"If everyone told the absolute truth in anyone's obituary, it would be a horror novel. 'Liked to chase women, cheat on his taxes, steal cars, and pick his nose.' People leave more out than in, and I don't blame them."

"I know one thing," Carole said. "I don't want our father's name in it. She'd have a fit, and rightly so."

"It's not hitting me yet. When does it sink in?"

"When you see them, I suppose. Do you want to see her?" When Carole glanced at her sister, she saw a frightened little girl. She reached over and held her hand.

"I'll be with you."

"Okay. I don't think I could do it alone."

For the first time they felt like orphans.

When Peggy called Sheena, Sheena howled. Peggy got a fright. "Are you all right, honey?"

"Gran's *dead*? I've never known anyone who died before! Why her?"

Peggy wanted to say, "Why not her?" She never did anything she was told and was living on borrowed time. It was a bit of a shock that Sheena was taking it so hard.

"It's okay, love," soothed Peggy. "Gran wanted to go. She was tired and unhappy."

"I'm tired and unhappy, but I don't want to die!" Sheena sobbed.

"Is everything all right with you and Drew?"

"Of course! Why do you always think something's wrong?"

"Why are you in hysterics?"

There was a pause. Sheena cleared her throat. "Sorry. That time of the month, I guess. When's the funeral? Maybe I'll come up and stay until Christmas. Drew can come before the holiday."

"That would be lovely. I can't wait to see you."

They had a small service in Sydney Memorial Chapel, with only family in attendance. They saw the body before the cremation and Carole took out a brush and fixed her mother's hair to her liking. Sheena sobbed through the whole thing while Mary hugged her. The minister asked them if they wanted to say a few words about their loved one. All eyes focused on Mary.

Mary walked up to the lectern and took a deep breath. "Gran was an original. She wasn't perfect and she drove us crazy, but we loved her and she loved us and in the end, that's all any of us can hope for. We will miss her."

They picked up Gran's ashes the next day and sat around Carole's kitchen table wondering what to do with them.

"I suppose we should buy a plot at Forest Haven," Aunt Peggy said.

Mary shook her head. "She'd hate that. Put her urn on the side table by the couch. I'll put her teacup beside it. Then she'll be happy."

They agreed.

In a bit of a ceremony, they placed the urn on the table and even poured tea in the cup. Mary threw in the last of the gin. Standing back to look, they knew they had the perfect solution. Until Liam and Will came tearing into the room and jumped up on the arm of the couch. The urn went flying and the teacup followed. There was Gran on the floor, soaking up the gin.

All of them stared at it, horrified, until Carole said, "How fitting."

They laughed until they couldn't catch their breath. Gran would've loved it.

Christmas Eve was vastly different from the previous year. Mary was invited to Daniel's parents' house for dinner, Carole was going to Jerry's to be introduced to his boys, Sheena and Drew were having drinks with his parents and their new partners, and Peggy and Ted were going out to dinner to celebrate his return.

Mary was a bit overwhelmed at the horde of people around Bob and Millie Hennessy's table. Daniel had six siblings and all of them were married with kids. It was a bit like being at an amusement park. Mary wasn't sure where to look first. She tried to remember everyone's names, but it was a lost cause. All his siblings looked alike, and they had an easy manner. Everyone teased everyone else and there was a lot of good-natured prattle between shouts of laughter. Mary found herself smiling all night.

She knew she'd passed the family test when Millie came over and handed her a recipe card. "I've written out Maman's sugar cookie recipe. She always said how much you liked them, and I thought you could make them for you and Daniel. And just between us, I've never seen Daniel so happy. I'm not a woman who gossips, but I have to say I was rather dismayed when I first met Amber. I knew it wouldn't last, but you can't tell your kids anything. Let them find out themselves, is my motto."

"Thank you, Mrs. Hennessy."

"Call me Millie," she said kindly. "Everyone does."

Carole was almost sick she was so nervous. What did she know about young men? At least she was bringing along the boys. Jerry suggested they come, perhaps to break the ice. His sons were home from out west and spending Christmas Day with their mother, so this was Jerry's chance to have a visit.

Jake and Joe seemed nice enough, both of them shy with her, but they came to life around Billy, Will, and Liam. Nothing like dogs to distract you from uncomfortable repartee.

Carole liked Jerry very much. Probably loved him, but couldn't quite say it or even admit it to herself. Her limited experience with the male species made her guarded and she kept waiting to be disappointed, but so far, Jerry hadn't put a foot wrong. He was loving and kind to his kids, a big softie with Ruth, and great with Carole's three dogs. Even her mother had liked him. So why was she afraid to admit that she'd fallen for him?

Because maybe he'd find out she wasn't a nice dog lady but a disappointed, bitter woman who had always lived in her little sister's shadow. The jealous kid in the family. When did you stop being who everyone thought you were? How late was too late? Was she a changed woman or was she just putting on an act for this man?

Why did he like her so much? What was wrong with him?

They sat in Jerry's living room, all of them with a beer. Jake lit a cigarette and Carole wanted to crawl over the couch and tackle him for it.

"Our mom is a hairdresser too," Jake said. "Seems like Dad has a type."

Carole looked at Jerry. "You never told me that."

"It's not important."

"She owns her own salon," Joe added. "She has ten people working for her."

Carole caught the look Jerry flashed his youngest.

"Do you have people working for you?" Joe asked.

"No, I don't. I work out of my dining room. I'm a one-woman operation."

He looked unimpressed.

"Anything else you want to know?" Jerry asked. "Like how much she makes a year, or if her teeth are real?"

Joe got his father's drift and excused himself. His brother followed him out to the kitchen.

"Sorry about that. You're the first woman I've brought home since the divorce."

"I get it. They hate me. It was bound to happen."

"They don't hate you. It's me. I didn't tell them about you until yesterday. I should've prepared them better for this."

"Yeah, you should have," Carole said acidly. "Thanks a bunch for throwing me to the lions."

"I'm new to this game too, Carole. It seems as a divorced father, I'm doing everything wrong."

Carole softened. "No you're not. I can tell they love you a lot. And they aren't being mean...just nosy. I'd be exactly the same way, so don't worry about it."

"Want to help me get supper ready? That's always a good strategy around boys: food."

Time to confess.

She took a deep breath. "I don't cook, Jerry. I'm sure you're aware of that fact since you've eaten frozen food every time you've been at my house."

"Everything you've served me has been delicious," he said seriously. He got up from the couch and made his way to the kitchen.

There was definitely something wrong with this guy.

Drew and Sheena were having a whispered fight in Sheena's old bedroom. They didn't want Sheena's parents to hear what they were saying.

"I think we should wait to tell our parents about the baby. I'm only seven weeks. Things can happen."

"I want to tell my parents so I can see their reaction."

Sheena snorted. "I know what your mother will say: 'my Drew is too young to be a father.'"

"This will be her first grandchild. You don't know how she's going to react."

"If you tell your parents then I'm going to have to tell mine."

Drew put a comb through his hair while looking in the mirror over Sheena's old dresser. "I can't believe you haven't told your mom yet anyway. It's not like you to keep a secret."

"I'm scared."

He turned around and sat on the bed beside her. "There is nothing to be afraid of. I'm with you."

"That's fine and dandy, Drew, but you don't have to give birth to a large ham. I hate pain."

"You're small and I'm not that big. Maybe we'll have a pork chop."

She bumped his shoulder with her own. "It's not fair to make me laugh when I'm trying to be upset."

Chuck Corbett and his new girlfriend, Elaine, lived in a condo overlooking Sydney Harbour. It was a beautiful, well-appointed spot. Sheena could tell that Drew was having a hard time seeing his dad with this woman, though Elaine was doing her best to win him over. The trouble was, she never sat down, constantly jumping up to offer platters of nibbles and snacks. She had enough food for twelve and looked disappointed when Sheena declined both the food and the drinks.

"Have a glass of bubbly." Chuck poured champagne into a flute for Sheena. "We're celebrating your first Christmas together."

"She can't have a drink, Dad."

"Why not?"

Elaine jumped in. "Are you pregnant?"

Chuck looked up. "What?"

Drew smiled at his dad. "We're having a baby."

Chuck put down the glass and gave his son a huge hug. "Congratulations, son! Well, well. This is quite something. The first grandchild." He loomed over Sheena, so she stood up and was caught in a tight embrace as well. "Thank you, my dear. You're giving us a wonderful gift." He turned to Drew. "Does your mother know yet?"

"Not yet. Even Sheena's parents don't know."

This put a big smile on Chuck's face. He looked at Elaine. "Imagine that. I'm the first one they told. I can't tell you how happy I am."

Seeing big Chuck so tickled gave Sheena a bit of a thrill. She'd forgotten about this aspect of the whole thing—how special she'd be to everyone in the family. Kind of like being a princess for nine months. Deep down she wished her first reaction hadn't been panic and uncertainty…hopefully over time that would lessen.

Somehow she doubted it.

Their next stop was Maxine and her boyfriend, Sherman. All the Corbett boys snickered over Sherman's name, but once they found out he was a retired detective, the laughing stopped. Sherm was a tank. A tank with a crew cut. Drew confessed to Sheena later that he rather liked the guy, even though he wouldn't want to meet him in an alley.

What surprised Sheena was how feminine and girly Maxine was around Sherm. She tittered at everything he said, and was almost a completely different woman than the one Sheena knew. Maxine must have been desperately unhappy with Chuck, because tonight she was as nice as pie.

And she was even nicer when she heard she was going to be a grandmother. She hugged Sheena and seemed genuinely thrilled. Drew was delighted by her reaction. Maybe mother and son would be closer now. The idea of a baby seemed to make everyone forget their petty differences.

Peggy and Ted went to Governor's Pub for dinner and Ted raised his glass to his wife. "To surviving an unforgettable year and to a new beginning."

"A new beginning." Peggy touched her glass to his and smiled as she took a sip of champagne.

It was over the escargot that Peggy told Ted she had considered divorcing him at one point. His eyes popped. "Excuse me?"

"I hated you for a while because I thought you were having an affair with the woman who called you Teddy."

"Are you kidding me? That's ridiculous."

"It wasn't ridiculous. I felt abandoned and alone and I thought you went halfway around the world to get away from me."

Ted buttered a roll. "If I wanted to get away from you, I'd just move across town."

"But you need to see it from my point of view. Have I ever come home and said, 'Ted, I'm going to China for a year. I hope you don't mind'?"

"Why are you rehashing this? It's over. I'm back." Ted took a bite of his roll and chewed it while shaking his head impatiently.

"So I'm not going to be allowed to discuss my feelings, is that it?"

"Peggy, it's Christmas Eve. I wanted a nice dinner with my wife. That's it."

Peggy sat back in her chair. "I'm not the same person I was when you left. The fact that you haven't noticed that is telling, don't you think?"

Ted leaned closer to her. "Can you just relax and enjoy your meal? I've only been home for a week. Give me a chance to settle back in."

They ate their steaks but didn't enjoy them. The atmosphere thawed somewhat over dessert and coffee, but once in the car, there was silence on the way home.

When they walked into the house, they heard the kids in the kitchen. It was a relief to have someone else to talk to. Sheena and Drew were popping popcorn in the microwave. When the noise stopped, Sheena took out the bag and shook it. "Guess what else is popping out soon?"

"I don't have a clue," Peggy said listlessly.

"A baby!"

"Whose baby?" Peggy and Ted said together.

"Our baby," Drew shouted. "Hello, Grandma and Grandpa!"

Peggy screamed right in Ted's ear, and then she jumped up and down in Ted's arms before racing across the kitchen to try and kiss Sheena and Drew together. Poor old Ted tried to get into the action, but Peggy was everywhere at once. She kissed all three of them over and over again.

Ted whispered, "I thought you hated me."

"Oh, shut your face, you big dope."

Once again, Ted shook his head. "Women."

On Christmas morning, Mary and Daniel exchanged a few gifts in their bed. She was going with her mother over to Aunt Peggy's for dinner and he was going home with his mom and dad.

Daniel gave her a triangle-shaped bracelet encased in silver wire with an elaborate clasp. Daniel pointed at it. "This is made of cement, if you can believe it. But it's really light. The girl at the store said it was the latest thing, so I wanted you to have it."

"No one has ever given me jewellery before. This is definitely something the girlfriend of a rockstar would wear. I love it!" She kissed him several times just to make her point.

Then she gave him his gifts, a Foo Fighters hoodie and a small framed picture of Weechee. He got choked up when he looked at the photo and put it on his nightstand. Roscoe went hairy in the gift wrap, proving yet again that the best things in life are free.

As Carole and Mary drove over to Coxheath, memories of last Christmas loomed large.

"Remember when we got stuck in the snow bank?" Mary smiled.

"Poor Ma almost froze to death."

"Because you had to have a cigarette."

"I know. What a bitch I was."

Mary did a double-take. "Did I hear you correctly?"

"I was wrong. I always say I'm wrong when I'm wrong."

"Then you have been wrong exactly once in your life."

"What can I say? I'm perfect."

Mother and daughter smiled at each other.

They didn't get in the door before Peggy came bounding from the kitchen with arms flapping, but Sheena managed to beat her to it by racing down the stairs and shouting, "I'm having a baby!"

Carole and Mary exchanged stunned glances. "Already?" they said in unison.

"Believe me, I cried when I found out. Me, a mother?"

"You took the words right out of my mouth," Carole said before looking at Peggy. "And you're okay with this?"

"No. I'm going to tell her to send it back. What kind of a reaction is that?"

Mary hugged her cousin. "I'm really happy for you both."

"Thank you."

Carole grabbed Sheena next. "I'm obviously happy for you as well. It's just a shock, that's all."

Peggy folded her arms. "Yeah, what a shock. A married couple having a baby."

Uncle Ted walked out from the kitchen. "Do you realize you both sound like Ethel? Now someone help me with this dinner."

As they eventually sat around the table, Sheena insisted on setting a place for Gran. "I read an article in *Cosmo* that spirits appreciate being remembered. Apparently the Kardashians do it."

"Then it must work," Ted said with a straight face.

Mary took a bite of stuffing to keep herself from laughing. "So are you two hoping for a boy or a girl?"

Sheena looked at Drew. "We both want a boy."

"I think Maxine would like a girl," Peggy said. "Having three boys, it might be a nice change to buy for a little girl."

"Are you ready to be a mom?" Carole wanted to know.

"Oh, Carole, is anyone ever ready to be a mom?" Peggy laughed. "I remember when you came home with Mary. I've never seen anyone as frightened as you were, and yet here she is, an absolute delight."

"More good luck than anything else," Carole said. "Ma always got up with her at night."

"Did she?" Mary asked.

Carole grinned at the memory. "I haven't thought about that in years. She used to take Mary out of the crib and sit with her in the living room. They shared many hours together in that old recliner."

When Mary thought about that on the drive home, it brought her a lot of comfort. Maybe that's why she and Gran had been so close. Buried memories still live within us and shape who we become.

When they pulled into the driveway there was an unfamiliar truck parked outside the house with the driver sitting in the cab. Daniel's truck wasn't there; he was still at his parents' house. It was a little unnerving to realize there was someone obviously waiting for them.

"Who's that?" Mary said.

"I don't know, do I? Take the car keys and put them between your fingers. I saw that on a cop show once."

The women got out of the car and started towards the back step. The truck door opened and a stranger emerged. He walked towards them in the dark unsteadily, as if he were drunk.

"Hello, Carole?"

"Who wants to know?"

A pause, and then: "It's me."

Carole peered into the darkness, eyes narrowed. Then she gasped. "D-Dave?"

He nodded. "And this must be Mary." He held out a hand. "Hello, Mary."

"Don't you talk to her!" Carole shouted at him.

Mary's spine tingled. "Dave? Dave from Alberta?"

"That's right. I'm your father."

CHAPTER SEVENTEEN

CAROLE GRABBED MARY AND PUSHED her up the back steps. "You stay away from her! Go on! Get lost!"

"Mom! Let me go." Mary turned and faced Dave. "I don't have a father, and you have no business being here. I suggest you leave us alone."

"You don't have a father because your mother doesn't want you to know me."

"My mother doesn't even know your last name! You were a one-night stand and that's all."

"Your mother knows my last name. I've tried over the years to make her see sense, but now that you're an adult there's nothing she can do about it."

"I've been an adult for years."

"I've been ill."

Carole walked up to Dave and pointed in his face. "How dare you? Get out of here. She doesn't want to know you."

"Mom?"

"He never wanted you! He left both of us. And now he comes crawling back when you're a grown woman? What do you want from her?"

"Nothing. I want her to know that she has a father if she wants one. I was young and foolish, and I ran away. I regret that. I'm trying to make things right."

Mary's head was spinning. "Did you two have a relationship?"

"No!" her mother yelled. "He was a sperm donor. End of story."

Despite this ridiculous situation, Mary wished she could see Dave up close. His face was hidden in the dark. Did she look like him? He wore glasses—she'd inherited his lousy eyes, if nothing else.

"Tell me the truth, Mom. How long did you go out with Dave here?"

"Two days."

"Two months," Dave answered.

"Why did Gran never tell me about him?"

"She did what mothers do. Protected me. This rat left when he found out I was pregnant. Do you really think I wanted him in our lives after that? He didn't deserve to know you and he still doesn't. So you can talk all you want, you miserable bastard. You're not her father and you never will be. Are you coming, Mary?"

Mary stood still. "Mom, go in the house—"

"Don't talk to him!"

Mary turned to her mother and pointed at the back door. "Go. I'll be with you in a minute."

Carole had no choice but to go inside, but she made sure she banged the door behind her.

Dave approached her and Mary held up her hand. "Don't. Stay there."

He looked at his feet and swayed. "I'm sorry it had to happen this way."

"What did you expect? You come here, on Christmas Day no less, and think you're going to be welcomed? My mother has never talked to me about you. All she said was that you were a guy named Dave who lived in Alberta. I pictured a cowboy or an oil rigger. You've occupied my thoughts for about ten minutes over the course of my life. I have no need for a father. I have a very loving uncle who has been like a father to me. So whatever you're looking for, you won't find it here."

"I have some medical information to pass along to you. It's important that you have it." Dave took a folded piece of paper out of his pocket. "It explains a bit about my condition. Unfortunately, it's hereditary." He held out the paper and waited for her to take it.

A feeling of dread washed over Mary as she stared at the paper. She wouldn't get any comfort at all from this man. Her tiny spark of curiosity about him vanished. She reached out and took the paper.

Dave looked contrite and shaken. "You don't know me, and that's my fault. I'm hoping that someday you might reconsider and at least want to talk to me. My number is there. I live back here now, to be closer to my sister. You look a lot like her."

Damn. Why did he have to say that? She turned away and started for the back stairs.

"Goodbye, Mary."

She didn't turn around, but at the last minute she said, "Goodbye."

Once inside the kitchen, Mary stood and glared at her mother, who was sitting at the table with Will and Liam in her arms. Billy sat in front of her, as if sensing she needed protection.

"What do you have to say for yourself, Mother?"

Carole's eyes welled up with tears. "I thought I was doing the right thing. I hated him for leaving us. What was the point of including him?"

"How long has he been trying to get in touch with me?"

Carole lowered her eyes. "Not long."

"Tell me," Mary demanded.

"Since you were twelve."

"Twelve! Are you crazy? So for *half of my life* he's wanted to be in it, but you erected a giant wall and kept me inside. Do you know how awkward it was to tell kids I didn't have a father? It made me feel different and uncomfortable. Did you think I'd love you less?"

Carole nodded as she sniffed. "I couldn't stand the thought of sharing you with him."

"If it wasn't for him, I wouldn't be here. He had parental rights."

"Why are you sticking up for him? You don't even know him."

Mary shook her head. "I don't know you, Mom. Just when I think we're getting close, another door is slammed in my face. You've been lying to me for most of my life. How am I supposed to feel about that?"

Carole brushed the dogs off her lap and stood up. "If he really wanted to be with you, he would have come before this. He knew where we lived. Don't pin this all on me! Don't hate me, Mary. Please don't hate me. I've lost Ma. I can't lose you too. I'd have no one."

"You have a lovely man who thinks you're swell. You should be with him. Then maybe you'll be happy. I've never managed to make you happy."

Carole stamped her foot in frustration. "That's not true. Just because you're mad at me right now doesn't give you the right to say things like that. You have no idea what it was like to be me. I did my best, and yes, maybe I made a mistake when it came to your father, but I thought I was doing the right thing. Doesn't that count for something?"

Mary looked at the paper. "I don't know."

"What is that?"

"He said I need to know about a hereditary medical condition."

"What? Oh my God…what does that mean?"

Mary sat at the table and opened the paper. "I assume it means I might have something wrong with me."

"That bastard! How dare he?"

"Mom. Just shush." Mary read the brief paragraph giving her his phone number and address and then his medical condition, which had only flared up a few years ago. Huntington disease. Children had a 50 percent chance of inheriting it from a parent.

Mary passed over the note. Carole's face went white. "Huntington's? That's bad, isn't it?"

Mary typed the word into Google on her phone and pressed the first link that came up. Her eyes scanned the first few sentences. Uncontrolled movements. Emotional problems. Loss of cognition.

"Yep. It's bad."

Carole slumped into the nearest chair. "It's my fault. God is punishing me."

Mary looked up at her mother. "I believe I'm the one who's being punished."

"We'll call Ted. He'll know what to do. We'll get you the best care possible. Oh, I'm going to be sick."

"I want you to do something for me."

Carole reached across the table and grabbed Mary's hand. "Anything."

"Don't tell Daniel."

Carole sat back in her chair. "Are you sure?"

Mary was determined not to cry in front of her mother. "Of course I'm not sure! But I need this to sink in. It's not enough to find out I've got a dad who actually wants me, but now I find out I might die a horrible death. Do you mind if I take a minute? Goddammit, Mom. Just do what I ask for once in your life!"

Mary could see the shock and hurt in her mother's eyes. Carole wasn't used to having a daughter who stood up for herself. But she had nothing to give her mother right now. She ran out the door and back into her apartment. The minute she threw herself on their bed, she wept. What was she going to do?

What was this going to mean down the road? How many good years did she have left? Would she be able to have children? Would she want them, knowing she might pass this condition to them? What about Daniel? Was it fair to affect his life like this? She didn't want him to stay with her just because he felt sorry for her. This was a disaster.

When she heard his footsteps on the stairs, she sat up in bed and tried to compose herself. She wasn't ready. She'd tell him about Dave but nothing else.

Roscoe rolled over on his belly in anticipation of Daniel's nightly rub-fest. Her wonderful guy came into the bedroom.

"My two favourite people." He smiled. "Did you have a nice dinner with the gang?" He flopped on the bed and reached over to caress Roscoe's soft belly fur.

"The dinner was nice. Sheena and Drew are having a baby."

"Already? That was fast."

"Why wait? Life can be over in a minute."

Daniel looked at her for the first time. "Hey, what's wrong? You okay?"

"I found out I have a father who's been trying to see me for twelve years."

Daniel sat up and stared at her. "My God."

"He showed up at the house when we came home from dinner. Mom kept yelling at him to go away. She always told me he was a one-night stand. Turns out they dated for two months, but when he found out she was pregnant, he bolted."

"Shitty. No wonder she didn't want him around."

"I guess so," Mary sighed, "but did it ever occur to her that I might want him around? That's the trouble with her. She only thinks of herself."

"What's he like?"

"I couldn't really get a good look at him. His name is Dave Cooper. I could've been Mary Cooper. That's so odd."

"Are you going to see him again? Now that you know he's been trying to meet you for a long time?"

Mary bit her lip. "This is so complicated. Too many years have passed."

"True. And you certainly don't owe him anything, Mary. Don't feel you need to connect with him if you don't want to."

"He said I look like his sister. I could be passing her on the street every day without knowing it. That's who I'm curious about. Is that weird? He was in front of me, but I'm wondering about his sister."

"The best thing you can do at the moment, is nothing. Sit with this for a while. You've had a nasty shock. I can't imagine what it must be like."

"It's scary."

"You're the bravest person I've ever met. You'll be fine."

She reached out and touched his cheek. "What would I do without you?"

"You and Roscoe would have no fun at all, I'm afraid."

Carole raced over to Peggy and Ted's the next morning. Luckily Sheena and Drew were out with friends. She recited the whole story while sitting in the family room, never touching the cup of coffee Peggy made for her.

"So now she hates me for not telling her about Dave, and then the impossible rat delivers the worst news ever. 'Hi, I'm your father. I've come to tell you that you have a fatal and horrific disease. Have a nice life.'"

"That's not necessarily true," Ted said. "There's a fifty-fifty chance she doesn't have it. And as harsh as it sounds, he did the right thing by telling her."

"Stick up for him, why don't ya!"

Ted held his coffee cup in both hands. "I'm not sticking up for him. I'm telling you he had no choice. Mary deserves to know her family medical history. As for whether you should have told her about her dad…well…."

"You're going to tell me I screwed up there too."

"No...."

"Don't lie, Ted. I know you too well. Your ears are getting red."

Peggy intervened. "You should have told her. You should have told me too! I didn't know anything about him."

"It was a summer fling. It wasn't serious."

"It was serious enough that you were heartbroken when he left, from what you're telling us now. Anyone who wants revenge badly enough to keep a girl's father from knowing her must have felt something."

Carole looked around. "Why did I come here? Do you have a cigarette?"

"You're not smoking!"

"Then give me one of your joints. I need something bad."

"I'm all out."

"I hate my life."

"Carole, you have to stay strong for Mary," Ted advised. "Don't make this about you. This is about your daughter. She needs you to be there for her."

"The worst part is that she doesn't want Daniel to know, so I have to pretend she's fine."

Peggy shook her head. "That's not good. She should tell him."

"She said she needed time."

Ted leaned forward in his chair. "Then for God's sake, do as she asks. Respect her wishes."

Peggy glanced at him. "How can she keep that from him? It's not fair to him."

"Ladies, just cool it. She found out exactly twelve hours ago. She might not even have the disease! Let her handle this her own way. The trouble with you Ryan women is that you go off half-cocked before you've thought things through!"

"Okay, you're right" Carole sighed. "But should I tell Jerry? He'll think I'm a horrible person."

"You're not a horrible person," Peggy said. "Stop with the dramatics. If it's going to bother you, then perhaps you should tell him. He'll want to know why you're distracted and upset."

"I'm always distracted and upset. It's the way I live my life. I don't know anything else."

Ted took a gulp of his coffee. "You should try yoga. It helps your body and your mind. I did it overseas and I couldn't believe the difference."

"I suppose Teddy-girl taught you," Peggy said.

"Knock it off, Peggy."

Carole leaned her head back on the chair and looked at the ceiling. "You know what would help me right now? A big fat cigar. I could smoke it or shove it up Dave's ass."

Talking to her sister and brother-in-law hadn't made Carole feel much better, and she knew that Jerry was busy with his boys, so she decided to go home and talk to Mary. She wondered if her daughter had slept. Carole had laid awake all night beating herself up. Why did every decision she made always turn out to be the wrong one? Maybe there was a Guinness World Record for that category.

The question now was how they should go forward. How in God's name would she cope if Mary had this awful disease? Having something happen to her daughter had never occurred to Carole. She had been consumed with imagining the worst for her mother her entire life. It seemed heartless that now she should have to worry about another family member. If she could trade places with Mary she would in a heartbeat. Mary was a good person who deserved the best. And Carole was a bad person for taking Mary for granted.

She thought about the night Mary had come through the door after walking home in the snowstorm, the night Mrs. Aucoin died. Why hadn't she taken the time to pick up her child? Who else would be selfish enough to let their kid walk home in a blizzard?

When Carole got home, she searched for a piece of paper and a pen. She wanted to write a letter of apology, but all she got on the page was "Dear Mary." The list of transgressions in her head became insurmountable and she balled up the paper and threw it away.

Goddammit.

She rang Mary's doorbell and Daniel answered the door. Carole was sure she saw annoyance in his eyes.

"Hi. Can I speak to Mary?"

"She's having a shower."

"I'll wait."

He opened the door and let her pass through. Once they were upstairs, Daniel offered to make her a cup of tea.

"No, thanks."

She sat on their sofa next to Roscoe. When she reached out to pat him, he jumped off the couch and marched out of the room.

"Even the cat hates me," she said mournfully.

Daniel sat at the computer desk. "Mary doesn't hate you. But she is reeling, and rightly so."

"I never meant to hurt her, you know."

"And yet she's hurt."

One part of Carole's brain wanted to punch Daniel in the nose. Another was glad that Mary had this champion in her corner. But her overwhelming feeling was envy. She had never had a man stick up for her like that. The envy obliterated everything else. She rose from the couch and walked out of Mary's apartment. Daniel watched her go without saying a word.

She went downstairs and sat alone in the kitchen. Looking around, she knew it was a dump. Not even the boys could make it nice. Their snoring was coming from her bedroom. Who would take care of them if she took some pills? How did one leave this planet on a whim? Everything was so long and involved and required careful planning, or at least a trip to the drugstore. She didn't have the energy for that.

When Daniel told Mary what had transpired, she went downstairs and walked into the kitchen. Her mother had her head in the oven. Mary reached over and shut it off. "We don't have a gas stove."

Carole emerged, red and sweating. "I realize that now."

"Get off your knees and sit down like a normal person."

Carole groaned as she got off the floor and plunked herself onto the nearest chair. "Now I know how a pot roast feels."

"Please do me a favour and stay alive. I really don't need to be worrying about anyone else."

"Daniel doesn't like me."

"Why do you care what he thinks?"

"No one likes me…except the boys."

"Jerry likes you."

"There's something wrong with him."

"What is it?"

"He likes me."

Mary opened the fridge door and took out a can of Pepsi. She tossed her head towards a can in the fridge but her mom shook her head no, so Mary sat at the table, opened the can, and took a long drink. Then she placed it in front of her. "Mom?"

"Yes?"

"It's time you grew up."

"What's that supposed to mean?"

"I'm tired of being your parent. I need someone to take care of me, especially now. I know I have Daniel, but you're my mother. Act like it."

"I told you I'm no good—"

"This is what I mean. You can't just say you're no good at something and absolve yourself of responsibility. You need to be better. I've never been able to lean on you. I need a place to lay my head. Please."

Mary waited.

Her mother eventually nodded her head. "Okay."

"Thank you."

"What can I do?" Carole asked. "What do you need?"

Mary got up off the chair and sat in her mother's lap, resting her head on her mother's shoulder. Carole put her arms around her daughter and didn't say a word.

Mary spent a lot of time with her Uncle Ted over the first few months of the new year.

He ran her through all the testing options. Testing, it turned out, was an incredibly complicated and emotionally fraught process. Not the blood work itself, or the neurological exam, or the pre-test counselling and follow-up, but the implications for the entire family, and their reactions to the results. Even Mary hadn't realized some of the major considerations for the future, like medical insurance and job security. It was a minefield that grew bigger exponentially, the more she explored the possible paths.

"What would you do if you were me, Uncle Ted?"

They were in his office. Sometimes Mary made an appointment with him just so they could sit uninterrupted. She always brought coffee for the both of them.

He sat at his chair and leaned back, cradling his cup. "I honestly don't know. It depends on your personality, I guess. If you're a worrywart, knowing might help you.

"Or not. If the test were positive, you'd just worry about that instead of wondering. And if you're laid back, knowing what's coming might make you anxious and you'd regret it. It's a miserable, unsolvable puzzle.

"I suggest you gather as much information as you possibly can, and make a decision based on that. I'll put you in touch with the appropriate medical people when the time comes. Obviously talk to your own doctor and stay as healthy as you can."

"Living with second-hand smoke all my life can't have helped. And then Mom quits because of the dog! Can you believe that?"

Uncle Ted laughed. "I have no explanation when it comes to your mother."

"Did you know she was jealous of Aunt Peggy when you first met her?"

"Instantly. But I also knew that she loved Peggy very much. She took me aside on our wedding day and said if I hurt a hair on Peggy's head, she'd come after me. I thought it was pretty cute."

Mary wondered what she'd ever worried about before, because now Huntington's coloured everything, running through her mind like white noise. At work, she smiled at her customers but was distracted and vague. She didn't even notice her favourite customer until she plunked a huge bag of French fries on the counter.

"Guess who I'm feeding today."

"Sorry?"

"These are for our crows. They adore frozen French fries."

"Oh. That's nice."

"Aren't you going to ask me what my lipstick shade is today?" She pursed her lips, then grinned.

"Sure."

"It's Candy Crush. Isn't that delicious?"

"Yes."

As Mary handed the change over, the woman patted her hand. "Everything comes out in the wash," she said sagely.

That night when Mary got home, Daniel and Roscoe were in front of the television sharing a can of Pringles. Roscoe loved to crunch up a chip or two while Daniel devoured the entire thing.

"Is that your supper?" she said.

Daniel nodded, his mouth full.

"Did you think to make something for me? You were off early." She threw her coat and purse on the nearest chair.

He looked at her quizzically.

"What? Is it so crazy for me to want something for dinner after working all day? I make supper for you all the time."

"What's the matter?" he munched.

"Nothing, Daniel. Forget I said anything."

She went into the kitchen and looked in the fridge. So much for eating healthy. There wasn't one vegetable or fruit to be seen. "Did you eat the last of the watermelon?"

"What?"

She shouted, "Did you eat the last of the goddamn watermelon?"

"Yes! I didn't realize it was just yours!"

"Perfect!"

Mary slumped into a kitchen chair. Daniel showed up in the doorway. "What is wrong with you? Lately all you do is get annoyed with me. I leave a towel on the floor in the bathroom and it's like I committed a crime. This isn't like you."

"Maybe my true colours are showing."

"Well, something is going on and it really bugs me that you're not telling me what it is."

"Why should I tell you everything? I'm a private person, Daniel."

"Fine. Be like that. At least Roscoe enjoys my company."

That night in bed, Daniel turned towards Mary and put out his hand to rub her back. "Still mad at me?"

"Yes."

He turned away.

The next day, without telling anyone, Mary contacted Dave and met him for coffee. When he sat opposite her at the table she took a good look at him. He seemed incredibly tired, but other than that he was neither handsome nor ugly. He wasn't short, but he wasn't tall. He had freckles and thinning hair and brown eyes with thick eyebrows. She would pass him on the street and not give him a second look. Dave was invisible. Until he smiled. Then she saw herself reflected back as clear as day.

"I want to ask you something," Mary began.

"Shoot."

"Did you get tested for Huntington's before you were diagnosed?"

"Eventually."

"Are you sorry?"

"I'm not sure."

"Okay. Now tell me about your sister."

He was taken aback, but obliged. He told her his sister's name was Bonnie and she had three kids and a firefighter husband. She sold quilts and raised chickens.

"Does she know about me?"

"No."

"Does anyone in your family know about me?

"No."

"Why don't you tell them?"

"My parents and grandparents are dead now. It doesn't matter."

Mary leaned back in her chair. "You were ashamed of me."

"I'm ashamed of the way I behaved towards your mother and you. It hasn't been an easy thing to live with."

"Are you married?"

"Yes."

"Kids?"

"No. We couldn't have any."

Mary saw pain in his eyes. "Too bad. I suppose I'm a secret from her too."

"At this point, yes. I didn't have the heart to tell her about you, not until you and I established a relationship."

Mary cupped her coffee and said softly, "I can't be your kid, Dave."

"I know that now. I don't have a lot of years left. If I'd been braver I would've stayed away from you altogether. It's not fair to make your acquaintance now."

"For what it's worth, I don't mind being your friend."

He smiled. "I'd like that."

Mary stood up and held out her hand. "It was nice to meet you, Dave."

He rose from his chair unsteadily and took her hand. "The pleasure was all mine."

"See ya around." She turned and walked away.

When she got home, Daniel was sitting in bed, leaning against the headboard and playing his guitar softly for Roscoe. Mary walked over, pushed the guitar away and curled up in his lap.

"I'm sorry."

"That's okay." He ran his hand over her hair. "You can tell me anything."

"I know."

CHAPTER EIGHTEEN

SHEENA WAS BESIDE HERSELF.

"No one in the history of the world has ever thrown up this much." She emerged from the bathroom and flung herself groaning onto their bed.

Drew grimaced for her benefit. "Except maybe William's wife."

"William who?"

"The future king."

"Oh, spare me. At least she has a prince or princess at the end of it. And apparently I don't have hyper...grav...something. That stupid doctor says it's *just* morning sickness. I'm nothing special."

Drew put his hand on her belly. "You are special, and so is this baby. You need to relax and enjoy this."

She got up on her elbows. "I cannot believe you just told me to relax. You have absolutely no idea what I'm going through. If you did, you wouldn't say such a ridiculous thing."

"I'm only trying to make you feel better."

Sheena grabbed his hand and kissed it. "I know...ugh."

"Hey, if I was throwing up twenty times a day, I'd be pissed." He pulled her off the bed. "We're going to be late for the ultrasound."

At least this was exciting. Maybe if she saw the baby, she'd forgive it for being so unbearably cruel up to this point. So far, the baby part was nebulous. The only sign was being nauseous around the clock.

One thing that did delight Sheena was the fact that Drew talked about the baby non-stop. He told people in the grocery store. He even bought her a T-shirt that said *BABY* with an arrow pointing at her stomach. She refused to wear it outside, but it made him happy when she wore it to bed.

By the time Sheena settled herself on the gurney in the darkened room, she had to pee so badly she thought she'd faint. Drew held her hand and tried to distract her.

"Please hurry up," she moaned to the technician. "I'm about to explode."

"I haven't had that happen yet," the girl said cheerfully.

Sheena wanted to hit her.

She and Drew peered at the screen but had no idea what they were looking at.

"Is it supposed to be in a muddle like this? Why can't I see a head?"

The tech didn't say anything as she manoeuvred the wand over Sheena's stomach. "Just bear with me for a moment."

Sheena looked at Drew and she could tell he was pretending to be brave.

"Are you going to tell us what's going on? Is there something wrong?"

"No, there's nothing wrong...."

Sheena began to relax again.

"Could you excuse me for a moment?" And she walked out of the room.

Sheena sat up on her elbows. "What's going on? Where did she go? Drew, do something!"

Drew stood up uncertainly, but fortunately the tech came back in the room with someone else. "This is Doctor Lee. I just want to verify something for you."

"You're scaring me!"

Doctor Lee smiled. "Am I really that scary?" He looked at the screen as the tech resumed her exam. "Yes, indeed. Well, this is your lucky day, folks. You have two babies in there. It's twins! Congratulations!"

The shock was so profound that Sheena forgot to breathe. It wasn't until Drew gave her a big smack on the lips that she inhaled and let out a screech. "TWINS?"

Sheena held it together in front of the technician and doctor, but after she was finally allowed to go to the bathroom and pee, which she did for two minutes straight, she opened the door and fell into Drew's arms. She cried all the way out of the hospital, through the parking lot, and into the house, collapsing on their bed and soaking the pillowcase.

Eventually, Drew called her mother.

"I don't know what to do," he started.

"Dear God...what's happened? Is Sheena all right?" Peggy asked.

"Yes...and no."

"Drew, I am going to strangle you right through this phone if you do not tell me what's going on."

"We went for an ultrasound today—"

"Is there something wrong with the baby?" Peggy yelled.

"No. But there are two of them."

"TWINS! Oh my God...Ted! Ted! Sheena and Drew are having twins!"

There was a huge commotion over the phone, with Peggy trying to put Drew on speaker phone so he could repeat what he'd just said.

"Congratulations!" Ted blustered. "Oh my, this is exciting!"

"It's just that Sheena's been crying since they told us, and she won't stop. Is that normal?"

Peggy laughed. "It's normal for Sheena. She once cried for three days because we missed a flight to Montreal to see a Britney Spears concert. She blamed me for the snowstorm."

"I'm worried she's hurting the babies."

"The babies! Did you hear that, Ted? You can hold one and I can hold the other. I'm so thrilled. I love you very much, Drew! Thank you for this."

"Well, thanks...I guess."

"Let me speak to her."

Drew walked up the stairs and stood in their bedroom doorway. "Your mom wants to talk to you."

"I didn't hear the phone ring." Sheena sat up then, her face red and ravaged. "Did you tell my mother about this?"

"I didn't know what else to do," Drew said. "I was worried about you."

"Thanks a lot. I wanted to tell her."

"The way you've been carrying on, I thought you'd never stop crying long enough to tell anyone."

"Drew, I have twice the hormones coursing through my veins at the moment. I'd stay out of my way for the foreseeable future."

"Done." He passed her the phone but gave her cheek a quick kiss. "You're Wonder Woman."

"Oh, please. Mom?"

Her mom and dad yelled in her ear about how extraordinary this news was and how their lives were going to be so much fun and just imagine dressing two babies and did she want fraternal or identical twins—all thoughts she hadn't had time for yet.

"Don't get overwhelmed," her mom instructed. "I know you. You're just like me. You get frazzled and panicked but there's no reason to."

"How on earth would you know, Mom? You only had one kid. How am I supposed to feed two at a time? What if I mix them up? I sure as hell won't be dressing them alike. That's so basic."

"You could have a boy and a girl. A perfect family with only one pregnancy. Who ever gets that lucky?"

"I'm going to be as big as a house!" Sheena sobbed.

"You'll look beautiful," her father said. "You've always been beautiful."

"Thanks, Daddy," she sniffed.

"Why don't Daddy and I come up on the weekend? We can go shopping for the babies! Oh, what fun!"

It was only after Sheena hung up that she realized something else. She yelled for Drew and he raced up the stairs. "Are you okay?"

"We have to buy a bigger house! We can't fit two cribs into these bedrooms. This is a disaster!"

He sat on the edge of the bed. "Please calm down. We have so much time to think about what we're going to do. Let's just enjoy this moment. We have two children right this minute—they're in this room with us. I'm over the moon, Sheena. Please enjoy this. Do you know how lucky we are? Chris and his wife are dealing with in vitro as we speak. He asked me not to say anything, but you need to understand that having two babies is a miracle. And you did this. You. I love you so much."

Sheena hugged him tight. This little speech was so much better than his wedding vows.

Peggy rushed over to Carole's to tell her the good news. Mary was having lunch with her mother when she arrived.

"You'll never guess what!" Peggy chirped.

"We never will, so you might as well tell us," Carole said.

"Sheena and Drew are having twins!"

Mary clapped. "What wonderful news!" Then she braced herself for her mother's response.

"That's amazing. I'm really happy for all of you."

Mary smiled. Carole had passed the test.

Her mother was trying hard to not default to her usual doom and gloom about how everyone else's life was so great. Maybe she was still grumbling about it alone, but she was on her best behaviour in front of Mary, and that was all Mary cared about. She'd even told her mother that she had met Dave for coffee twice. Carole managed to keep quiet.

Peggy told them that she and Ted were going to Halifax to see Sheena. Carole suggested she and Mary buy something for the babies so that Peggy could take the gifts with her. It was a spontaneous gesture and it felt good to rush into Peggy's car together and hightail it to the mall. Mary went straight to the bookstore and bought the classics: *Pat the Bunny, Goodnight Moon, The Runaway Bunny,* and *Blueberries for Sal.* Then she spied *Bedtime for Frances* and grabbed that too.

What fun it would be at their next Christmas dinner. The babies were due in August, so they would be about four months old. Mary already knew that Aunt Peggy would be the best grandmother in the world. And the fact that she sewed meant Sheena would be up to her eyeballs in handmade outfits. But knowing Sheena, she might not want anything handmade. Designer label was more her speed.

When Peggy dropped them back home, Carole asked her in for another cup of tea. Having nothing better to do, Peggy said yes. The minute they got in the kitchen, Carole pointed at the dining room.

"It's been a year since Sheena's wedding. You have yet to come to me for a hair appointment. Don't think I haven't noticed. Despite this wonderful news about your grandbabies, it doesn't get you off the hook. Why aren't you coming to my salon, when you said you would?"

"I thought it was obvious," Peggy said. "I was as high as a kite when I made that promise."

"What a horrible thing to say. Did you hear that, Mary?"

"I have to go. See ya." Mary left in a hurry.

"Carole, don't be mad. You're a very good hairdresser, but Sheila and I are like old slippers. We're just comfortable with each other."

"I don't think your hair is flattering."

"Oh, you don't? And why is that?"

"It makes your face look droopy. You need to cut off five inches at least." Carole marched into her salon and came out with her scissors. "Let's do it."

"Are you crazy? Don't you dare come near me with those things!"

"Do you love me or not?"

"Carole! What is wrong with you? You've lost your mind. I have to go!"

Peggy hightailed it out the back door and zoomed away in her Lexus. Carole watched her go though the kitchen window and laughed and laughed.

"Did you see that, Ma? She thought I was serious."

In April, Jerry asked Carole if she'd like to go to dinner at his place. He planned on barbecuing steak, despite the cool weather.

"Bring the boys too."

Carole was very impressed. He presented her with a thick rib steak, crispy baked potato, sautéed mushrooms and onions, and even a Caesar salad on the side. She was about to say that she couldn't eat another bite when Jerry presented her with a fancy piece of cake that was obviously made in a bakery.

"Gosh, this looks nice."

Jerry sat down opposite her with sweat on his lip. Carole noticed it but didn't say anything. His whole face was flushed by the time she took her first bite.

"Delicious," she murmured.

He stared at her.

"Aren't you going to eat?"

He quickly took another cake out of the box and shoved a piece in his mouth. "Mmm."

She ate the rest of the cake while he kept glancing at her plate. It was strange and became very uncomfortable.

"What's wrong, Jerry?"

"Eat that final piece."

"Why?"

"Because."

"You're scaring me." She put her fork in the remaining mouthful and ate it. "There, are you happy?"

Jerry looked confused. Then he took his fork and mushed up his dessert. There on the plate was a diamond ring covered in chocolate. "Bloody hell. I gave you the wrong piece."

Carole looked at it and couldn't process what was happening.

He picked up the ring, dropped it in a glass of water, and then fished it out with his fork, finally drying it off and presenting it to her. "This is for you."

"You wanted me to eat a ring and perhaps choke on it?"

"It seemed romantic when I saw it in a movie. Obviously I'm a big dope."

The penny dropped. "Is this...an engagement ring?"

"Yes. I was hoping you'd marry me and Ruth."

Carole's mouth dropped open. She didn't know what to say.

"I'm sorry," Jerry stammered. "I'm not really good at this sort of thing."

"But your boys—"

"My boys live across the country. Of course they'd like to see their mother and me together, but that's not going to happen. Their mother left me for another man."

"Do they know that?"

"No. I don't want them to. It will come out eventually, but I don't want to be the one to tell them."

"Oh, Jerry. You don't know what you're asking. I'm the last person you want in your life. I'm not a good person."

Jerry looked like he was ready to explode. "Why do you keep saying that? Do you have a dead body in your freezer?"

"I'm selfish."

"I have yet to see a selfish bone in your body. You love your dogs. You love your daughter. You loved your mother. You have nothing to prove to me. I'm not perfect either. I crack my knuckles and I snap my gum, which used to drive my wife up the wall."

It came out in a rush: "I didn't tell Mary that her father was trying to see her for years. That's how horrible I am!"

"I don't understand."

"Of course you don't! Who would do that? He left me when I was pregnant, and when he wanted to see Mary years later I told him no, and I kept it all from her."

Jerry reached for her hand. "That must have been very difficult. It doesn't mean you're a horrible person."

Carole got up from the table and walked over to his living-room window. "I didn't want to tell you, because I knew you'd never do something like that. And anyway, I would enter this marriage with nothing. I have nothing to contribute."

"That doesn't matter."

She turned around. "It matters to me. I'm sorry, Jerry. It's a lovely offer and I'm very grateful, but I can't marry you."

Carole grabbed her coat and purse then whistled for the boys and the four of them headed out the door.

Drew had a week-long business trip and drove Sheena to Cape Breton to be with her parents while he was away. Peggy and Maxine had already discussed at bridge what a great opportunity it would be to look around for baby things while Sheena was in Sydney.

"Mom, I can't believe I'm saying this, but you're going to have to stop buying baby gifts. We don't have any room as it is."

"Don't be a party pooper. I'm having a blast and so is Maxine. Did you know we went out for lunch the other day, just the two of us? Lynne had to cancel at the last minute and we had a great time anyway. She's hoping these babies are girls, just like I predicted. I said I wanted one of each."

Sheena rocked in the recliner, her hands resting on her protruding belly. "I can't believe you and Maxine like each other."

"She's a lot of fun now that she's not with Chuck. I assume Drew told his dad about the twins."

"Yeah. He's like a big kid. Already wants to buy them two of those horrible tyke-sized Cadillacs."

"Bless him."

"I was thinking...."

"That's a first."

"Oh, ha ha. Maybe Drew and I should move home to be closer to you guys. I'm afraid to manage these babies on my own."

Peggy's eyes opened wide. "I'd love that, but Drew won't."

"Right now he'd do anything for me."

"That's blackmail."

"I was just thinking out loud."

"Don't make him feel guilty. That's the worst thing you can do in a marriage."

Sheena stopped rocking. "Are you serious? You make Dad feel guilty about going away every chance you get. Don't think I haven't noticed, and I don't even live here anymore."

Peggy got defensive. "It was a rash and thoughtless thing for him to do on the spur of the moment. If he'd given me more time, maybe I would've dealt with it better. My reaction was the same as yours when Drew told you about moving to Halifax. It hurts not to be consulted."

"But Mom, haven't you noticed that you're so much happier than you were before he went? You actually have a life. I think he did you a favour."

"Maybe. Still rankles though."

Later that night, when Peggy was upstairs sewing, Sheena wandered into the family room. Her dad was watching *Power and Politics*. He muted the television as she sat beside him on the couch. He put his arm around her shoulder and she buried her face in his shirt. Her dad always smelled nice and clean.

"How are you feeling, sweetheart?"

"Overwhelmed."

"That's natural. But remember, you don't need to know everything right now. Life has a way of taking its time; you'll adjust."

"Did you ever picture me as a mother of twins?"

"No, I can't say I did."

"I'm too young."

He kissed the top of her head. "Don't wait for anything. Whatever life puts in front of you, accept it. That's why I said yes to going overseas. I didn't want to miss the chance."

"I suppose." Sheena played with the button on his shirt. "Do you want to know how to get Mom to stop bellyaching about that?"

"Please tell me. I'd be forever in your debt."

"Buy her a very expensive ring. Let her know you're grateful she let you go, but even more grateful that she waited for you to come back."

Ted squeezed her shoulder. "Who says you're not smart?"

She looked up at him. "I don't know. Who says I'm not smart?"

Her father's ears turned red. "That didn't come out right."

Peggy was raking the front yard when Ted's car came up the driveway. He got out and gave her a wave.

"You're home early."

"Going to take you to dinner."

Peggy smiled. "Well, this is a nice surprise. Where are we going?"

"Your choice."

"Let's go to that new restaurant, A Bite of Asia. They say it's fabulous."

"Perfect."

While Peggy was in the shower, Sheena saw her father putting on a tie. "Where are you going?"

"We're going to that new Chinese restaurant."

"Oh goody. I wanted to try it."

"You're not coming."

Sheena pouted. "Why not?"

Ted patted his jacket pocket. "I took your advice."

Sheena clapped her hands in excitement. "Let me see it."

He took the velvet box out of his pocket and opened it. It was a diamond ring surrounded by emeralds. "Do you think she'll like it?"

"She'll love it! Good choice, Daddy."

"Thank you."

Peggy was disappointed Sheena didn't want to go to dinner, but she insisted she was just tired and wanted to put her feet up.

The new restaurant was a nice change. They both ordered the shrimp pad Thai, but the waiter convinced them to try the Thai sweet chili fish as well.

Ted took a big bite. "It's not something my grandfather would've eaten, but I love it!"

Peggy agreed. "It's wonderful being able to try different food."

Over their green tea ice cream they sighed contentedly at what the future held.

"We need to travel, Peggy. The world is just begging for us to come and visit."

"But we'll be so busy with the babies."

Ted put the last spoonful of ice cream in his mouth. "How's that? They're in Halifax."

"Sheena thinks maybe she and Drew should move home."

"That's not a good idea."

"Why not?"

"He finally has Sheena out of your clutches. If she comes back, she'll depend on you to do everything with those babies. It's not fair to you."

"I'd be thrilled to look after my own grandchildren."

"Not if we want to have a second honeymoon."

"Ted Henderson. What has gotten into you?"

Ted pulled out the velvet case and put it in Peggy's hand. "I want to let you know that I love you and want to spend the rest of my life with you."

Peggy's spoon clattered on her plate. She opened the box and her hand flew to her mouth. "Oh my God. This is gorgeous!"

"Try it on."

She slipped it on her right-hand ring finger and watched it sparkle in the light from above. "Ted, I don't know what to say."

"Say that you want to travel the world with me."

"But your job—"

"I'm going to share a practice with the new doctor in our office. It's a way of still working but having family time too. I need to include you in my plans."

Peggy got out of her seat and hugged her husband when he stood up. "I love you so much. Thank you for this wonderful gift. I can't believe you thought of this yourself."

CHAPTER NINETEEN

IT WAS NOW JUNE. DANIEL would be starting his course in the summer and only a few months after that, Mary would be going to school too. Aunt Peggy was right. The year had gone by in a flash.

But Mary's excitement about the future was muted. She pretended it was great when Daniel would talk about their plans, but privately she often cried in the shower. It wasn't that she felt sorry for herself; it was her indecision about taking the test. Keeping it from Daniel was her way of protecting him, but he often looked at her sadly, as if he knew something had changed.

One morning Mary saw a gooey Facebook meme about mothers and daughters. On a whim, she went downstairs and let herself into the house. Her mom was talking to a client, so she plugged in the kettle and got out two mugs for their tea. Billy, Will, and Liam surrounded her with dog love and she spend a happy fifteen minutes patting them. Her clothes were completely covered in Billy's fur in a matter of moments, but it didn't matter. He was beyond adorable; she could see why her mother had fallen in love with him.

She chatted a little with the client, who said that Mary looked wonderful and that Carole must be so proud. Carole agreed and they said farewell. Her mother sat at the table while Mary poured tea. It gave Mary a chance to look at her mom and she didn't like what she saw.

"To what do I owe the pleasure?" Carole said.

"No reason. Do you have any cookies to go with this?"

"Arrowroot."

Mary found them in the usual spot and put the box on the table. She dunked a cookie in the tea. "You're looking tired. Are you all right?"

"Just getting over a cold. How have you been?"

"Fine. Counting down the days until I leave Sobeys. I'm really going to miss Janet."

"I'm going to hate to go in that store if you're not there. I always knew where to find you."

Mary laughed. "You've never come looking for me in your life. Now, Aunt Peggy, she's another story."

Carole frowned but didn't say anything.

"Sorry, I shouldn't have said that."

"Why not? It's the truth."

"Have you been talking to Aunt Peggy or Sheena lately? Sheena called me out of the blue one day and we had a great chat about how she's so fat she can't fit in the tub anymore. I find that hard to believe."

"I talked to Peggy. She and Ted went to Quebec City for a week last month."

"That's nice. Did he have a conference?"

"No, just a holiday. She sounded really happy. Have you seen the ring Ted bought her? It's quite something."

"Speaking of men, how's Jerry?"

Carole avoided Mary's eyes. "I wouldn't know."

So this was why she looked miserable. "What happened? Did you guys break up?'

"He asked me to marry him."

Mary almost spat out her tea. "What? Well, that's terrific! Why aren't you over the moon?"

"I said no."

Mary sat back in her chair, dumbfounded. "Why?"

"I don't know. It seemed like the right thing to do."

"The right thing for who? If he asked you then that must mean he wants to be with you. And you always seem so happy when he and Ruth are around."

Carole sighed. "God, I miss that dog."

"I'm hoping you miss the man too."

"Of course. I just…."

"What?"

"I'm not good enough for him. He'll find out what I'm really like and he'll throw me out."

"What are you really like?"

Carole jumped up and started to pace. "It's like you said. I've never once come looking for you in my life. I didn't pick you up that night of the blizzard. I never took you shopping or went to the movies with you. We never did mother-daughter things like Peggy and Sheena. I feel bad about that now."

"Mom, all that might be true, but you have to remember, you were holding down a full-time job and looking after Gran, which was another full-time job in itself. She didn't make it easy for you. You were hurt and resentful most of the time, and I probably would've been too in your position."

Carole's eyes started to fill up. "I'm trying hard not to be that person anymore. I'm happy about Sheena's twins, I'm happy that Peggy is back in love with Ted, I'm happy you found Daniel. But I feel I need to pay for my mistakes."

Mary jumped up and held her mother's shoulders. "Stop punishing yourself. You don't owe any of us anything. Why shouldn't you be happy? Jerry is a lovely person. Ruth is a lovely dog. Why can't you have them in your life?"

"His boys aren't crazy about me."

"So what? That didn't stop Jerry from asking you to marry him. Mom! A man asked you to *marry* him! That's exciting and wonderful."

"But I've got nothing to contribute. I'm not worth anything. I don't want his sons thinking I'm taking advantage of their father."

"Oh, bullshit. Jerry knows how and where you live. That didn't stop him from coming over here to be with you."

"It's like I'm looking for a sign."

Mary shook her. "Here's your sign: stop being a big idiot and call Jerry immediately."

"What if he hates me now? I said no."

"That's a risk you'll have to take. I'm not worried. Jerry doesn't seem like the type to hold grudges. Mom, if you don't do this, you will regret it forever."

"I'll think about it."

Mary kissed her. "I better go." She turned to leave.

"Mary?"

Mary turned around.

"If I need to be brave, then so do you. I think it's time you told Daniel about your dilemma. He told me the other day that he was worried about you. He wondered if he was doing something wrong. For him to say that to me took a lot. Now that's not fair, is it?"

"No," Mary whispered before she disappeared.

Carole sat at the table. It was easy for youngsters to be optimistic. They still had the rest of their lives to fix things if they had to. She was positive that she'd hurt Jerry very badly and he wouldn't forgive her. Once again, the old negative thoughts whirled around in her head. She wasn't good enough for him. Everyone else deserved happiness, but she'd thrown hers away and had no right to complain.

Later that night as she got ready for bed she opened her mother's bedroom door. She found it hard to go in there. It still smelled like Ethel, and that wasn't always pleasant. Carole hadn't done a thing to the room. It's not like any of them were interested in dividing up her belongings. Everything she owned was fit for the landfill. Most of her clothes were too badly stained and worn to give away to charity and she didn't have any jewellery or perfume they could share.

Carole still missed her mother's presence. She missed fighting with her and arguing about nonsense. And Ethel had done one heroic thing in her life: Kicked out the man who planned on hurting her kids. That was noble, even if she drank to cover up the hurt he'd caused her.

And then she remembered that her mother had liked Jerry. That was a sign right there. Her mother hadn't liked anyone.

She looked around and knew that she had to clean out this room and bring it back to life. It was depressing to see it so sad and neglected, and she was tired of being surrounded by dreary things. Mary was right. Carole deserved as much happiness as anyone else. And even if Jerry never wanted to see her again, that didn't mean she had to live like this.

Carole started with the bed. She ripped off the blankets and sheets and pulled up the mattress to grab the dusty bed skirt. Paper fluttered to the floor. She reached down and realized she'd just unearthed a hoard of scratch tickets.

"Ma, you were a friggin' squirrel."

She looked at the dates and they were still viable. No time like the present. She left the house, much to the dismay of the dogs, and walked up to Dotty's Dairy. The pimply kid was still in charge of the store.

"Could you check these for me? I just found them under my mother's mattress."

He put the tickets into the lottery terminal and suddenly a terrific racket sounded. Carole looked around confused.

"You won, lady."

"I won? A free ticket?"

"No, you won five thousand dollars."

"Are you serious?"

She grabbed her ticket and the kid said she had to call Atlantic Lotto in Moncton and they'd let her know what to do. She thanked him and ran out the door, bursting into the house to tell the boys first. Then she ran into her mother's room.

"You wonderful, crazy-ass woman! I hear ya, Ma! I hear ya!"

She banged on Mary's door and opened it before they had a chance to answer. She charged up the stairs yelling. Mary was at the top, with her hand over her heart.

"What's wrong?"

"I won five thousand dollars on one of your Gran's scratch tickets!"

"No way! Daniel! Come here!"

The three of them looked at the precious piece of paper.

"What are you going to do with it?" Daniel asked.

"I don't have a fucking clue, pardon my French. This is my sign, Mary. I better go find Jerry!

"Good luck, Mom."

Carole hurried down the stairs and out the door, then back in the front door to her place. She hollered for the boys. "We gotta go see Jerry and Ruth!"

The boys wagged their tails and gathered by the back door. Carole grabbed a sweater and her purse and car keys. Billy jumped onto the back seat and Will and Liam flew over the seat into the front. She didn't have a thought in her head other than that she needed to be with Jerry.

"Do you think he still loves me?" she asked the fellas.

They barked yes.

When she pulled up into his driveway, Jerry was in the backyard working on his fence with Ruth supervising. When Carole let the boys

out of the car there was a mad dash and squeal-fest between the canine friends. Jerry stayed where he was and looked stunned when
Carole ran over to him waving a piece of paper over her head.

"Jerry! Jerry! Look! I won five thousand dollars! I can marry you
now. I have a dowry." She laughed. "I'm so sorry I said no. Please
forgive me. I would love to marry you and Ruth!" She reached over
and held him, hammer and all, in a firm embrace, willing him to say
something, to give her an indication that he didn't hate her.

She finally let him go, because he wasn't saying anything. She'd
blown it. She'd had a dream for about ten minutes and it was over.
When she let him go, she couldn't look at his face. It was too hard.

"I'm sorry," she whispered. "Everything I do is wrong. I shouldn't
have come here."

"Carole," he croaked.

When she looked up she saw that he was crying tears of happiness.
He held out his arms and she found her way back in.

Their dogs jumped around them in a frenzy, sensing that this was
a pretty great moment.

Back at the apartment, Mary and Daniel were still laughing at her
mom's excitement over the lottery ticket.

"You'd think she won fifty thousand dollars!" Daniel said.

"I don't think she's ever felt lucky before. I've definitely never seen
her that happy."

Daniel pulled at a loose thread unravelling on his sock as they sat
on the couch. He kept his head down. "I wish you were happy."

Her mother was right. She thought she was protecting Daniel, but
what she was doing was lying to him—acting just like her mother.
Mary needed to be better than that. She reached over and held his
hand. "I've been keeping something from you since Christmas."

Daniel's head snapped up. "I knew it! Please don't tell me you've
met another guy, because—"

"Don't be ridiculous! I never want anyone but you, ever! Do you
hear me?"

He looked relieved. "So what's wrong?"

"My father has Huntington disease. There's a fifty-fifty chance I might have it too. I'm trying to decide if I should get tested to find out if I do." She let go of his hand and looked down. "I'm so scared, Daniel. I don't want this for you. You want to get married and have kids one day, right? I don't think you can do that with me. I don't want to ruin your chances of having a normal life."

The look of disbelief on his face frightened her. Daniel reached over and pulled her into his arms. He held her tight as he choked out, "And you've been keeping this from me this whole time?"

"I'm sorry."

He pushed her back so he could see her face. "Babe, I'm here for you. These are the things that we need to decide together. I hate that you felt you had to protect me. And what the fuck is a normal life without you? I don't care if we get married or don't get married. I don't care if we have kids or don't have kids. The only thing in this world that I care about is you. And whatever happens to you is always my business. Don't ever hide anything from me again!" He hugged her again. "Christ! At one point I thought you were having a fling with Donny, that's how crazy it got!"

She snuggled against him once more. "I love you, Daniel. I don't deserve you."

"You deserve everything."

Carole didn't sleep a wink when she finally trudged home after midnight. She relived that moment in the garden over and over again. Had it really happened to her? She even sat on her mother's bed and told her about it.

She was too happy to sit and do hair all day so she decided to take the day off. A few customers were put out, but so what? She wanted to tell Peggy her good news, so after a hot shower she drove to Tim Hortons and picked up a coffee and a muffin. When she got to her sister's, Sheena's Jeep was in the yard.

Does that girl ever stay home? Carole wondered.

The front door was open, and she hollered into the foyer, "It's only me."

"Come into the kitchen, me," Peggy yelled back.

When Carole saw Sheena standing by the stove she did a double-take. "Oh God! Are those babies due today?"

"Very funny, Aunt Carole. I can't help it if I'm as big as a house. The doctor said they're going to be huge."

"Who knew they'd take after me?" Peggy grinned.

"Why are you here? Don't you ever stay home with Drew?"

"We're up here together. His cousin, Faye, is getting married."

Carole held out her left hand. "She's not the only one."

Peggy dropped the colander she was holding into the sink. Chickpeas went everywhere. She screamed like a little girl. "Oh my God! Carole!"

She hugged her sister as tightly as she could. Both of them cried and Sheena howled, because she cried at cereal commercials now.

"When are you getting married?" Peggy asked.

"I don't know. I can't think straight."

"Well, why wait? You should do it now."

"I have to plan, don't I?"

"What's to plan? Buy a dress, get married at the courthouse, and we'll go to dinner afterward."

Carole sat at the island. "That sounds boring."

"This is his second marriage, we have no relatives, and you never darken a church door."

Sheena wiped her tears. "Mom, you're not being very romantic. This is Aunt Carole's first marriage. Why shouldn't she have what she wants?"

"Are you going to wear a white wedding gown?"

"Yes! And a veil."

Peggy and Sheena exchanged looks.

"What?"

"Maybe not the veil," Sheena said. "You're a little old."

"Thanks a bunch."

"Don't worry. I'll help you pick out something."

"Sheena, you don't live here," Carole reminded her.

"I know. I can send you ideas over the phone."

"I'll look forward to it."

Peggy ran to the fridge. "Sorry, Sheena, but this calls for a glass of wine." She pulled out a bottle and poured two glasses. "To Carole and her new life."

Carole took a sip and smiled. "Oh yeah, and I won five thousand dollars at Dotty's Dairy!"

"You never buy lotto tickets."

"I found some of Ma's under her mattress and one of them hit the jackpot."

"Go to Paris and take me and we'll pick a dress there!" Sheena shouted.

"I can't. I'm going to use it to fix up the kitchen. Jerry suggested it. He'll do the work for free."

Peggy went back to gathering up the chickpeas. "That's a wonderful idea. Mom would be super happy."

Sheena tried to fit her bulk on a stool but thought better of it. "You still need to save a little for yourself."

"I already know one thing I'm going to buy, but it's a secret."

"For my babies?"

"No, as a matter of fact. You don't need anything. I just saw the dining-room table covered with baby paraphernalia. Are you taking all that back to Halifax?"

"I can't get Mom or Maxine to stop shopping."

"Do you know what you're having?"

"We decided we didn't want to know. I don't want to be fighting about kids' names just yet."

"I hope one of them will be called Carole."

Sheena laughed. "Of course. And I'll call the other one Ethel."

Carole and Jerry asked Mary and Daniel downstairs for supper one night. Jerry did the cooking, so there wasn't a Kraft Dinner box in sight. It was a lovely pot roast with a chocolate cake for dessert. Mary kept wondering what they wanted to talk about, but they didn't seem in any hurry to get to it. Only when they were finishing up their tea did Carole clear her throat.

"We have a proposal for you both."

Mary and Daniel looked at each other. "Okay," said Mary warily.

"Once Jerry and I get married, I will live in his house, which I still can't picture because I've never lived anywhere but here."

"That will be strange for you, Mom."

"But his house is much better for the dogs, with the big backyard and everything fenced in. What we were wondering is whether you two would like to live here rent-free. Jerry is going to fix up the kitchen with the money I won and you can rent the upstairs apartment and bring in some income for yourself."

"But don't you want that income?"

Jerry spoke up. "Your mother doesn't need it now that she's marrying me. I make good money and I don't even want her working, unless she'd like to. I think she should take a few years off and just relax for the first time in her life. We plan on travelling to dog shows around the country. We have lots of great things planned, don't we, Carole?"

Carole reached out her hand and stroked his forearm. "Oh, yes. A whole lifetime of doggie adventures."

Mary wanted to weep with happiness. Her mother was beaming at the prospect of her future with this man. When Mary looked at Daniel, she could tell he was pleased for them too.

"I think that would be a great idea. Don't you, Daniel?"

"Hey, it's a lot bigger than upstairs. And you'll get your wardrobe back."

Mary laughed. "Yes, indeed. A perfect solution. Maybe we can even find a Mrs. Aucoin to rent the upstairs."

"Then it's settled."

As Mary and Daniel were leaving, they thanked Carol again for her generous offer. Just before they went out the door, Carole held Mary back for a moment. "Did you tell Daniel yet?"

"Yes. I should've done it the moment I found out. I feel so much better now."

"Have you decided anything?"

"No, but that's okay."

Her mom kissed her cheek. "You are the best thing that ever happened to me."

CHAPTER TWENTY

PEGGY TRUDGED INTO THE HOUSE one day in July and collapsed on the family-room recliner. Ted put down his paper.

"What's wrong?"

"Why did I ever think it would be fun to go wedding-dress shopping with my sister? Sheena was a thousand times easier."

"What's the problem?"

"The problem is she's trying to dress like she's twenty-one. She wants to wear a big white dress and veil. It will be ludicrous."

"To whom? You? Let her do what she wants."

"I don't want her to be a laughingstock."

"Is she getting married in front of hundreds of people? As far as I know it's only us and Mary and Daniel. Sheena's getting too big to go anywhere. Are his boys even attending the wedding?"

"He doesn't know yet. But what about wedding photos? She'll regret it."

"I hate to say it, darling, but you're turning into an incredible snob."

"I always was a snob. Are you just noticing?"

Peggy felt compelled to call Mary. "How can we keep your mother from looking like a cake topper?"

"If she wants to wear scuba gear, it's okay with me. Why does it bother you so much?"

"Because I know what she *can* look like, and I want her to see herself as I see her. If only she'd trust me."

"I'm not fighting this battle, Aunt Peggy. I don't have the strength."

"All right. I'll do it on my own."

Somehow, Peggy convinced Carole to make a hair appointment with Sheila at Vallie's.

"If you don't like it, you can stand under the shower when you get home. I promise."

"I'm only doing this to shut you up."

"That's fine. I'll never mention it again after today."

Sheila was her usual bright blond self, looking fabulous with the latest hairstyle and perfect makeup. Peggy had warned Sheila that Carole would be a tough nut to crack, and not to worry if Carole scowled through the whole process. Sheila never backed down from a challenge.

Two hours later, the results were in and even Carole couldn't wipe the smile off her face. She had a perfect bob with highlights and lowlights and even bangs that brushed over her forehead, looking perfectly messy and carefree.

Peggy grabbed a tissue from her purse and wiped her eyes. "You see? What did I tell you? You look ten years younger."

Carole stood up and gave Sheila a great big hug. "Thank you. Just thank you."

"My work here is done!" Sheila laughed.

"I'll be back in six weeks."

Peggy knew that Sheila had another customer for life.

Apparently Jerry almost fainted when she saw his fiancée later that night. She didn't get home until the wee hours of the morning.

Now it was just the damn dress standing between a beautiful bride and a cartoon.

"But I want a veil."

"You can have a veil. A sweet little birdcage that will cover your face but not your hair. You simply cannot hide your hair. It's your crowning glory."

"But—"

Peggy grabbed her sister by the elbows. "Please let me show you. *Please!*"

"For God's sake, Peggy. You're like a dog with a bone."

"That's me. Now let me chew it."

So Carole relented and let Peggy drag her into clothes shops to look for elegant dresses fit for a wedding. There was one dress overlaid with lace in a soft eggshell shade that really was scrumptious. As soon as Carole put it on, Peggy knew it was the one.

"This is it, Carole. As God is my witness, you will never put on anything that will make you more beautiful. It's breathtaking, and it looks appropriate. You don't want to look like Sheena on your wedding day.

You are a mature bride, but no less stunning. I wish I had worn something like this. Instead I looked like I had an eagle's nest on my head."

Carole had to admit she did look pretty spectacular. She was glad she'd told Mary to stay away from dress shopping. She wanted to surprise her daughter as well as her future husband.

Carole bought the dress with her own money. She knew her mother would want her to.

In the end, she and Jerry were married in his backyard by a justice of the peace, surrounded by the dogs. His sons showed up, which meant the world to their father. Carole met his close friends for the first time. Mary, Daniel, Peggy, and Ted were Carole's only relatives there, but several of Carole's regular customers were invited, and all of them wanted to know where Carole had had her hair done, which pissed her off big time.

Peggy kept taking pictures of Carole and sending them to Sheena, who cried because she wasn't able to attend her aunt's wedding. She even called on the cell and cried as she talked to Carole, raving about how beautiful she was and how Sheena was so incredibly happy for her. Carole was genuinely touched until she remembered that Sheena was currently crying every minute of every day. Still, it was sweet.

Mary made sure she had a moment with her mother before the guests left. "You were a beautiful bride, Mom. I so wish Gran could've seen you."

"She probably did. She was awfully nosy, if you remember."

"Yes, she was that."

"I hope one day I can see you and Daniel get married."

"I don't think that's in the cards, Mom. I'll be with him forever, but right now, it's not something either of us needs."

"You'll change your mind. You don't know everything when you're twenty-five."

"Let's agree to disagree."

"Why change things now?"

Sheena couldn't get comfortable, no matter which way she turned her body. She was due in two weeks but kept wishing the babies would just come early. They were more than big enough now, but the doctor said he didn't want to interfere unless he had to.

"Typical man!" Sheena shouted at her mother, who was now living in a hotel room in Halifax to be close at hand, seeing as how Sheena's house was too small for a guest room.

"We really should've bought a bigger house," Sheena whined. "I told Drew that, but he said we'd be fine. Well, we're not fine. You have to stay in a hotel instead of being here with me."

"Now is not the time to worry about moving. I'm perfectly happy in a hotel room, but I'll sleep on the floor if you need me here."

"Mommy, rub my feet."

That's all Sheena wanted. Someone to rub her feet and for Drew to take her on drives in the air-conditioned car to buy ice cream. She'd gained sixty pounds. Drew was sworn to secrecy about that little detail.

The babies' room had been prepared for months. Drew had painted animals on the wall. Peggy made the curtains, the babies' blankets, and the cover for the baby table. Everything was in shades of soft greens and yellows. The cribs were white ovals, pushed into the middle of the room. Peggy thought it looked ridiculous but she kept her big mouth zipped. Sheena had seen it in a celebrity magazine, and the fact that this room was ten times smaller didn't dissuade her. Peggy knew the minute real life intervened the cribs would be pushed against the walls so they had room to move around. Let Sheena find out the hard way.

"Mom! Why is it so hot?"

Peggy stood over Sheena, who was splayed on the couch with her feet on the coffee table. She fanned the mother-to-be with a magazine. "I'm not responsible for the weather, my love."

"Any other summer it's freezing out, but not this one. The gods are against me."

The doorbell rang.

"Oh no. Send whoever that is away. I look like a beached whale."

Peggy opened the door and was delighted to see Mary and Carole. "What are you two doing here?"

"We decided to take a spur-of-the-moment trip to Halifax to see Sheena before her big day."

Sheena held out her arms. "You're allowed to see me as long as you didn't bring any paparazzi with you."

Mary kissed her cousin. "You look amazing."

"I look amazingly fat. My ass is getting bigger by the day and my stupid doctor doesn't think that's a problem. Next time I am definitely getting a female doctor."

"Next time?" Carole said. "Will there be a next time?"

"You're right. Forget I said that. I doubt I'll ever want to do this again."

Peggy went to get lemonade for all of them. When she returned, Sheena was opening more gifts. Mary had knit two mice wearing shorts for the babies. Sheena cried when she held them.

"These are my favourite things in the whole world! How did you do this?"

"I saw it online. It took me forever to finally get them right. Roscoe ate the first one I made. He's still in detention for that one."

Carole gave Sheena stuffed toys, a Newfoundland dog and two Chihuahuas. "To remind you of home."

Sheena smiled. "Remember when we first saw them and they chased Gran around the yard? That was so funny."

"I wish Ma was here. She'd get a kick out of seeing these babies," Carole said.

They nodded together, each with their own memories.

Peggy took a sip of lemonade. "So tell me, Carole, what's it like living in your new home?"

"Surprisingly, I love it. I don't miss the old place one bit. And the dogs are happy there. They play in the yard all day. Sometimes they're even too tired to go for a walk."

"Have you stopped hairdressing?" Sheena said.

"Yes. I've retired, and I can't believe what a difference it makes to wake up in the morning and have the whole day in front of me to spend how I like. I still have to pinch myself sometimes."

"Why don't we go out for lunch? Are you feeling up to it, Sheena?"

"Mom, the only pleasure I have in life at this moment is eating."

They bundled Sheena into the car and went to the Park Lane Parkade, rather than try to find a spot on Spring Garden Road. As they herded themselves into the small elevator, Sheena had a thought. "After lunch, why don't we go see a movie here?"

Peggy said. "Good idea. It'll be at least three years before you get to see another one."

"Hardly. You'll be babysitting," her daughter said with a grin.

They all faced forward and the elevator started normally but three seconds into the ride it stopped abruptly.

"Okay, that's weird," Sheena said.

They waited for something to happen.

"Push the button again," Carole told Peggy.

Peggy pushed it four times for good measure, but nothing happened.

"This isn't good."

Mary put her hand on Sheena's arm. "It's okay. Mom, press the call button."

Carole pressed it, but again, nothing.

"Oh, my God. We're going to be stuck in here!" Sheena wailed. "I'm going to have my babies in this elevator!"

Peggy looked around in a panic. Mary knew she better defuse the situation. "Look, guys, we're fine. They will notice the problem and get us out. This is a very busy elevator. Someone will come along in a minute. And by the way, Sheena, you're not due for two weeks. I doubt very much we'll be in here that long."

"But what if we are? Drew isn't here with me! I mean, I love you guys, but I really want my husband with me when our babies come into the world. I have to call him!"

"NO!" three voices said all together, causing Sheena to jump.

"Don't do that, honey," Aunt Peggy said. "We don't want to frighten him. We're fine. Right, Mary?"

Mary nodded. "Right."

Carole put her face up to the door and yelled, "Help!"

Only silence.

Peggy joined her. "Get us out of here! Can you hear us?"

Sheena started to breathe quickly. "I can't believe this."

Again, Mary stroked her arm and made soothing noises. "Don't panic. We're fine."

"We're not fine! We're stuck in an elevator!"

"Sheena, why don't you sit down?"

"On this dirty floor? Are you crazy?"

"You can sit on my sweater. I just don't want you to wear yourself out."

Both mothers agreed, so Sheena gingerly slid her bulk down the back side of the elevator wall. Mary squatted beside her and held her hand. "Now just rest until help comes."

Peggy whispered to Carole in front of the crack in the elevator doors. "Thank God Mary's here. I'm trying not to faint. What if we can't get out?"

"Is it my imagination, or is it getting hotter in here?"

Both Carole and Peggy went back to shouting through the door. Mary wished they'd stop but even she felt a little bubble of panic as the minutes dragged on.

And then the unthinkable happened. Sheena looked down and saw a circle of liquid oozing across the elevator floor. "My water just broke! What do I do? Tell me what to do!"

Mary now had three hysterical women to deal with. Everyone was hyperventilating. She finally had to put her fingers in her mouth and whistle sharply. They stopped and looked at her.

"Everyone, knock it off! This isn't like the movies! Sheena isn't going to have the babies this instant. She's not even in labour yet."

"I am—I can feel something."

"You're not feeling anything. You're imagining it."

"I am?"

"Yes! Water breaks all the time and you could still have hours or days to go. The calmer you are, the better for the babies. Do you hear me, Sheena? You have to stay perfectly calm and your babies will stay put. I promise."

Mary had no idea if what she was saying was true, but it had the desired effect. Sheena started to take slow breaths and actually listen to her.

"Mom, Aunt Peggy, keep yelling through the door and keep pressing every button. Bang on something too."

Mary took a bottle of water out of her purse and put it up to Sheena's lips. Then she rubbed the small of Sheena's back in soft, circular motions. She even hummed—anything to bring Sheena comfort.

"Remember when we were little girls and we'd play Barbies together?"

Sheena nodded.

"We'd always have Barbie in some kind of danger and she was always rescued before anything bad happened."

"Not quite." Sheena hiccupped. "Remember the day you cut off Barbie's hair?"

"That happened once."

"It still happened."

"Forget I said anything."

"Yeah. You better shut up about the Barbies. It's not making me feel better."

And then Sheena moaned. Mary couldn't believe it.

"What is it, honey?" Aunt Peggy shouted.

"I think that was a contraction." Sheena looked at Mary. "Was that a contraction?"

"No. Definitely not."

Peggy looked around frantically. "Oh my God, my poor baby! What do I do?"

"Call Drew," Mary said. "And tell him where we are. Ask him to get help."

"I'm calling Ted too!"

"Ted is in Sydney," Carole pointed out. "What's he going to do?"

"He's going to drive down here and hopefully be here when the babies pop out." Then she almost passed out. "My phone has a low battery. Who else has one?"

Sheena took hers out of her purse. "I'm too shaky. You do it."

"Aunt Peggy, why don't you call Drew instead of text? It'll be faster."

Sheena groaned and leaned forward, rubbing her belly. "Are you sure this isn't a contraction, Mary?"

"Positive. You're sitting in an awkward angle, that's all."

God strike her dead for lying.

Peggy yelled into the cell. "Is that you Drew? You have to come. I—I—"

Mary stood up and grabbed the phone. "Drew? It's Mary. Sheena and I and our moms are in an elevator at the Park Lane Parkade. It's stuck. We haven't moved for ten minutes, but it seems like an hour. Sheena's water broke. I want you to send for an ambulance and I'll be in touch. You can come here, but if they get us out they'll take us to the IWK right away so I'll let you know. Yes, I'll tell her."

Mary cut the connection and looked at Sheena. "Drew says he loves you and you're going to be fine. He's sending help."

"Thank God," Sheena cried. "He's my hero."

Eventually they heard a louder commotion somewhere below them. Voices called out asking if they were okay. All of them shouted back to say hurry up.

By the time they had the elevator moving, too slowly for their liking, Sheena's contractions were coming at a pretty steady rate.

"Are you sure these aren't the real thing?" Sheena panted.

"No. They're Braxton Hicks. I read up on it," Mary assured her.

"Well, they sure feel like the real thing."

"You've never been pregnant before. Remember that."

"True."

When the doors finally opened, they were four feet above the floor. There were service people, a police officer, an ambulance crew, and Drew waiting impatiently below them.

"You're going to have to pass her out," the paramedic said.

"Drew! Are you there?"

"I'm here, sweetheart! You're going to be fine!"

Mary, Carole, and Peggy knelt on the floor of the elevator and pushed Sheena towards the door, her feet hanging in the air until several people grabbed her limbs and slowly brought her forward.

"I can't believe this!" Sheena shouted. "I'm as big as a cow. It's taking ten guys to lift me out."

Mary patted her head. "Think of the great story you'll have to tell your kids."

Before she disappeared, Sheena shouted, "These are so real contractions, Mary!"

"I know!" Mary shouted back.

The paramedics and Drew disappeared as soon as they got Sheena onto the stretcher. Drew shouted that they'd be at the IWK. It took a good five minutes to get the other three women out, all of them unceremoniously dumped on the ground outside the elevator. They quickly thanked the staff and raced for the stairs, Peggy's arms flapping.

"Mary, call Ted! Tell him to get here fast."

Peggy raced through traffic and almost caused several fender benders. Both Mary and Carole had to yell at her to slow down.

"That's all these twins need on the day they're born. A dead grandma!"

After all that rushing, they were in the waiting room for hours.

Ted, Maxine, Sherm, Chuck, and Elaine all made it from Sydney on time. Peggy regaled them with the frightening elevator situation and how Mary had saved the day once again.

"This child is going to make a terrific nurse!"

Everyone clapped. Mary was so embarrassed.

Just when everyone was starting to fade, and truthfully begin to worry a little, Drew came out of the delivery doors. Everyone crowded around the beaming father.

"We have girls! They're identical!"

The entire group encircled Drew and everyone hugged and kissed with abandon. Mary found her face wet with tears. She was so unbelievably relieved that nothing had happened to Sheena or her babies. If there had been a real emergency, who knows what would've happened? All she wanted to do was call Daniel and hear his voice.

Much later, Peggy, Ted, Carole, and Mary were allowed in for a quick peek. The girls were bundled up, one in Sheena's arms and the other in Drew's. They looked like little pink munchkins with blond fuzz sticking straight up out of their scalps. Even wrapped up they looked alike. Peggy couldn't stop crying as she kissed first one head and then the other.

"Did you pick names yet?" she sniffed.

"Yes," Sheena said. "Isobel and Katherine."

Peggy looked delighted. "What lovely old-fashioned names! I love them."

"We're calling them Kat and Issie."

Peggy's face fell slightly. "Oh. That's nice."

Before Mary left, Sheena called her over. "I knew you were lying to me, but I felt better with you there. Thanks for everything."

"I'm glad I could help, cousin."

Sheena reached up and gave Mary a big hug. "You're the best."

CHAPTER TWENTY-ONE

ON MARY'S LAST DAY AT Sobeys, the staff had a small party for her before her shift, with a cake and a card wishing her well on her new adventure. Everyone said they'd miss her, especially Janet, who handed Mary a gift. "It's just a little something."

Mary opened the box and inside was a red sweater and cherry red lipstick.

"Oh, Janet! Thank you. I love it. You have no idea how this sweater changed my life."

"Yes, I do. His name is Daniel, and he's gorgeous."

"He is, isn't he?"

While they were cleaning up, Mary noticed an open *Cape Breton Post* on the table. The obituaries caught her eye. There was a picture of Dave.

She sat on a chair and brought the page closer. He'd died of pneumonia three days earlier. Her eyes scanned the obituary. "Survived by his wife, Denise, and sister, Bonnie." There was no mention of her. Dave must not have said anything to Denise after all. Or maybe he had, and his wife chose to ignore it. Mary wasn't sure what to feel. It was sad, but it didn't feel personal. She'd lived her whole life without him. She was used to it. Still, it seemed such a waste that after all this time, they hadn't had a chance to really connect.

Towards the end of the day, Mary noticed her favourite customer standing in line with a large tray of sweets and one of sandwiches, the kind you can order beforehand. She gave Mary a sad smile.

"Are you having a party?" Mary asked.

"No. Some people are coming back to the house. My brother died."

"I'm so sorry."

"Thank you, dear."

Mary reached out to take her money when her heart started to pound. "Is your name Bonnie?"

"Yes."

"Was your brother Dave Cooper?"

"Yes, did you know him?"

A shiver ran through Mary's body. This wonderful person was her aunt. This woman she'd admired and joked with was her blood. It was as if her father had left her a gift.

"I knew him a little."

Mary was aware that customers were waiting behind Bonnie. She quickly made the change and put it in Bonnie's hand. "This is my last day here. I might never see you again. Would you mind writing down your phone number so I can call you? Maybe we can meet for coffee. I have a story to tell you about your brother."

Bonnie looked taken aback, but she opened her purse and passed her a card. "Here's my business card. I sell quilts. My number is on it." She looked into Mary's eyes. "I'll look forward to hearing from you."

Mary walked back to the house slowly to get some air. She breathed in all the familiar smells: leaves on the trees, the grass, the car exhaust, and the faint smell of KFC. The sounds of traffic and radios playing through open car windows, the far-off noise of a lawn mower and kids shouting. Just a typical day in the city, and yet this miracle had happened.

How lucky was it that she'd made the connection with her aunt on her very last day of work? Someone had to be responsible for it. Maybe her dad, Gran, and Weechee were conspiring.

Daniel was home when she walked in. They were living happily downstairs now. Even the mess that Jerry was making with the renovations wasn't enough to quell their excitement about all the extra space. Mary loved restoring the dining room to its proper function. No one was more delighted to see the old sink and hair dryer tossed in the trash.

She sat at the table while Daniel filled her in on his day at school, but he eventually noticed she wasn't paying much attention.

"Your mind is elsewhere."

"My father died."

"Oh jeez." He took her hand. "I'm sorry."

She passed the paper to him and he read the obituary. "No mention of you," he noticed.

"No.

"Are you okay?"

"I felt a bit empty and then the most amazing thing happened." She told him about Bonnie.

"You mean the woman you always talked about, the crazy one with the lipstick? She's your aunt?"

"Can you believe it?"

"Did you tell her who you are?"

"No. There wasn't time. I'm going to get in touch with her. She gave me her card."

"Maybe that's why you always liked her. Does she look like you?"

Mary thought about it. "You know, I think she does. She certainly has my freckles."

"If she's as nice as you say she is, you're going to love her."

"Do you think she'll love me?"

Daniel grinned at her. "What's not to love?"

After they had their supper, Daniel said, "Why don't you go tell your mom?"

"Maybe I will."

She got in the car and drove over to Jerry's house. It was a really nice place in Sydney Mines. He took good care of it, too. Jerry was capable of anything. It was a miracle he'd crossed paths with her mother. Mary thanked the heavens for him every day.

After the slobbery dog welcome, Mary sat at the kitchen table and told her mom about Dave. She showed her the obituary.

"Oh dear. Oh, I'm sorry, Mary. I feel so guilty—"

"Don't feel guilty," Mary interrupted. "It's all in the past now. You did your best and so did he. So did I, for that matter." She sighed and folded her hands on the table in front of her. "It wasn't meant to be and I'm okay with it. I just felt like being with you right now. Tell me what he was like when you knew him."

Carole put down the paper. "He was cute, and he had a nice laugh. He also had a great body, which is why I was so desperate to be with him. I don't think my girlfriends at the time thought I was good enough for him. Turned out they were right. I knew from the beginning he wasn't serious, but when you're young and think you're in love, your imagination takes over, and I let myself get carried away. He never promised me anything or told me he loved me. He didn't lead me on, as they say. Getting pregnant was an accident that turned out to be the best thing I ever did. I'm sorry now I didn't let him enjoy you too. He didn't have any other kids, did he?"

Mary shook her head.

"I was wrong. I should've let him know you."

"Maybe."

Carole reached out and took Mary's hand. "Life is made up of chapters. This chapter is closed. You have so much ahead of you. Say your goodbyes and move on."

Mary smiled. "That's the most profound thing you've ever said."

"I'm not a complete asshole."

"No, just partial."

Carole snorted. "Charming."

Then Mary told her about Bonnie.

"Why don't you just move on? Do you really need to connect with this woman?"

"Mother. You just said you were sorry you didn't include Dave in my life. Now you're telling me that I shouldn't try and get to know my aunt?"

Carole frowned. "Well, when you say it like that…."

"What are you worried about?"

Carole looked out the dining-room window at the dogs prancing around the yard. "I remember you talking about her. Your favourite customer. And now you want to meet her. I'm afraid you'll like her more than me."

"I probably will," Mary joked, "but you're my mother. I'm stuck with you, aren't I?"

"That's true."

It took a week for Mary and Daniel to scrub the apartment upstairs and get it ready for a new tenant. Mary was in charge of picking the right person.

"I remember the night I met you," she grinned. "I wanted you to move in so badly."

"Not half as much as I did. I wanted to kiss you the moment I saw you."

"I wonder what ever happened to Amber."

"I'm sure she's out there making some other guy miserable."

"That's not nice. You obviously just weren't meant to be together."

"I hope she has a nice life—just very far away from mine."

The doorbell rang.

"Here goes," Mary said.

There was something about the first guy that Mary didn't like, and Roscoe growled when he came to the door. That was good enough for her. The second person was a girl who had forty earrings in both ears. She was perfectly pleasant, but Mary couldn't look at her ears.

When the doorbell rang a third time, Mary kept her fingers crossed. As soon as the door opened, she knew her prayers had been answered. It was an older woman.

"Hello, dear. My name is Ethel."

"The apartment's yours."

"But I haven't even seen it."

"You'll love it here."

Mary did take her upstairs and show her around, and Ethel was very pleased with the whole arrangement. "Oh, I get a nice feeling when I'm in this kitchen."

"Please say you like to bake cookies," Mary said.

"I'm a cookie expert."

"I'll buy whatever you're making."

"Land's sake, child. I'll give them to you."

"No, that's not fair. I'll pay for three dozen cookies a week. Daniel is a cookie junkie."

"Sounds like a lovely arrangement. Now I must tell you, I do own three cats, but they are very well-behaved elderly gentlemen who stick close to home."

"That's perfectly fine. We love cats. Roscoe will no doubt be up here to visit."

"How marvellous." Ethel smiled.

❧

Mary waited a couple of weeks to contact Bonnie. She didn't want to intrude on her grief, but she also didn't want Bonnie to think that she'd forgotten her. They arranged to meet at Starbucks. Mary had fond memories of that place.

They settled down with their coffee. Bonnie insisted on buying them. Today she was wearing bright orange lipstick and purple shoes. Her knitted cardigan had chickens all over it.

"What an odd thing," she said. "My favourite checkout girl knew my brother."

"I was your favourite?"

Bonnie laughed and waved her hand in the air. "By far! Didn't you notice that your line was always the busiest? That's because everyone liked coming to your counter. You were always so kind to the old hens, as I call them. The little old widows who come to the store for their daily jaunt. It did my heart good to see that in a young person. I always wondered who your parents were, that you turned out to be such a lovely girl."

Mary gulped. "Well, funnily enough, that's why I wanted to speak to you. There's not a delicate way to say this...." Mary took a deep breath. "It turns out your brother was my father."

Bonnie was in the middle of a sip of coffee. She gulped it down and coughed into her napkin. Her eyes were like saucers. "Excuse me?"

"This is no doubt a shock. I only found out myself at Christmas."

"But I don't understand."

"He came to our house last Christmas to tell me that I was his daughter. I never knew anything about him." And then the story came spilling out: "My mother always insisted I was the result of a one-night stand and said she didn't even know my dad's last name. Then Dave told me that he and my mom went out together for two months, but that when she got pregnant, he took off. He did say he was ashamed of his actions and that years later he tried to contact me but my mother wouldn't let it happen."

Bonnie was thunderstruck. "My God. I never knew any of this. But I thought he couldn't have children. That's what his wife always said. Although she always had a tendency to blame him for everything."

"The main reason he wanted to get in touch with me was to tell me about his Huntington's diagnosis. He felt I should know. I was very upset, obviously, but after a few months, I agreed to meet with him a couple of times. I told him he couldn't be my father but I'd like to be his friend. He seemed happy with that."

Bonnie put her napkin over her face. She didn't say anything as she tried to compose herself. She finally put down the napkin and took a deep breath. "I think you were more than generous with him."

"He never told anyone about me. That makes me sad. You had no idea?"

Bonnie shook her head. "None. If I'd had an inkling he had a child somewhere, do you think I'd have stayed away?"

Mary smiled. "I don't know you very well, but I don't think so. Which is why I felt it was okay to have this conversation with you."

Bonnie reached over and touched Mary's arm. "What are the chances that we would meet? That you found out about me on your very last day of work? To think that I might have gone through my life without knowing you! It doesn't bear thinking about!" Bonnie sat back and thought for a moment. Then she brightened and said, "Oh, Mary! You're my niece! I've always wanted one! This is a dream come true. Wait until I tell my family!"

"I keep thinking that maybe Dave made it happen."

"Who's to say? Do you want to see pictures of your cousins?"

"Cousins! I never even thought of that. I have more cousins!"

Bonnie rummaged through her bag. "Oh boy, do you." She brought out her wallet and retrieved some school pictures. She handed them to Mary. "Here's Damien. He's eighteen and exactly like his name, a bag of trouble, but we love him." Mary flipped to another portrait. "This is Jamie, she's sixteen and thinks she knows everything. She rolls her eyes constantly and sighs heavily every time I open my mouth." She flipped to another. "And this little devil is Nigel. He's twelve and all I want to do is kiss him, which makes him run for cover." Mary flipped to the last photo and Bonnie said, "Oh yes, and here's my husband, Simon. He's my rock."

Mary was overwhelmed. "These people are my family. I can't believe it."

"Yes! You belong to us now. You can't ever escape!" Bonnie clapped her hands with glee. "I came here feeling so lonesome and sad and now I feel as though Dave has come alive again. Thank you for this. You have no idea how this has changed my life."

Mary handed back the pictures. "What about Dave's wife? Will she want to know me?"

Bonnie made a face. "She might and she might not. That's not for you to worry about. I'll tell her and if she wants to meet you, fine. But if she doesn't, that's her right too. She'll be very angry at Dave for not telling her about this, and I don't blame her. She's allowed to feel what she feels; don't you agree?"

Mary nodded. They sipped their coffee and grinned at each other, both of them astonished at this turn of events. And then Bonnie looked suddenly serious.

"I'm so very sorry that you had to find out about Dave's illness like that. It couldn't have been easy."

"At first I was angry with him, but like my Uncle Ted said, he owed it to me to tell me."

"Yes, absolutely."

"Do you have it too?"

"I don't know."

"So you decided not to be tested?"

Bonnie looked away for a moment and then smiled at Mary. "My brother and I were very different people. He felt he wanted to know, so he eventually took the test. When it came back positive, I saw a little life drain away from him at that moment. I decided I didn't want that to happen to me. Life is so uncertain anyway, you know? Who knows what will happen tomorrow, let alone twenty years down the road? Why tie yourself down like that? That's what I tell my kids, anyway. The choice will be up to them some day."

"You never felt guilty about having kids?"

"No. As far as I'm concerned, I don't have the disease. I didn't have it the day they were conceived or the day they were born. That's how I live my life. We are just stupidly happy with our lot today."

Mary felt a massive weight vanish from her heart. There was no decision to be made. She didn't have Huntington's on this glorious day.

All she had today was an Aunt Bonnie, an Uncle Simon, and three more crazy cousins. An Aunt Bonnie who said, "Wait until you come to the house! I'm making a new quilt, and I know just who I'm giving it to!"

Mary was still smiling three days later when she and Daniel heard someone at their back step. They looked outside to see her mother and Jerry coming up the stairs with a big box tied with a red ribbon.

"Hello! Anyone home?"

Mary got up from the table and opened the door. "Hi, come on in. Would you like some tea?"

"No thanks," Carole said. "We just came to give you both your housewarming gift."

Daniel got up as well. "That wasn't necessary. It's enough that you're letting us live here."

"Oh, you need this," Jerry said. "No home is complete without one or two of these."

Now they were curious.

"What is it?" Mary asked excitedly.

Jerry put the box on the kitchen floor and Carole untied the ribbon. She opened the top and Mary and Daniel peered inside.

Two little Weechees looked back at them.

Both Daniel and Mary squealed and rushed to picked them up in their arms, both pugs kissing and grunting and nuzzling them immediately, their silly pink-tongued grins and crossed eyes looking every which way. Daniel grabbed Carole and Jerry with the dog still in his arms and gave them big hugs.

"This is amazing! Where did you get them?"

"They're from Ontario. They flew in today," Carole said.

Mary began to sob. She reached out and hugged her mother while trying to keep the little black devil in her arms.

"They're perfect!" she cried. "Thank you for thinking of them. Now it feels like home!"

They spent a good two hours just watching the pups run around and chase poor Roscoe in and out of the kitchen. They both had scratches on their noses before the evening was over, but they deserved them.

"What should we call them?" Daniel wondered.

"Thing One and Thing Two," Jerry laughed.

After she kissed Mom and Jerry goodbye, Mary went out into the living room. Daniel was in the old recliner, his puppy completely zonked from all the excitement. "Is this not the best day, little guy? Wait until I tell you the stories about your big brother Weechee."

Roscoe sat on the back of the sofa looking miffed.

Mary took her puppy out onto the porch and introduced him to the neighbourhood. "This is a nice place to grow up. You'll love it here."

As she stood there, Mary looked back on her life. Playing with friends in the yard, listening to her mom and Gran holler and laugh at each other through the open windows. Seeing Gran charge over to Dotty's Dairy for lotto tickets. The excitement of waiting for Aunt Peggy, Uncle Ted, and Sheena to come to her birthday parties, always with amazing gifts in their hands.

And now here she was with her fur baby, knowing Daniel was inside waiting for her, and a nursing career about to begin.

There was no point in *what ifs*. Life was what it was.

Spectacular.